VINYL
RESTING
PLACE

ALSO BY OLIVIA BLACKE

Killer Content
No Memes of Escape

VINYL RESTING PLACE

OLIVIA BLACKE

St. Martin's Paperbacks

This is a work of fiction. All of the characters, organizations, and events portrayed in this novel are either products of the author's imagination or are used fictitiously.

First published in the United States by St. Martin's Paperbacks, an imprint of St. Martin's Publishing Group.

VINYL RESTING PLACE

For information, address St. Martin's Publishing Group, 120 Broadway, New York, NY 10271.

www.stmartins.com

ISBN: 978-1-250-86008-8

Our books may be purchased in bulk for promotional, educational, or business use. Please contact your local bookseller or the Macmillan Corporate and Premium Sales Department at 1-800-221-7945, ext. 5442, or by email at MacmillanSpecialMarkets@macmillan.com.

Printed in the United States of America

St. Martin's Paperbacks edition / January 2023

10   9   8   7   6   5   4   3   2   1

Espresso Yourself

CHAPTER 1

The best part about working for the family business is that they can't fire me without causing all sorts of unwanted drama. The worst part is I can't ever quit, not unless I want to hear about it every single Thanksgiving for the rest of my life—although I would put up with a whole lot for a plateful of Uncle Calvin's deep-fried turkey. And as a bonus, at the family record shop I get to work with my two older sisters.

"Juni! It's been too long." An older Black woman shuffled toward me, arms outstretched for a hug.

My full name is Juniper. Juniper Jessup. But most folks around here call me Juni.

"Miss Edie!" I exclaimed, folding myself into the shorter woman's embrace. Growing up in Cedar River, Texas, all the latchkey kids found their way to Miss Edie's after school. Even though my mother was usually home or at the family record shop, at least once a week I invented an excuse to join the other kids at Edie's. "You're looking amazing."

"Don't you know it?" she agreed with a wide grin. She let go and stepped back to clasp my hands. As usual, she was dressed in bright, garish colors held together with elastic and Velcro. Her curly white hair was cut short and her grin was genuine. "Just look at this place! You and your sisters done good, kid."

"Thanks," I replied with a blush. I looked around Sip & Spin Records, the record shop/coffee bar my sisters and I owned, and felt a surge of pride.

The back wall behind the barista station and cash register was rough exposed red brick, lending an air of industrial chic to the crowded store. The side walls were a silvery gray, but I could barely make out the paint underneath a layer of vintage concert posters and framed albums. Above us was a second-floor loft ringed with a wide balcony, where shelves full of records were mounted to walls and bins, with even more albums lined up against the shiny black railing. The front wall was enormous panes of glass decorated with our logo on either side of the main entrance, the door to which was currently propped open to welcome customers and friends.

It was almost half past ten, and the grand opening of Sip & Spin Records was in full swing. Upbeat music and happy overlapping conversations filled the room. I didn't know why I'd been so nervous that the party would be a bust. We were packed to capacity, with people filling the main floor and the balcony overhead.

Although to be fair, that probably had at least as much to do with the free-flowing beer kegs set up near the coffee station and the complimentary taco truck out front as it did with our advertising campaign or the resurging interest in vinyl records. Then again, there were plenty of people browsing our carefully cultivated collection. Hopefully that would convert into future sales and repeat customers.

"I see some folks I need to talk to, but now that you're back in town, you come see me soon, hear?" Edie said.

"I most certainly will," I agreed. I felt bad that I hadn't gone around to see her already, but things had moved at a frantic pace ever since I moved back home. We'd worked constantly to get the shop ready for tonight's opening, so I hadn't had much time to myself. Besides renovating the space and filling it with records, my oldest sister, Tansy, had come up with the idea of setting up a small coffee shop in the back corner, which had wreaked havoc on our permits, but in the end we got it all done by working together and calling in every favor we'd ever collected.

Out of the corner of my eye, I saw my middle sister, Maggie, dash toward a patron who was leaning over the Golden Oldies section, a glob of guacamole oozing ominously from the end of their taco. She swooped in with a napkin to avert disaster with the skill of someone used to cleaning up other people's—and by other people's I mean my—messes. Out of the three of us Jessup girls, Maggie was the most fastidious. We shared a bedroom growing up. Her side was neat as a pin. Mine, well, was significantly less so. She had a lot of practice picking up after me.

It felt like déjà vu, not only being home in Texas and watching Maggie in action but also being back in this familiar record store. As the baby of the family, I'd felt the need to spread my wings farther than either of my older sisters. I'd left home soon after graduating from college (Hook 'em Horns!) to make my own way in the world. But now, six years later, I was right back here in quiet Cedar River, just outside of Austin, the live music capital of the world.

And, with a lot of hard work and a little luck, maybe we could make Sip & Spin the capital of vinyl records, too.

My grandparents used to own a record shop in this very storefront, back in vinyl's original heyday. My mother and her brother, my uncle Calvin, grew up in this shop. And later, after Mom met our dad not six feet away from where I was standing right now, my sisters and I grew up here, too. By then, we sold cassette tapes and CDs, too, but eventually Napster and iTunes put us out of business.

Then the miracle happened. Millennials discovered vinyl. Between a wave of nostalgia and the desire to experience music without commercials, records were back in a big, big way. And my sisters and I were poised to make the most of it.

A man's booming voice cut through the happy party chatter. "Excuse me, folks. If I can have your attention, please?"

I made my way around the checkout counter to turn down the background music playing over the shop's sound system. Conversations faded as our guests focused their attention on the makeshift stage we'd erected where the café chairs and tables would go when we opened for real tomorrow.

Mom's brother, Calvin Voigt, stood tall and proud as he lifted a red Solo cup. It didn't have the same effect as a glass flute, but tonight wasn't about putting on airs. Tonight's grand opening was about celebrating with friends and family, which equated to beer kegs, not champagne bottles.

"Thank y'all for coming out tonight," Uncle Calvin said, leaning into the microphone, not that he needed it. He had a booming voice to match his large frame and even bigger personality. A white man in his sixties, he was wearing what I considered Texas formal attire—dark pressed-denim blue jeans and a long-sleeved green-and-gray-checkered shirt fastened up to a bolo tie featuring a silver long-horned cow skull, topped off with a lighter shade of denim jacket. His salt-and-pepper—more salt than pepper these days—mustache was combed to perfection, and unless I was mistaken, he'd gotten a trim for the occasion. He pushed back the brim of his cowboy hat to survey the crowd.

"This here record shop will forever hold a special place in my heart. As you may or may not know, even though Thomas Edison is credited with inventing the phonograph way back in 1877, the origin of vinyl records can actually be traced to Frenchman Léon Scott in 1857. . . ." The crowd let out a collective groan, knowing that they were about to be treated to one of Calvin's long, rambling stories.

We'd begged our uncle to take it down a notch, just for one night, but apparently our pleas had fallen on stubborn ears. Then he turned to me and winked. "But while tonight *is* historic, I'm not gonna bore y'all with a history lesson. We're here tonight to celebrate the grand opening of Sip & Spin Records." He paused for a smattering of applause and lifting of Solo cups in the assembled crowd. "So without further ado, I'd like to turn the festivities over to my three beautiful nieces, Tansy, Magnolia, and Juniper Jessup."

"Maggie," the three of us corrected him in unison as we headed for the stage. Even though all the women in our family were named after flowers, Maggie had always resented her name. Anyone who dared call her Magnolia against her wishes had to answer to the Jessup sisters.

We took our places on the stage. Uncle Calvin kissed my oldest sister, Tansy, on the forehead as she passed and started to do the same with my middle sister, but she stopped him cold with a fierce glare. If looks could kill, he'd have needed to wear a Kevlar jacket instead of a denim one to escape unscathed from the faux pas of calling her by the wrong name. I gave her a gentle nudge to get her moving again. Her knee-length floral dress—she had a closet full of completely interchangeable ones just like it—swished as she walked.

"You might want to lock your doors tonight," I warned my uncle with a smile to show him I was at least half joking.

"Don't you worry yourself. I ain't scared of your sister. Much."

He tossed Tansy the microphone before hurrying off. It probably wasn't necessary. The store was packed, but small, and my oldest sister's voice carried. That hadn't changed since we were kids.

"Hey, y'all," she said, waving as if she had just won the Little Miss Texas pageant and had the place of honor in the lead float for the Fourth of July parade. Again. She wore a pink pastel twinset over a long denim skirt for the occasion, and her ultra-short brown hair was done in soft waves. "I can't tell y'all what it means to us for everyone to be here tonight. Uncle Calvin calls it a grand opening, but in truth, it's a grand *re*opening. Nearly sixty years ago, our grandparents opened a record shop in this very storefront, and it's been such a huge presence in all our lives as long as I can remember. When their record shop closed in 2005, it was the end of an era for Cedar River. Well, I'm here to tell y'all that a new era begins tonight."

Tansy's speech was met with tremendous applause. She continued, "Seeing it now, restocked and packed with friends and family . . ." I heard the hitch of emotion as her voice trailed off. Unlike myself, Tansy loved the spotlight, but if I didn't intervene quickly she would turn on the waterworks. Neither myself nor her mascara wanted that, so I slid past Maggie, wrapped one arm around Tansy's shoulders, and pried the microphone out of her quivering hands.

I swallowed down my stage fright, reminding myself that the crowd in front of me was made up of family and friends I've known for a lifetime. Then I cleared my throat and said, "We all hope that Sip & Spin will become the greater Austin area's premiere location for discovering new music, finding great local musicians, and exploring the joy vinyl has to offer, all while sipping your favorite caffeinated beverage with friends. Be sure to swing by tomorrow when we officially open for business, when the drink special of the day will be Java B. Goode."

That had been Maggie's brilliant idea, to combine our love of caffeine with our love of music to create unique specials with memorable names. We sat up many a night coming up with the perfect blend of musical references and coffee drinks that we couldn't wait to serve to our customers.

"Thanks again to everybody for coming out tonight," I continued, trying to ignore the way my hands were starting to sweat. I was usually more than happy to let Tansy have the limelight while I worked behind the curtain, but I could get through this. "Enjoy the beer and tacos, and don't forget to tag your pictures with the hashtag SipAndSpinRecords—all one word—on social media." I switched off the microphone and, instead of replacing it back in the stand, clutched it for dear life.

If I left the mic on the stage, we'd eventually be treated to impromptu drunken karaoke, which was *not* the vibe we were going for tonight. Although I made a mental note to revisit the idea later. Anything that drew customers into the shop was good for business.

"Look at the three of you girls, all grown-up and together again," my mother gushed, gathering us all up in a group hug as we exited the stage. Begonia Jessup, known by most as Bea, had an eye-catching blend of dark and light gray hair, with a few strands of silver acting as natural highlights. When I was a kid, it was usually in a long braid, but she'd since cut it to shoulder-length, somewhere between Tansy's ultra-short and Maggie's medium haircuts, only my sisters' hair was chestnut brown like mine. Mom's features had sharpened with age and her skin wasn't as taut as it used to be, but every time I saw her it was like looking into a mirror from the future.

"Just having y'all home is a gift," she went on. Like any family, my sisters and I had our share of spats when we were younger, but a few years and a lot of miles apart had made us appreciate each other in a way that being forced to wear matching outfits in the annual Christmas portrait never had. "And Juni, I'm so proud of my baby girl. Speaking in public? I never thought I'd live to see the day. You didn't speak a single word until you were nearly six years old, you know."

"I know, Ma." I'd heard the story enough times. Everyone in Cedar River had. Shucks, I wouldn't be surprised if everyone in Austin had heard it at least once. People assumed that my lack of speaking was because I was shy, which was only partially true. Between Tansy naturally gravitating to the spotlight and Maggie's middle child FOMO, I could never get a word in edgewise.

"Now y'all get together. I need a picture of this for Facebook. Calvin! Get over here. Family picture time."

We put our arms around each other and scrunched together in a familiar pose. Mom was in the middle, standing proud. Tansy stood on her right. She was the tallest of the three of us sisters. Her hair barely brushed the top of her long, thin neck. Even though her beauty pageant days were long gone, she still had a sharp jaw and delicate features. Maggie stood on the other side of Mom. Her jovial smile never looked forced, and set off the pleasant roundness of her cheeks and deep dimples.

Then, on the end, was me. I wasn't as tall as Tansy but had a few inches on Maggie. My hair was longer than either of my sister's, reaching the middle of my back with barely a hint of wave even when it was wet. I envied Maggie's armpit-length spiral curls. I'd tried to replicate it with an at-home perm once, and let's just say it took a long time for my hair to recover.

Even with Mom's hair gone gray, we shared the same big brown eyes and heavy, arched brows. There was never a question that we four were closely related, something that bothered my dad to no end. Out of three kids, he would have liked it if even one of us had taken after him. Much to his chagrin—and our relief—he didn't get his wish.

Although I did inherit his eyesight and as a result had worn glasses ever since I was little. My sisters used to tease me about them, but these days they were my favorite fashion accessory. I had several pairs, each with colorful frames. To-night's were a pink-and-black-speckled pattern.

Mom thrust her phone at the nearest partygoer. "Make sure you get us all in the picture," she instructed him.

"Yes, Miss Bea," he replied dutifully. He snapped a few pictures and handed her phone back to my mother to inspect them.

"Juni!" she exclaimed. "What have I told you about giving your sister bunny ears?"

I grinned and wiggled my bunny ear fingers. "Old habits die hard, I guess."

She shook her head, but her smile never faded, so she couldn't have been too upset at my familiar antics. Our family albums were stuffed full of goofy poses and bunny-eared sisters. She posted the picture online before slipping her phone back into her purse. "I wish your daddy was here to see this. He'd be so proud." She smiled wistfully.

He'd been gone two years now, and he wouldn't have wanted to cast a shadow over an otherwise perfect family moment. So instead of letting myself dwell on what we'd lost, I grabbed a fresh Solo cup and filled it halfway. I lifted it in a toast. "To Dad."

"Hear! Hear!" my sisters echoed, clinking our plastic cups together.

"Now, as much as I love seeing all my girls together, y'all can't just keep standing around ignoring your guests," Mom said. "It's rude. Go. Mingle. You too, Juni," she added as if I was still that little girl who refused to speak.

"Sure thing," I replied. Like my sisters, I'd been working tirelessly getting the shop ready for customers. I'd helped organize and advertise our grand reopening and wanted it to be a raging triumph. I was as invested—literally and figuratively—as everyone else in the family with making Sip & Spin Records a success. I'd been saving up for a house I could call my own, but I'd just lost my job when Tansy announced that this storefront was available and suggested that we revive the family record shop. We jumped on the idea and I contributed all the money I'd earmarked for a down payment without any hesitation.

Or rather, without too much hesitation.

It wasn't a lot of money in the grand scheme of things, not going-to-space-for-funsies money, but it was every penny I had. Both of my sisters chipped in the same exact amount, ensuring we three were equal partners. It wasn't quite enough to get the shop off the ground, but Mom still had a little left over from Dad's life insurance policy, and our uncle Calvin tossed in the remainder that we needed on the condition that he remain a silent partner.

Did we know how to open a family business or what?

The record shop was crowded, which was a good thing. Balloons dangled from the high ceiling and clustered under the balcony ledge. Crepe paper streamers decorated the displays. A grand opening banner hung across the back wall. The long, shiny bar near the register that held the complicated espresso machine and a tray full of mugs with the Sip & Spin logo on it was littered with discarded Solo cups and crumpled-up taco wrappers. An informal line snaked around the shop, ending at a keg of local craft beer that was on its last dregs.

Mixed in with the vintage rock 'n' roll posters and framed vinyl records lining the walls were autographed and rare albums encased in glass protectors. Normally, there would be several racks filled with records in the center of the shop, but we'd temporarily relocated them to the stock room in the back to make room for a crowd.

We just weren't expecting quite this many people.

It was a good problem to have. The party spilled out of the store and onto the sidewalk out front, where a taco truck was parked at the curb. We'd handed out tickets to the first hundred guests for free tacos. I felt into the pocket of my jeans, where two tickets remained. Thank goodness. I'd been too nervous that no one would show up to the big event to eat anything earlier, and now I was ravenous.

I made my way through the crowd, stopping briefly every few feet to say howdy and make sure everyone was enjoying themselves. By the time I got to the sidewalk, I was ready to chew off my own arm if I didn't get something to eat soon.

Luckily, the line was short, and I queued up at the back of it. Finally, it was my turn. As I pulled the tickets out of my pocket, the man inside the taco truck reached out to slide the window closed. "Hey, wait, I haven't ordered yet!" I protested.

"Sorry, lady, we're all sold out."

"How is that even possible?" I asked.

He shrugged. "What can I tell you? People love tacos." The man had a point. He closed and latched the window. A few minutes later, the truck rumbled away. I watched the food truck retreat, my stomach grumbling almost as loud as its muffler.

"Juni?"

I looked up to see who was calling my name and saw a Hispanic man on the sidewalk heading my way. He was maybe an inch over six feet tall, not counting his ostrich cowboy boots or a well-worn cowboy hat that looked like it had once been brown but was bleached and weathered by years of exposure to the brutal Texas sun. "Just look at you. I hoped I'd catch you tonight."

"Teddy!" He went in for a hug. I extended my hand for a shake. We bumped into each other and ended up settling for an awkward half embrace with my arm trapped between us before we each took a step back. "It's so good to see you."

He grinned again and removed his hat. His hair was short on the sides and brushed back on the top, held in place with enough product that it withstood being crushed by his hat but not so much that it didn't still look soft and manageable. It wasn't fair. Even when we were awkward, scrawny pre-teens, Teddy always had the best hair. And he wasn't awkward or scrawny anymore.

"Juniper Jessup, back home in Texas at long last. I heard the rumors, but I had to see for myself."

"Teddy Garza, how have you been, my old friend?" I'd known Teddy since about forever. We'd been best friends from grade school until we drifted apart when we went to separate colleges. Despite its nearness to Austin, and the metropolis' tendency to gobble up nearby towns, Cedar River was a tight-knit community. Most people lived here all their lives and knew everyone else. Myself, I was third generation. If my sister Maggie ever had children, they would be the fourth.

"Same ole, same ole," he replied. "Nothing ever changes around here. Not like you, though. Last I heard, you were out in California or something?"

"Oregon, actually," I corrected him. "Working for a tech company. We developed digital footprint aggregation software." His eyes glazed over, as most people's did when I tried to explain what I did for a living. "Or at least we used to."

"What happened?" he asked.

"Bankruptcy. Layoffs. Same old story." That was the short answer.

IT changed so rapidly that by the time I excelled at a new skill or programming language, it was already obsolete. My company was on top of the game for a few years, but once it got overtaken, the restructuring began. I was still holding out hope that we'd get gobbled up by another, bigger company when everything crumbled and the owners took off without so much as a backward glance.

"Sounds rough. Wanna talk about it?"

I shrugged. "For years, I gave them ten hours a day, six days a week. And they didn't even have the decency to fire me properly. I just showed up on Monday and the doors were locked."

To add insult to injury, I worked from home most of the time, but that particular Monday I'd driven all the way in to the office, in rush hour, in a skirt and suit jacket instead of my normal jeans and a T-shirt, because we had a client coming in. Some days, it just didn't pay to shave my legs.

I worked at a record shop now. A record shop that I partially owned. It was scary, knowing that my grandparents' record shop had gone out of business just like my old tech company had, but my sisters and I were determined to make it work. There was a bit of irony buried in there somewhere, and I didn't mean the Alanis Morissette song. Technology forced the original record store to close when physical media was replaced with downloadable MP3s and streaming services, but when my job writing the kind of computer software that made digital music possible went belly-up, I found myself right back here in Cedar River at the rebooted record shop.

Everything old was new again.

I wondered if feather bangs were next in line to make a comeback. I sincerely hoped not. I looked truly horrific with bangs.

"So you're back in Cedar River now?" Teddy asked. "For good?"

I nodded. "Yuppers. I'm back."

CHAPTER 2

Downtown Cedar River hadn't changed much since I was little. The awnings on the storefronts got new logos every couple of years, and the town council had added a bike lane on Main Street. That was about it. Tonight, cars were parked along the curb as far as I could see as people rotated in and out of our store.

It was a welcome twist of fate that we'd managed to open Sip & Spin in the original location of our grandparents' record shop, right between Cedar Spines Bookstore and Boot Scootin' Dance Studio. This coveted storefront—located conveniently in the middle of the block where foot traffic was the thickest—had housed a frozen yogurt shop, a day care, a shoe store, and most recently a yoga studio. Maggie pointed this out as evidence that the location was cursed, but I think it was just waiting for us to return home.

Our new logo—a vinyl record with "Sip" arching around the top, "Spin" curved along the bottom, and a giant ampersand in the center, all in bright orange disco-era lettering—was painted on the windows and duplicated again on the lighter orange awning above the entrance. The grand opening banner flapped in the breeze. Our new sidewalk signs were invisible in the mingling crowd.

I let out a sigh of contentment. It felt right to do something together as a family. The timing was perfect, during the height of the vinyl revival. The location here in this specific shop, so close to the famed Austin music scene, was ideal. This was gonna work. We would *make* it work.

We had to.

"You okay?" Teddy asked, casually draping a comforting arm around my shoulders. He'd misinterpreted my sigh for something else. A conflicted reaction to moving back home, maybe. Or just the everyday stress of owning my own small business.

"Yup. Never better." My stomach grumbled again. He laughed at the embarrassingly loud noise. "A little hungry, maybe."

"There was a taco truck here earlier." He waved at the recently vacated spot on the curb, which had already been claimed by a shiny new Prius and an ancient, banged-up Dodge pickup truck. If that wasn't a perfect analogy for Texas—at least Austin—I didn't know what was. The old and new, coexisting more or less peacefully, side by side. "You should have grabbed some tacos while it was here. They were just the right amount of spicy and fresh, with no boring filler."

"Don't rub it in," I said.

"Come on." He turned, paused at the curb to check for traffic, and dashed across the street. I was right on his heels. The sidewalks downtown normally rolled up by nine o'clock. It was approaching eleven now, and while the rest of the block was quiet, the party at the record shop was still going strong.

We reached the other side of the street without incident. A car slowed down, did a U-turn in the middle of Main Street, and crept slowly behind us, hoping to snipe our parking spot. I waved the late partygoer on before he could get too disappointed that we weren't leaving and freeing up a space. There was a municipal parking lot at the end of the block, but for some unfathomable reason, everyone preferred to parallel park on the curb. Personally, I'd rather walk the extra block, but maybe that was because I failed the parallel-parking portion of the driver's exam three times before the haggard DMV employee took pity on me and gave me a license anyway.

"Is anything still open this late?"

Instead of answering, Teddy pulled open a door. The smell of hot pizza wafted over us. I felt weak in my knees. There might have been drool. Inside, the air conditioner was blowing full blast, but it couldn't keep pace with the coal pizza ovens behind the counter. I could only imagine what the temperature would be in this place at the height of summer.

The woman behind the cash register dabbed her brow with a napkin. "What can I get y'all?"

I hadn't realized how much I missed that word until I got back home. When I said "y'all" in Oregon, people looked at me like I'd grown a third head. It hadn't stopped me from using it. I just got used to the perplexed stares. Here it was as common as breathing.

"Three slices, plain," Teddy ordered.

Even after all the time that had passed since we'd last seen each other, he'd remembered my favorite—not that it was particularly unique. "Oh, I couldn't possibly eat three slices," I protested.

"Who said anything about you? This is for me."

I poked him in the ribs with my elbow. It was simultaneously comforting and strange, being back home after so long away. After six years of living on my own, I was now staying with my sister Tansy. My poor Civic would never have made the long drive from Oregon, so I'd sold it before moving back to Texas and relied on my family or my bicycle to get around town.

Except it's not a bicycle. It's an adult tricycle, to be precise. It's long and low, with a giant basket mounted between the back two wheels. My trike is perfect to cart groceries home from the farmer's market and is painted a sensational shade of lime green. It's got an ergonomic seat that's ten times more comfortable than the old Schwinn I used to ride in high school before I got my license and enough gears to handle most paved roads with ease without being overly complicated.

Back in Oregon, I only rode it on the weekends, but now it was my primary mode of transportation. It was a lot to get used to—everything about moving home at twenty-eight was, to be honest—but at least I got to see my family every day and could reconnect with friends I'd left behind, like Teddy.

Three slices of hot pizza were shoveled onto overlapping paper plates and slid onto a red cafeteria tray that we carried to a table. Teddy dumped a heap of Parmesan cheese and a sprinkle of red pepper flakes on top. He grabbed one slice, folded it in half, and took an enormous bite. I snagged one of the other pieces.

It tasted as good as it smelled. My eyes rolled back into my head, and Teddy let out a snorting laugh around a mouthful of pizza.

"Good, right?" he asked.

I nodded, too intent on gulping down my slice without burning the roof of my mouth to respond. He pushed the tray toward me. "You sure?" I asked, then snagged the last piece before he could change his mind. I didn't slow down until even the crispy crust was gone. "Thanks. I needed that."

"No kidding." He stood. His chair made a metallic scraping sound as the legs slid across the tile floor. "But shouldn't you be getting back to the party?"

"Yuppers." We headed back toward Sip & Spin Records in that companionable silence that only ever existed between old friends. As we drew nearer, I saw that the crowd had thinned out considerably in the short time it had taken us to eat. Then again, it was getting late. People had to drive back to Austin or take the babysitter home before turning in for the night. "Thanks again for the pizza."

"Anytime." Teddy waved at someone, and they waved back. "I'm gonna call it a night, but I'll see you around?"

"You know it."

"Man, it's good to see you again, Juni," he said, patting my shoulder before walking away. I watched him for a second before returning my attention to the reason I was here. I wove between the guests, making small talk as I went. I exchanged hugs with acquaintances I hadn't seen in ages and even a few folks I didn't recognize at all but who appeared to know exactly who I was.

"Where did you disappear to, little lady?" my mother asked.

"Who, me?" I tried to look innocent.

As usual, she saw right through me. She gave me a knowing smile. "I saw you sneak off with Teddy Garza. He's a good boy. And single, you know."

"Uh-huh," I agreed. Teddy *was* a good guy. I agreed with that with my whole heart. He was also my friend and had been as long as I could remember. In school, we were in all the same classes and clubs and even rode the bus together. He used to pull my pigtails and tease me about my braces. But since I'd been gone we'd both grown up, and now I was starting to see him in a new light.

"You should ask him out. Or you know what? I'll arrange something. There's a dance down at the civic center next month. That's the ticket." Her eyes sparkled with excitement.

"Thanks, Ma, but I'm good." She meant well, and I wasn't opposed to the idea of dating, but if I let her have even the tiniest opportunity, the next thing I knew, she'd be fixing me up with the mailman or some rando passing out hot dog samples at the mall. I pushed my glasses up the bridge of my nose. "I see someone over there I need to talk to." I indicated a small clump of people with a jerk of my chin, as an excuse to wiggle out of this conversation.

"Well then, hurry up, dear. People are leaving."

It was almost midnight before the last guest left. We locked the door behind them. Sometime in the last few minutes of the party, our mother managed to slip away unseen, leaving my sisters and me alone to clean up. That was so like her. Then again, it was our store. Our mess, our responsibility.

"That taco truck was a great idea, Juni. What a hit! But I still think we should have asked them to keep the food outside," Maggie said. She'd already filled one trash bag. An outsider might think she was complaining, but I could hear the unmitigated delight in her voice. Cleaning up after a messy gathering? This was Maggie's happy place.

"What's a party without food?" Tansy countered, her voice floating down from the loft, where she was haphazardly cleaning upstairs. The open second floor made the shop feel larger than it was and gave us more space to display albums. It more than made up for the floor space we'd sacrificed to create a coffee nook.

"And beer," I added, emptying Solo cups and stacking them together. Were Solo cups recyclable? I certainly hoped so. I took the trash bag from Maggie, tied it up, and carried it down the narrow hallway that led to the dumpsters in the back alley. I opened the back door and a flash of orange barreled into my legs.

"Hello to you too, Daffy," I said as the skittish cat dashed past me.

Daffodil—Daffy for short—was an enormous white-and-orange tabby cat that looked like a fluffy, novelty-size candy corn. He'd adopted us when we were first setting up Sip & Spin, and decided to make this his home. We'd put up flyers and had him checked over at the vet, but he wasn't chipped and no one came forward to claim him. He didn't like strangers but had already bonded with my sisters and me. I guess that meant we had a cat now.

So I wasn't surprised he'd disappeared during the party. He might eventually adjust to what I hoped would be a steady stream of customers, but I was resigned to him disappearing every time the front door opened. Which might be a good thing if the health inspector ever dropped by to check on the coffee bar.

The dumpster was already nearing full. We'd done an awful lot of work getting Sip & Spin Records ready for the grand reopening, which resulted in an abundance of construction waste. The garbage company would come by in the morning. In the meantime, I tossed the bag over the lip and it landed with a wet thud. Hopefully we could finish the cleanup without overflowing the bin.

As I let myself inside, Maggie called to me, "Grab a broom, will ya?"

"Sure thing."

I opened the door in the narrow hallway where we stored cleaning supplies, coffee filters, and other miscellany. I flipped on the light and shrieked. I slammed the door to the supply closet.

Maggie looked over at me, one eyebrow lifted. "Is it a mouse? Tell me it's not a mouse. Daffy! Daffy, get in here and take care of this mouse."

"It's not a mouse," I said, my voice trembling. My mind was racing, trying to make sense of what I'd seen.

"Then what is it?"

I took a deep breath. "There's a dead body in our supply closet."

"There's not a dead body in our supply closet," Maggie said. She rolled her eyes. "Move, Juni. I need that broom."

Being the surprise baby of the family had its advantages.

By the time I came along my sisters were old enough that I never got stuck with their hand-me-downs. It had its drawbacks, too, such as still being treated like an incompetent kid even though I was in the home stretch of my twenties. I was used to not being taken seriously. "I'm telling you . . ."

My sister cut me off and in a shrill, mocking voice said, "Hi, I'm Juniper and I'm a lying liar."

"Maggie, I'm serious." I pressed my back against the closed door.

"What's taking you two so long?" Tansy asked. She'd come down the stairs and joined us in the cramped hallway. She looked tired. We all were. It had been a long day. "Seriously, I don't know what I'm gonna do with y'all."

"There's a dead body in the supply closet," I told her.

"Of course there isn't a dead body in the closet," Tansy said. Maggie crossed her arms and smirked at me. "See?"

"Fine. You asked for it," I said. Don't get me wrong, Tansy and Maggie were my best friends. They would always be there for me, as I would for them. They brought out the best in me. And the worst. Sometimes at the same time. I turned the doorknob, pushed the door open, and stepped back.

My sisters gasped. "There's a dead body in the supply closet," Tansy said.

"Told ya."

CHAPTER 3

The three of us stared at the body in the supply closet.

There appeared to have been a struggle. The closet was in disarray. There was a pool of blood and a dead woman on the floor. Her long honey-blonde hair covered most of her face. I didn't recognize her. She was white, around twenty or so years old, and wore a white shirt and khaki pants with white tennis shoes—the generic uniform of a service-industry job. There was a bright orange canvas tote on the floor beside her. I tried to recall if I'd seen her during the party. I didn't think so, but I'd talked to so many people tonight.

"What's she holding?" Maggie asked. I wondered if she realized she was whispering.

I shivered and took a step back. I'd already seen quite enough, thank you very much.

"There's a piece of paper in her hand," Tansy agreed. "We should take a closer look."

None of us moved.

"At the very least, someone needs to call the cops," Tansy said.

I took another step back. At this rate, I would be in the alley before we came to a consensus.

"I'll call J.T. He'll know what to do," Maggie said. She'd

married John Taylor Taggart, J.T. to almost everyone, in college and helped put him through law school. He was now the go-to legal counsel for everyone in town. Most of his work came from civil cases. Despite our proximity to Austin, Cedar River wasn't exactly a hotbed of crime; it certainly wasn't known for having dead bodies in supply closets. "He's not answering." She stared down at her phone.

"Was he at the party?" I asked. "I don't remember seeing him tonight."

"He had to work late," she replied.

"Lucky for him." I looked at my sisters. "What are the chances that if we close the door and wish real hard, the, um, problem will go away?"

Tansy shook her head. "Oh, Juni." Always the responsible sister, she walked over to the checkout counter, lifted the shop phone, and dialed 911.

♪ ♫ ♪

Half an hour later, my sisters and I huddled together outside as the police ran yellow crime scene tape around Sip & Spin. Maggie shivered. Tansy took off the outer sweater half of her twinset and wrapped it around our sister.

Unlike my Texas-climatized sisters, I was used to the colder weather up north and barely noticed the unseasonable chill in the early-spring air. I was perfectly comfortable in my jeans, cowboy boots, and well-worn retro concert T-shirt. Tonight it was my favorite Nine Inch Nails shirt, advertising an album that had come out before I was born. The tee had originally belonged to my mother. She might not look like it these days in her sensible blouses and linen slacks, but she was quite the rocker back in her day.

In front of us, a steady stream of emergency personnel circulated through Sip & Spin Records. EMTs had gone in a while ago, but now they waited outside in the ambulance for the all clear from the crime scene techs. Despite the late hour, the sidewalk behind us was packed with people attracted to the sirens and flashing lights who wanted to get a glimpse of the action.

One thing I could say with certainty about small towns was we sure knew how to make our own entertainment.

Another thing about small towns was that everyone knew everyone. Especially if you'd lived there for generations. It seemed like every person, from the chief of police to the skinny photographer, nodded at us as they passed. "Tansy. Maggie. Juniper." In turn, we'd nod and return the greeting. Not even death was an excuse for bad manners, our mother always said. Although when she said that, she'd been talking about a goldfish. Not a murder scene.

Maggie groaned.

Automatically, I asked, "What's wrong?"

"What isn't wrong? The record shop, *our* record shop, is an active crime scene." She'd always been the most pessimistic of the three of us—although she preferred to call herself a realist—but I had to admit in this particular instance, she had a point.

"It's gonna be okay," I said, trying my best to reassure her.

"What if it's not?" Maggie asked. We stood in silence, letting the ramifications of that sink in. We'd invested an awful lot of money and hard work into the store.

Another police car pulled up. There were no spots left at the curb, so the driver simply parked in the middle of the street. It was angled so the ambulance could leave, but no more cars could navigate down Main Street. Which was fine. As far as I could tell, practically everyone in town was already here.

"Ladies," the latest arrival said, touching the brim of his police-issued cowboy hat.

Contrary to popular belief, not everyone who lived in Texas

owned a cowboy hat, but those of us who did never had just one. We had a formal cowboy hat. A casual cowboy hat. A working cowboy hat and a going-out cowboy hat. Some of us, like the white man standing in front of us now, even had an official uniform cowboy hat.

Beauregard Russell, or Detective Beauregard Russell, according to the badge clipped to a chain around his neck, was the One Who Got Away. Or, to be perfectly candid, the one who ripped my vulnerable young heart into itty-bitty pieces and then fed the pieces into an industrial shredder.

On either side of me, my sisters tensed, worried I was going to dissolve into a puddle of teenage angst. As if. I'd matured considerably since the last time I'd spent any real time in Cedar River, but I couldn't blame my family for not realizing that since I was only around for holidays. FaceTime was no substitute for sitting around a dinner table together every night.

My sisters had nothing to worry about. I was fine. Honest.

"Tansy," he said. His voice, his specific drawl, sent shivers all the way down to my toes. "Maggie." The pizza I'd scarfed down with Teddy did cartwheels in my stomach. "And unless my eyes deceive me, Miss Juniper Jessup."

Dark stubble shadowed his face. His big, dark eyes met mine and I was transported back in time to when I was very young, very naïve, and very much in love. "Beau," I said. My voice came out a lot steadier than I felt. Go, me!

I knew moving back to Cedar River meant bumping into Beau eventually. Frankly, I was surprised it had taken this long. But nothing had prepared me for running into my ex at a crime scene.

A Black woman in a uniform opened the door and poked her head outside. She was around my height, with broad shoulders and a no-nonsense expression. She oozed authority and her voice commanded attention. "Been waiting for you," she said to Beau. "What took you so dang long?"

"Hold your horses, Holt," Beau told her. Then he turned back to us. "Don't y'all go nowhere. I'll be needing to talk to y'all in a bit," he said. There were three of us there, but I felt like he was speaking to me specifically.

"We're not going anywhere," Tansy replied for all of us. When he was gone, she turned to me. "You okay, baby sis?"

"Yup," I assured her, nodding confidently. I'd gotten over Beau a long time ago. That was my story, and I was sticking to it. "Never better."

"That's our girl," Maggie said, squeezing my hand.

An increasingly chilly hour or so later, Beau reemerged with the female officer by his side. "Y'all can go home as soon as you give Officer Holt your contact info. I'll want to talk to each of you tomorrow."

"It *is* tomorrow," Tansy pointed out, tapping the delicate watch on her slender wrist. "Has been for quite some time."

"Go on home," he repeated.

She drew herself up to full height and put her fists on her hips. "We've got an awful lot of valuable merch inside, and if you think I'm gonna leave our shop unlocked overnight, you're sorely mistaken, Beauregard Russell."

Beau took his cowboy hat off and knocked it against his knee, as if to clear off imaginary dust, and flashed a grin at my older sister. His teeth were pearly white and laser straight. Forget the gun in his holster, that ridiculously handsome smile of his was his most dangerous weapon, and he knew it.

"Can I talk to Juni for a minute? Alone?" he asked.

"No," my sisters said in unison, edging forward to form a physical barrier between me and Beau. The only thing more overprotective than an older sister was *two* overprotective older sisters.

"Fine. Be that way. Any idea where I might find your uncle, Calvin Voigt?" He rubbed his forehead with the back of his hand before resettling his hat.

"At home. In bed. Asleep," Maggie suggested.

"He's not answering his phone."

"Why should he?" Tansy asked. "It's the middle of the night. And what's he got to do with anything, anyway?"

"Need to have a few words with the man. Odd that he's not here."

Tansy glanced down at her watch again. She was one of the few people I knew who still wore a watch that didn't double as a heart monitor, step counter, and social media tracker. "You're surprised that a sixty-something-year-old man isn't standing around in his nightie on Main Street at two a.m.?"

"Everyone else is," Beau said, gesturing to the crowd behind us. It had thinned out considerably as people got tired, bored, or cold and wandered home after making their neighbors swear to call them if anything interesting happened. "Why isn't Calvin?"

Tansy shrugged. "You'll have to ask him." She glanced around at the gathered townspeople. "I'm sure I could name a number of others who aren't here, either." She turned her attention to us. "Maggie, we don't all need to stick around. Mind dropping Juni off on your way home? I'll stay and lock up."

Of course she would. Tansy was the responsible one. Maggie was the organized one. I was, well, I wasn't 100 percent sure what I was. The tired one, tonight. "Yeah, that sounds like a plan," I agreed.

Beau nodded and returned to the shop. *Our* shop. Maggie and I started to leave, but Officer Holt stopped us. "Ladies, I'm gonna need a few things from you first."

Maggie's shoulders slumped. "Yeah, sure. Sorry. It's been a long night."

"I know what you mean," she replied. The officer turned to me. "Jayden Holt. I don't believe we've met. You're the youngest Jessup sister, aren't you?"

"Sure am. Juniper. Juni." I gave her my cell number and she

wrote it down. "And thanks for coming out here in the middle of the night to take care of all this."

"Just doing my job."

After Maggie gave her contact information to the officer, we got into the car and carefully navigated our way away from the crowded street. "She seems nice," I said.

"Who, Jayden? She sure is. Smart as a tack and twice as tough. When she first came to town, I thought for certain the good ol' boys in the Cedar River Police Department were gonna have her for breakfast, but turns out she's got things under control."

"Good for her." I liked women who stood up for themselves. Coming from the IT industry, I knew what it was like to be outnumbered in a male-dominated profession. I respected her instantly.

"J.T. has gone up against her in court a few times. Lost because of her testimony every time. She's good."

J.T., my brother-in-law, was tough and almost as competitive as Tansy. It was hard to imagine him losing, much less losing gracefully. After he finished law school, he could have gone anywhere, but he and Maggie settled back in Cedar River, where he hung out his shingle. Most of his practice revolved around writing wills, settling land disputes, and defending folks in traffic court. It might not have been as glamorous as being in a big-name practice in the city, but it was enough to pay for the Lexus we were riding around in tonight.

Maggie headed toward Tansy's house, where I was staying in one of her spare rooms. Living under my sister's roof after being on my own for so long took some getting used to, but we all agreed it was for the best. It kept money in the shop rather than wasting it on rent when there was a free place for me to live.

My oldest sister never had much use for boyfriends. Every-one tripped all over themselves vying for her attention, but she never gave them the time of day. Her buying a house of her own as a single, independent woman was a loud and clear declara-tion that she was going to live life on her own terms. What could I say? Tansy was the bomb.

Then Dad died. Mom rattled around that old ranch-style house we'd all grown up in, complaining about being lonely until Tansy practically begged her to move in with her. And now I'd come back home, too.

Tansy's house had a detached mother-in-law cottage around the side of the house where Mom stayed, and thank good-ness for that. After living on my own, I didn't think I could have handled sharing a bathroom with anyone, especially my mother. Sharing a living space with my sister was enough of a readjustment.

Nestled in the foothills of Central Texas, Cedar River was a small town, and it was shrinking every day as nearby Austin kept pressing against its borders and swallowing up its neigh-bors. Main Street ran straight through downtown, with side streets and neighborhoods blossoming off it like a dandelion gone to seed. With the river—raging this time of year, but it would be dry as a bone in a few months—to the east and rocky hill country to the west, Main was the only way in and out of town unless you had a horse or a four-wheeler. And what self-respecting Texan didn't have one or the other?

Okay, technically I had neither, but I had a trike. That had to count for something.

Maggie wound her car through the maze of streets toward Tansy's neighborhood in the southeast. Working-class fami-lies lived here in solid brick one-story two- and three-bedroom homes with dirty trucks and sun-bleached cars parked in the driveway or under rickety carports. Many of these houses had once had garages, but they'd long ago been converted to extra bedrooms or game rooms for families looking to escape the brutal Texas summer when going outside for longer than it took to check the mail was unbearable.

We passed my uncle's house. It was dark, which was to be expected. It was, after all, an unreasonable hour of the morning. His car, an aging Bronco with enormous tires and mismatched paint on the doors, was parked in the driveway. "Wait. Go back," I told Maggie.

She yawned. "You're gonna wake Uncle Calvin up in the middle of the night to tell him the cops want to talk with him? You trying to give him another heart attack?"

"Just go back. Please?"

There was no one around, but instead of reversing down the street, Maggie made a clean three-point turn and headed back to our uncle's house. She turned off her headlights as she pulled into the driveway so they didn't shine through the front windows.

I hopped out and hurried to his front door. I knocked. Nothing. Pounded on the door. Rang the doorbell. Nothing. I pulled out my phone and called him. It went to voicemail. I turned toward Maggie's car and shrugged as I got back in. "He's always been a sound sleeper," I said, buckling my seat belt.

"Not that sound," she said with a frown.

"He could've had one too many at the party," I suggested.

"Maybe." Maggie drove me the remaining three blocks to Tansy's house. The front porch light was on. Mom's little cottage was dark.

"Thanks for the lift." I unbuckled my seat belt and stretched across the seat to give her a quick hug. There were times I wished I had a car, but it really was an unnecessary expenditure, at least until our record shop took off. I could have walked home from the store if I'd wanted to—it wasn't far—but I was tired and appreciated the ride. Besides, the coyotes always came out this time of night. They wouldn't attack a grown adult, but it was still spooky when they stalked me from the shadows. Another thing I'd almost forgotten about Texas living.

I let myself inside and headed for my room, where I collapsed facedown into my bed. It had been a long day. I kicked off my shoes but didn't bother getting undressed. I blinked, and the next thing I knew, sunlight was streaming in through my window and my cell phone was jangling and bouncing on the pillow beside my head.

CHAPTER 4

I blinked the sleep out of my eyes and reached for my phone before it could dump the caller into voicemail. "'Lo?" I asked. My throat was dry and a little sore, probably from being up too late and talking to so many people yesterday. I missed the days of staying out with my friends until the wee hours and still getting up for work a few hours later all bright-eyed and alert. Lately, it took two cups of coffee and a cattle prod just to get me going in the morning.

"Where's your uncle?" a man's voice on the other end of the phone asked.

I pulled the phone away and glanced at the caller ID. It was fuzzy. I put on my glasses and still didn't recognize the number. "Who's this?"

"You know who this is, Juni," he said.

There was something about the familiar mixture of exasperation and good-natured humor that clicked into place. I'd deleted his number from my contacts ages ago, but I knew that voice. "Beau."

"Who else were you expecting?" he asked.

"I don't know, literally anyone else?" I sat on the edge of the bed. After six years of radio silence following the abrupt end to our relationship, it seemed surreal to be casually chatting with

Beau on the phone as if nothing had ever happened. Although, come to think of it, there was probably nothing casual about it. This wasn't the same as getting a Facebook friend request from a long-ago ex. He was calling about a murder investigation.

Not exactly something I had on this year's bingo card.

I sat up in bed and shielded my eyes. My sister's guest bedroom was decorated very much like her childhood bedroom had been. Frilly bedspread on a four-poster bed. Pink floral wallpaper. A shelf along the wall displayed beauty pageant trophies and crowns. Sheer lacy curtains that did nothing to block out the morning sun hung in the window.

I'd been home almost a month, but the closest thing I'd done to putting my own touch on the room was spreading the contents of my suitcases across every surface, even the rattan vanity in the corner. I stood and staggered over to the mirror. My eyes were bloodshot. My hair was plastered to my head on one side and frizzed on the other. I pinned my phone between my chin and my shoulder as I removed one of the ever-present hairbands from my wrist and pulled the whole lot of it up into a messy bun.

"Juni? You still with me?"

"I'm here. If you're calling about Uncle Calvin, I have no idea where he's at. We stopped by his house on the way home last night. His truck was in the driveway, but he didn't answer the door."

"And you don't think that's a little weird?"

"Not as weird as you calling me at this unearthly hour of the morning." It had been, at most, four hours since I got home, and Beau was still at the record shop when we left. "Did you get any sleep at all?"

He laughed. "Nah. But thanks for asking. You always did look out for me." He lowered his voice. "Listen, Juni, this is important. I need to talk to your uncle. ASAP."

"Why? What's the big deal?" Someone started pounding on the front door and then rang the doorbell several times in quick succession. "Hold on." I padded barefoot down the hall as the knocking grew louder. At this rate, whoever was at the door was gonna wake my sister *and* the neighbors. I threw the door open. "Sheesh. Do you know what time it is?"

Beau leaned against the doorframe, grinning. His stubble was thicker than I ever remembered seeing it before, and he had shadows under his eyes. He'd had a long night. We all had. "Well? You fixin' to invite me in or what?"

I hung up my phone and opened the door wider. Without extending a formal welcome, I headed toward the kitchen. I heard Beau knock the dirt off his cowboy boots on the threshold and close the door after himself.

There was a yellow sticky note on the coffeemaker. "Don't talk to the cops without J.T. present," it read, in my sister's handwriting.

It was too late for that, but I could at least try to follow instructions. I texted my brother-in-law: "Beau Russell's in my kitchen, asking questions."

I started a fresh pot of coffee and pulled two mugs out of the cabinet. My sister had the cutest mug collection. Today I chose one covered in dancing giraffes and another that looked plain white but once filled with hot coffee would undoubtedly sport a funny saying. "What's so important that it couldn't wait until after breakfast?" I asked, turning to see that Beau had made himself at home at Tansy's kitchen table. Behind me, the coffeemaker gurgled and let out a whiff of divinity. I breathed deeply, hoping I could get a caffeine hit off the scent alone.

"I need to talk to your uncle."

"So you said." It was oddly familiar, the way that Beau and I fell back into a domestic routine as if we'd never been apart. We'd had plans to get a place together once upon a time, but that had been a lifetime ago.

"The dead woman, the one from your store, she was holding Calvin's business card."

I shivered at the memory. It was weird that the dead woman had my uncle's card, granted, but it wasn't exactly a smoking gun. "Calvin and Mom are both silent partners at Sip & Spin." Not that my mother was ever silent about anything. So far, she'd been content to let my sisters and me make all the decisions, but I doubted that would last long. Although, to be fair, she had more experience running a record shop than we did and we'd be wise to listen to her. "We all had a bunch of business cards made up. We were passing them out like candy last night."

"This wasn't a Sip & Spin Records business card," Beau said. "It's an older one. His number was crossed out and rewritten in pen." He pulled a plastic evidence bag out of his pocket and laid it on the table where I could see it. The business card was worn around the edges. I recognized the Prankenstein, Inc., logo. Before Calvin had abruptly quit a few weeks ago, he'd run an online prank store with his friend/business partner, Samuel Davis. Last I heard, Samuel was still sending anonymous gag gifts to anywhere in the U.S. The most popular item was a glitter bomb, which had been my uncle's evil idea.

If I was being 100 percent honest with myself, I'd have to admit that while Calvin had a big heart, his moral compass wasn't screwed down as tight as it could have been. The prank store had been a perfect outlet for him where he could straddle a fuzzy line between right and wrong. I was as surprised as anyone when he walked away, leaving his brainchild in Samuel's capable hands.

"That Calvin's handwriting?" Beau asked, pointing to the number written in ink.

"Could be. Hard to tell." I couldn't remember the last time I'd exchanged written correspondence with my uncle outside of emails or text messages. I used my camera phone to zoom in and snapped a picture so I could look at it closer. "Maybe."

My phone rang. According to the screen, it was my brother-in-law, J.T. I picked up. "Morning."

"I know you're not talking to the cops without me present, are you?"

"Who is it?" Beau asked.

"My lawyer," I replied.

"Put him on speakerphone," Beau said in one ear as J.T. said, "Put me on speakerphone," in the other. I put the phone on speakerphone and set it down on the table.

"Morning, J.T.," Beau said.

"My client's not going to say another word to you. If you want to question Juniper, or anyone in the family, you can call me and I'll arrange a sit-down at my office." I didn't know if my brother-in-law's law firm had ever handled a case with stakes higher than a parking ticket before, but I knew I'd do well to heed his advice.

"I got all I need for now anyways," Beau said, standing and stretching before gathering up the business card. "Any chance I could get that coffee in a to-go mug?"

"Don't forget to bring it back," I said as I poured his drink into a travel mug, which was plastered with stickers from local Austin bands, only half of which I recognized. I added sugar and cream just like he liked it, and handed it to him.

"I'm gonna need you to get ahold of your uncle and tell him I want to talk to him. J.T., you're welcome to be present, but I'll tell you what, if I have to go chasing him down, it won't look good for him."

"We hear you," I said, disconnecting the speakerphone. I made a shooing motion at Beau. "Now get out of here."

"I hope we're gonna be seeing a lot more of each other, now that you're back in town."

I took a second to think about that. There had been a time

when I thought I couldn't live without Beau Russell in my life. But if the last six years had taught me anything, it was that I could. I shrugged. "Maybe. We'll see."

He grinned like someone had just handed him a winning scratch-off lotto ticket. "Ain't no maybe about it."

I fought the urge to return his grin. Beau was self-confident enough without me encouraging him. Besides, I hadn't had a chance to brush my teeth yet, much less reexamine ancient history. "Don't get your hopes up," I said, walking him to the door.

"You can't avoid me forever, Junebug."

"I'm not avoiding you. And don't call me Junebug." I closed the door. I watched until he got in his car and drove away.

What I really wanted to do was go back to my room, toss a sheet over the curtain rods to block out some of the light streaming in through the windows, and try to get a few more hours of sleep. Instead, I went to the kitchen and popped a slice of bread into the toaster. Once it was ready, I sat at the kitchen table sipping my coffee—delicious!—and nibbling my breakfast, but I couldn't put yesterday's bizarre events out of my head.

Even though I was the one who had found the body, in my own store, I knew very little about what was happening. I hadn't recognized the dead person, but when I closed my eyes I could picture her. She was in her late teens or early twenties. That meant she hadn't been much more than a kid when I'd left Cedar River, assuming she was a local. She was dressed like she was going to work instead of a party. I wished I'd thought to ask Beau what her name was. Now I'd have to talk to him again to get it and I wasn't a hundred percent sure how I felt about that.

To keep from thinking about Beau, I decided to review what I did know. My sister Maggie was fastidiously neat, but the supply closet had been a complete mess. There had to have been a struggle. I didn't remember hearing anything, but the party had been loud and I'd stepped out for a minute with Teddy. I'd noticed a pool of blood on the floor near the woman's head, but there was no wound that I could see. I shook myself to clear the image out of my head and mentally focused on her hands instead.

Why was she holding my uncle's business card when she died? It was certainly his phone number. It might have been his handwriting; it might not have been. It was hard to tell with numbers. At least I'd snapped a picture of it.

How on earth was Uncle Calvin involved in any of this? Where'd he go after the party? And where was he now? I tried his cell phone again. It went to voicemail like it had last night.

And why did the woman have to die in Sip & Spin Records? There'd been so many people in and out of the store during the grand reopening I couldn't even begin to list everyone who'd attended, but it was a very public place for such a private act. Between the music and the crowd, it was loud, but loud enough to cover the sounds of a murder? All I knew for sure was that there hadn't been a dead body in the supply closet before the party and there was one after.

I needed to talk to my uncle.

I could have woken my sister and asked to borrow her car. The keys were hanging on a hook next to the front door. I could have taken her car without permission and it probably wouldn't have bothered her, but I didn't feel right about that. In the end, I decided to throw on clean clothes and ride my trike to my uncle's house, since it was only a few blocks away.

When I got there, two police cruisers were parked out front. Jayden Holt, the officer I'd met last night, was escorting my uncle out the front door. He was in handcuffs.

Despite the early hour, his neighbors were milling about on their front lawns watching the show. Even Miss Edie was there, with a little beige dog with a curly tail on a pink leash.

At least Miss Edie had the common decency to pretend to be walking her dog, unlike the other lookie-loos. When I was younger, her front yard looked like a playground with scattered toys all over the grass and porch. That much hadn't changed. I didn't know how she found energy at her age to be the neighborhood busybody and still watch over half the kids in town, but I guess that's the power of multitasking.

Unlike Edie, the neighbor to Calvin's left had abandoned all pretense and had dragged a lawn chair out so he could see everything in comfort while he sipped his morning coffee. I was surprised no one had their phones out to record the scene and post it on the internet later, but then again, Calvin was one of the youngest people on the block and most of his neighbors were more likely to have flip phones than TikTok accounts.

I jumped the curb and rode my trike up onto the lawn, where I left it on a scrubby patch of dry grass—chores dealing with external appearances like lawn care weren't high on Calvin's to-do list. "Stop that! What's going on? Where are you taking him?" I asked as I hurried toward my uncle.

"Juni! They're arresting me!"

"I can see that." I pulled out my phone and called J.T., who answered on the first ring. "They're arresting Calvin," I said.

"Tell him to keep his trap shut. We'll see him at the station," my brother-in-law replied.

"J.T. says not to say anything until he gets there," I relayed the message to my uncle.

"I didn't do nothing!"

"I know that, Uncle Calvin, but don't say anything else, okay? Please?"

He scowled and nodded.

"Why are you arresting him?" I asked Jayden, trying to stay calm.

"Talk to the boss," she said, nodding toward the open door as she guided Calvin into the back of her patrol car.

"Thanks." I hurried into the house. Beau was standing in front of the long, low credenza my uncle emptied his pockets onto whenever he came into the house. He was rifling through the drawers, which I knew held light bulbs, paper clips, screwdrivers, and other such items that tended to accumulate in odd spots when you lived somewhere long enough. "You don't have permission to do that," I said.

I felt betrayed. Not even half an hour ago Beau had been sitting in my kitchen telling me he wanted just to talk to my uncle. He must have come straight here afterward, which meant he already had an arrest warrant when he showed up at Tansy's house to bum a coffee. In any event, he didn't have the right to rummage through Calvin's stuff.

"I'm sorry; I really am. I tried to do things the easy way."

I took out my phone and snapped a photo of Beau standing next to the open drawer, holding a stack of unopened mail. "That's not in plain sight. You need to get out of here and come back with a proper search warrant."

"Suit yourself." Beau set the letters down and scooped up the key ring.

I held out my hand. "You'll be giving me those."

He frowned at me. "Just need them to lock up. You wouldn't want anything bad happening to your uncle's house while he's in custody, would you?"

"I'll lock up," I said between gritted teeth. Once upon a time, I would have trusted Beau with my life, but I hardly recognized the man standing in front of me. It was bad enough that he hadn't warned me that he was planning on arresting my uncle. If I hadn't shown up when I did, would he have gone through Calvin's unopened mail without just cause? I liked to hope he wasn't that kind of cop, but I was starting to think otherwise.

He tossed me the heavy key ring. "Sure thing. You know

me. I'll see to it that Calvin gets a fair shake. I tried to talk to him, didn't I? Thought it'd go easier if he turned himself in."

"Turn himself in for what? He didn't do anything," I insisted, outraged at Beau's implication. I knew my uncle. He played fast and loose with the legal gray areas that he didn't necessarily agree with. He would bend the law in a heartbeat, but he wouldn't break it, not when it counted.

"It just so happens that your uncle has a substantial amount of unpaid moving violations and has had a bench warrant out for his arrest for three months."

"Oh, you've got to be kidding me. That's what this is all about? Outstanding speeding tickets?"

Beau had the decency to look sheepish. "I need to question him, and he's dodging me. You understand. This isn't personal."

I shook my head. "I most certainly do not understand, and it feels pretty personal if you ask me." I folded my arms over my chest.

He sighed. "We'll get this cleared up and I'll have him home in time for lunch. Look, Juni, it's long past time we clear the air between us. What do you say to dinner tonight?"

"Beauregard Russell, you're out of your stinkin' mind. You just arrested my uncle for a bunch of unpaid traffic tickets. And now you want to, what, take me on a date?"

"Can we just start over, Junebug?"

I blinked at him. "Start over? Seriously? When you dump your girlfriend with a text message, you don't get a do-over just because you decide the statute of limitations has expired." I took a deep breath and reminded myself that this was *not* the time for this conversation. "You're not to talk to Uncle Calvin without his lawyer present. And stop calling me that."

He winked at me. "Whatever you say, Junebug." He brushed past me, out into the sunshine. I made sure that the lights were off and nothing was on the stove before locking up and heading back to Tansy's, where I hung Calvin's keys on a hook next to the front door.

My sister was awake when I got back to her house. She was pacing around the kitchen wearing a long yellow robe, looking more frazzled than I could remember seeing her before. Even when we were kids, Tansy was the stoic one, the one who never needed a nightlight like Maggie and never got into fights on the playground like me. "Have you heard? They arrested Uncle Calvin," she said.

"I know. I was there when it happened."

"What are we gonna do?" she asked.

I shook my head. In any other circumstance, I would say we let the police do their job. That was what they were there for. But I wasn't confident with Beau in charge. He could have warned me that he was going to arrest Calvin if I couldn't get him on the phone, but he didn't. If I hadn't shown up when I had and interrupted him, would he have conducted an illegal search?

Taking Cedar River High's football team to state finals two years in a row might have made him a hometown hero, but if Beau had turned into the kind of cop who cut corners and railroaded innocent people I couldn't trust him to do the right thing. Besides, what did he know about leading a murder investigation? The most exciting thing to ever happen for Cedar River P.D. was a string of B and Es a few years ago, and if memory served, they'd needed help from the State Police to solve those.

With my uncle's future in jeopardy and a killer on the loose, the stakes were too high to sit back and hope for the best. "I don't know. But we may need to take matters into our own hands."

CHAPTER 5

Tansy and I stared at each other over the table. She broke the silence first. "You're kidding, right? We're not going to interfere with a police investigation."

"Who said interfere?" I asked. "I didn't say interfere. You didn't say interfere. Well, you kinda did, just now. And me, too, just now, I guess, but you know what I mean."

"Yeah, I know what you mean." Tansy checked her phone. She must not have seen anything interesting, because she turned it facedown on the table. "Juni, I know you mean well, but we are possibly the only people in Texas less equipped than Beau to solve a murder. We could hire someone. A P.I. maybe."

"With what money?" I countered. Every penny I had was invested in the shop. I didn't know how Maggie was doing, but Tansy barely had enough to cover her mortgage and car payment.

Tansy nodded reluctantly. "If there's one thing I know, it's that Uncle Calvin didn't kill that poor girl. The police will figure that out soon enough."

"Yeah, totally," I said, every bit as sarcastic as my teenage self would have been. "Which is why there's not a single innocent person sitting in jail right now." I rested my elbows on the table and leaned forward. "We've gotta do something. Anything."

"We *are* doing something." She tapped her phone with one long, perfect fingernail. "We're waiting to hear back from J.T. With him and Elroy on the case, Calvin has the best lawyers in Cedar River." Elroy was J.T.'s old frat brother and current law partner. And other than our brother-in-law, he was the *only* lawyer in Cedar River.

I stood and pushed the kitchen chair back under the table.

"Where are you going?" she asked.

"I don't know. I'll have my phone on me. Call me if anything happens." I let myself out the front door and got on my trike, hoping a bit of exercise would help clear my head.

I saw movement behind the window of the guest cottage, presumably my mother looking out at me. I waved; then I got on my low-slung tricycle and took off down the street, eager for some time to myself.

Cedar River might be a small town by any standards, but it wasn't without entertainment. There was the river. The shops on Main. The foothills. And everything in between. Who was I kidding? There was nothing to do in this town.

Almost as if I was drawn there magnetically, I found myself cruising toward Sip & Spin Records. My middle sister must have had the same idea, because her car was parked at the curb. She was sitting on the front stoop, drinking from a reusable water bottle. Daffy the cat was curled up in her lap, rubbing his head against her hand. I hopped my trike over the curb and dismounted. At least I had someone to talk to now.

"What are you doing here?" Maggie asked.

It was a Saturday morning. I was wearing a vintage B-52's concert shirt with denim shorts. I'd planned to wear it on my first official day at work, but with the record shop closed, I had no plans. "Looking for a distraction while we wait for your husband to save the day. You?"

"I thought I'd finish cleaning up." She waved her hand at the front door. There was a bright yellow sticker covering the lock. I leaned in to read it.

"We're not allowed inside. Not until the police release the scene," she summarized for me.

I sat down next to her and rested my head on her shoulder. I reached over to pet the cat and was rewarded with a loud purr. "If it would make you feel better, we can sneak in, clean, and then reseal the door when we're done," I offered.

Knowing I was joking, Maggie smiled. "You'd do that with me?"

"Of course."

"You just want Beau to show up and handcuff you."

"I do not," I said, a little too emphatically. Maggie twisted away from me, startling Daffy. He hopped off her lap, gave her an angry glare, and proceeded to groom himself. I straightened. "What?"

"Oh my gosh. You still like him. After all this time. After what he did to you."

"I most certainly do not." I'd admit I might have felt *something* when I saw him last night, but I'd just scarfed down two greasy slices of pizza, so it was probably just heartburn. It was annoying enough how he'd shown up unannounced this morning and made himself at home, but then he went and arrested my uncle on trumped-up charges instead of just talking to him. I'd forgotten how infuriating he could get, but there was a nagging voice in the back of my head that wondered if Beau might be onto something. "You don't think Uncle Calvin . . ." My voice faded away.

"Absolutely not," Maggie said with certainty.

"Beau said he just wanted to talk to him because the victim was holding his business card. Then they went and arrested him on bogus traffic tickets. They had a warrant, Maggie." I shook my head. "It doesn't smell right."

"You're afraid just because Cedar River is a little hick town filled with hick town cops that they're gonna try to railroad Calvin into taking the fall?"

"Yeah," I admitted. It still bothered me that Beau had been rifling through Calvin's credenza when I interrupted him. What had he hoped to find? "I just have a bad feeling, that's all. Is that silly?"

"Not even a little bit." She dug through her purse and pulled out a small spiral-bound notebook and a purple gel pen. She flipped past grocery lists and what looked like a handwritten softball or volleyball schedule. Either was equally likely.

My sisters both got the sporty gene from our dad. Tansy preferred solo events where she was going up against the only person she thought was worthy competition—herself. She ran 5Ks for fun and completed at least one marathon a year. Right now, she was training for a triathlon. Her bicycle looked like something from outer space compared to my well-loved trike.

Maggie liked teams. Volleyball. Softball. Soccer. Bowling. If it had uniforms, she played it or watched it. Maggie was a joiner, like Mom.

I liked sports, too. Spelling bee was a sport, right? They aired it on ESPN, so it must be.

"What are we doing?" I asked.

"What does it look like we're doing? We're making a list. We're gonna solve the murder and clear Uncle Calvin's name," Maggie replied, voice as firm as ever.

I chuckled. While I was away, I'd almost forgotten the little things that made my sisters unique. Like the way that Tansy still used her Little Miss Texas smile even though she'd gotten out of the beauty pageant circuit decades ago, or how much Maggie liked lists. "I'd like to hear Calvin's side of the story, but there's no telling when he'll be released," I said. "In the meantime, where do we start?"

She blinked at me. "Guests? Timeline? Motives for murder?"

"Guests," I agreed. "But there were so many people at the party. It might be easier to list the people who weren't there. Like J.T."

"And Beau," she pointed out.

Come to think of it, that *was* odd. This morning, Beau had accused me of avoiding him, but he hadn't been at the grand opening. Surely, he had to have known about it. It was all anyone in town had talked about all week. We'd posted flyers in all the windows of the shops downtown. I hired Roadrunners, the local delivery service, to include our flyers with their deliveries. Mom had made an announcement at every club, group, and organization she was a member of—which was plenty. I even posted on the Cedar River Nextdoor and Facebook groups.

Beau would have had to be hiding under a rock to have not known about the party, which was interesting but not very helpful.

"Seriously, Maggie, there were over a hundred people at the party. I talked to lots of folks, some I don't even know. We were there. Mom. Uncle Calvin. I saw his old business partner, Samuel Davis. I talked to Miss Edie, Jen Rachet, and the lady who used to own the ice-cream parlor . . ."

"Martha," Maggie supplied helpfully.

I nodded. "And her oldest daughter. Joy Akers with there with her husband. I saw Sue that used to live down the street from us and Teddy Garza, for starters." Maggie scribbled furiously, trying to keep up with me, but it was useless. Even if she could write as quick as I could talk, off the top of my head I could barely name a dozen of the partygoers. "What about the security system? Surely we got plenty of footage."

"Assuming the police didn't take it last night. Besides"— Maggie gestured at the Sip & Spin door—"we're locked out." She scribbled a few more names in the notebook. "You know what the real problem is, don't you? These are our friends. Our neighbors. Our family. People we've known for most of our lives. Do you really think someone from Cedar River is capable of murder?"

"Anyone is capable, I suppose," I mused. Trying to lighten the mood, I added, "I seem to remember a time or two growing up that I thought you might murder me."

"That's different. You were a real brat that never did learn to stay out of my side of the room." She chuckled. "Remember that time that you took all of Tansy's expensive pageant makeup and mixed it all together with orange juice to make muffins?"

"It wasn't muffins. It was unicorn cakes," I corrected her. "And man, they tasted awful."

"I don't think you're supposed to eat makeup."

"I don't suppose you should," I agreed. It was nothing short of a miracle that my sisters and I got along now as well as we did. Tansy and Maggie were only two years apart, right at that sweet spot that all the baby books recommended. I came along as a surprise five years later. It was one thing to drag your infant sister to show-and-tell at school but another thing completely when I was old enough to follow them around, and I followed them *everywhere*. I was still in junior high when my sisters were both off in college dorm rooms.

And can you believe that as much as we looked alike, *neither* of them would loan me her driver's license to get me into the cool concerts in Austin? Rude.

"Thanks," I said.

"For what?"

"For being on the same wavelength. Tansy seemed to think we should sit back and hope for the best."

"Are you kidding me? My husband's a lawyer. J.T.'s always complaining about cops taking shortcuts. We're not gonna let it happen this time, not to Calvin."

"No, we're not," I agreed.

Maggie's phone buzzed. She checked the screen. "We're needed at the courthouse." She got up, dusted off her skirt, and offered me a hand.

"What does that mean? Surely they questioned Calvin and now they're letting him go, right? Maybe he just needs a lift home?"

"I doubt it. J.T. could drive him home if that was the case. I have a bad feeling about this, Juni."

♪ ♫ ♪

I hated it when my sister was right.

J.T. and his partner, Elroy McGibbons, met us outside the courthouse. Elroy was a lanky beanpole in his thirties with ruddy cheeks and slicked-back hair. Today he was in an expensive-looking suit. In contrast, my brother-in-law was in slacks and a blue polo shirt—not exactly standard courthouse attire, not even on a Saturday.

"Elroy," Maggie said, but there was confusion in her voice.

He tipped an imaginary cowboy hat in our direction. "Maggie. Juniper."

"I asked Elroy to take the lead, so there wouldn't be any conflict of interest," J.T. explained. "If I represent family in court, it looks wonky, but if my partner does it, it's all aboveboard."

"Oh. That makes sense," Maggie said, sounding relieved. "Where's Calvin?"

"Well, that's gonna be a problem," Elroy said. "We sat down as asked and answered Detective Russell's questions. Didn't hold anything back. Was kinda expecting leniency for his cooperation, but the on-call judge declined to release Mr. Voigt on his own recognizance."

"What does that mean?" I asked. "In English, please."

J.T. interpreted. "Beau said your uncle would get off easy about the tickets if he played ball. Calvin held up his end of the bargain. But the judge won't cut him loose."

"That rat fink," Maggie fumed. "I've got a few choice words I'd like to say to Beauregard Russell."

"Hold your horses, Mags," J.T. said, touching her elbow gently. "Beau did put in a good word, but your uncle has quite a lot of unpaid moving violations."

"How much is a lot? No way is the judge going to make a sixty-something-year-old upstanding citizen with strong ties to the community spend the night in jail over a few measly tickets." To be honest, Calvin wasn't exactly textbook upstanding, but he wasn't a hardened criminal, either. "Can we just pay the fine and bring him home?" A voice in my head whispered that I didn't have even a few measly dollars. Until the record shop started turning a profit, I was going to have to rely on the generosity of my family or go hungry.

"You got sixteen hundred dollars lying around, Juni?"

I goggled at Elroy. "For speeding tickets?"

"Speeding tickets. Parking tickets. Driving distracted. Late fees. Service charges. Court costs. Legal representation." At least Elroy had the good sense to look sheepish at the last bit. "Plus, he was driving without a valid license with no insurance. It adds up."

"Is there some kind of payment plan?" Maggie asked.

"He's gonna be sitting in jail for fifteen days, and when he gets out, he still is going to owe everything, plus another fifteen days' worth of interest," J.T. explained.

"That's not fair," I said. "How can he pay the tickets when he's in jail because he hasn't paid the tickets?"

"Oh, he's not in jail for the tickets. He mouthed off to the judge," Elroy added.

"Now *that* sounds like Calvin," Maggie said. I nodded my head in agreement. Our uncle called himself a free spirit, but "scofflaw" was more accurate. This wasn't the first time that his temper had landed him in trouble, and it probably wouldn't be the last. My sister let out a long-suffering sigh. "What are we going to do?"

"You could bail him out," Elroy suggested.

"With what money? Everything we have is in the record shop," Maggie said.

I blinked at her. "I thought y'all were doing well?" She was driving around in a leased Lexus and her husband had his Beemer. No offense to my wonderful trike, but we weren't exactly in the same tax bracket.

"We are. We were. We, um . . . ," Maggie hedged.

J.T. finished for her. "Elroy and I bought out our third partner recently. What with the shop opening and all, times are a little lean, that's all."

"Mom, then. She used what was left over from Dad's life insurance to invest in Sip & Spin, but what about the house? She had to have made a pretty penny when she sold."

Maggie grimaced. "You'd think, but between a second mortgage, what it cost to fix the place up before putting it on the market, and back taxes she hadn't paid because Dad always took care of such things, there wasn't much left over. Maybe if she'd held on to it a little longer, it would be a different story." She shrugged. "I'm surprised she didn't have to pay someone to take it off her hands."

I took a deep breath. "That just leaves the shop."

There were nods all around. Apparently, I wasn't the only one to come to that conclusion. The only way to secure bail for our uncle was by putting Sip & Spin Records up for collateral.

"We need to call Tansy and make sure she's on board, but yeah," Maggie said.

We called our sister, who came downtown to join us. The three of us, with our two lawyers in tow, headed to the bail bonds office to get Calvin released. An hour later, he was a free man. We offered him a lift home, but he said he'd rather walk to clear his head.

I didn't blame him. I could use some head clearing myself, but instead of a healthy walk, I choose candy therapy. After the morning's drama, the siren song of the Sweet Shoppe on Main was calling my name. I was standing in front of the self-serve candy trying to decide between chocolate malted balls and something called Unicorn Poop when Beau burst into the store. "Had a feeling I'd find you here," he said.

I glanced around, hoping that maybe he was talking to someone else. No such luck. The only thing near me was a lollipop almost as tall as I was, the kind with a big circular swirl of bright colors mounted on a round stick. It was probably about as old as I was, too. I wondered about the expiration date on giant novelty lollipops. I rapped the hard sugar and it responded with a hollow thud. How about that? In all this time, I'd never realized that of course it was made of resin instead of sugar. Sure, five-year-old me would have been fooled, but twenty-eight-year-old me should have known better.

"If you're done assaulting the lollipop, we need to talk," Beau said.

"How'd you know I'd be here?"

He gestured at the floor-to-ceiling shelves of decadent treats. "I know you, Junebug. You've got a sweet tooth."

"I do not," I argued. Although, to be completely fair, he wasn't wrong. "If this is about us . . ."

He cut me off. "It's about your uncle. And before you tell me to talk to your lawyers, I wanted to give you a heads-up. For old times' sake."

"Oh yeah?" I raised my eyebrows. I wasn't sure how much that was worth. Old times' sake hadn't kept him from arresting Calvin in the first place. "I'm listening."

"He's gone. Disappeared."

I couldn't believe my ears. "He what?"

"He jumped bail."

"This isn't funny. And it's nonsense. How can he have violated the terms of his release when he's not even due back in court for weeks?"

Beau took the empty candy bag from me, partially filled it with blue jellybeans—my favorite—popped two in his mouth, and handed it back to me. "Few years ago, the department spent their end-of-year surplus on ankle monitors." He gestured around at the Sweet Shoppe, which was a throwback to a simpler time. "Crime in Cedar River being what it is, we don't have a lot of need for them, so the judge likes to use them whenever she can. Put one on your uncle. He hadn't had it fifteen minutes before he ditched it in the middle of the street, halfway between the courthouse and his house."

"He wouldn't do something like that," I insisted. Thumb his nose at the rules? Absolutely. Actually breaking the law? Not so much.

Beau shook his head. "We both know that's not true. As soon as he removed the monitor it set off all sorts of alarms, and now every officer in Travis County has a BOLO for him. It doesn't look good for your uncle, Juni."

"I'm sure this is all a misunderstanding. You know Calvin; he's probably at the track right now, betting on a sure thing so he can pay off his tickets." Not that it would help him get out of this situation, I reminded myself. Calvin's luck generally ran toward the bad kind. Which was, as I thought about it, why he was in this situation in the first place.

"It's not about the tickets anymore." He lowered his voice. "Is there someplace we can go to talk?"

I hadn't realized it until then, but everyone in the store was staring at us. It was a gorgeous Saturday afternoon, and the Sweet Shoppe was a popular place for haggard parents to bring their kids and for worried twentysomethings like myself to look for a chocolate fix to improve their mood. "We are talking, Beau."

"Someplace with a little privacy?"

I shook my head. Being anywhere private with Beau sounded like more trouble than I cared to get myself into right now. "Just say what you've come to say."

He sighed. "Tampering with an ankle monitor is a felony, but that's the least of his problems." Beau paused and stared at me, checking for any sign that his words were sinking in. He must have seen what he was looking for, because he continued. "Running off in the middle of a murder investigation looks bad. Real bad. Your uncle needs to turn himself in before it gets any worse."

CHAPTER 6

"That's not funny, girls. What do you mean Calvin jumped bail and skipped town?" Mom asked, looking as bewildered and betrayed as we all felt as we sat around Tansy's kitchen table discussing the latest development.

"The cops wanted to question him because the body we found in the supply closet was holding Uncle Calvin's business card when she died," I said.

"When they ran his name through the system, an alert popped up that he had a warrant for outstanding tickets," Maggie added.

"Which is why Beau arrested him," I said.

"That Beau Russell really is a handsome fella, isn't he, Juni?" Mom asked. Clearly, the seriousness of the situation hadn't yet sunk in for her if she was more interested in my love life than her brother's whereabouts.

"Now's not the time to play matchmaker, Ma," Tansy said. "Besides, Juni's over Beau, right?"

"Right," I agreed, automatically.

"I still can't understand why Beau went and arrested Calvin over a few silly little tickets. Isn't that a little extreme?" Mom asked.

"Over sixteen hundred dollars' worth of tickets," I clarified. "Besides, didn't you tell me that the new Cedar River sheriff ran on a 'No crime is too big or too small' platform?"

"I can't believe I voted for him," Mom said, now looking horrified.

"Well, I certainly didn't, for all the difference that makes," Tansy said. "I feel sorry for Calvin. We all do."

"Didn't seem right, putting an old man in jail for moving violations," Maggie added.

"Who are you calling old?" Mom asked. "He's only three years older than me."

"I didn't mean it like that," Maggie said quickly. "It's just with his health scares, it just wouldn't seem right to make him spend the night in jail."

Mom nodded. "Y'all know your uncle. He's . . ."

"Reckless?" I suggested.

"A rule breaker?" Maggie said.

"A juvenile delinquent that never grew up?" Tansy contributed.

"Impulsive. He's probably freaked out right now, and needs some alone time to process. As soon as he comes to his senses, he'll come back and apologize for all the trouble he caused. When's his arraignment?"

"In two weeks," Maggie said.

"That's plenty of time. I'm sure Calvin will be back before Sunday dinner. If the judge had thought he was a flight risk, they never would have let him out on his own recognizance."

Deafening silence filled the room.

Mom sighed. "Oh, girls, what have you done?"

I glanced at my sisters. One of the best things about being the baby of the family was I didn't get in nearly as much trouble as either of my older sisters. Near as I could figure, by the time I came along my parents were already worn-out from raising the two of them and most of what I did slipped through the cracks. I was allowed to stay up later, make bigger messes, and stomp around louder. Embarrassing as it was to admit, I was the kid who could run around at the town picnic with mud on my face calling anyone with white hair Santa.

When I put a frog in my sister's pillowcase or got sent to the principal's office because I'd punched a little boy who pulled my pigtails, I never got in trouble. At least not from my parents. My sisters, on the other hand, were always ready and eager to keep me in line. Which, looking back, was probably the only reason I didn't turn out more like my uncle. "We bailed him out," I admitted.

"How on earth did you do that? None of y'all have two pennies to rub together. . . ." Her voice faded as realization of what we'd done dawned on her. "You put the record shop up as collateral?"

We all nodded sheepishly. "He would have done the same for any of us," I pointed out. Then again, the worst thing I could remember doing was sneaking dollar-store candy into the movie theater. If I could afford concession stand M&M's, I would buy them, but until then, I'd stick with purse snacks.

"I know I taught y'all that family comes first, always. But this is going too far."

"We're gonna get him back," Maggie said, resting her hand on Mom's elbow.

"How?"

"Don't worry. We have a plan," I said. "We're gonna get Calvin off the hook."

Mom looked confused. "What aren't you telling me?" Mom asked. She'd raised three daughters. It was hard to slip anything past her. "Juni, what's going on?"

"It's nothing. A misunderstanding, really. The cops think Calvin took off because he knows more about the murder than he's saying. Nothing to worry about. Circumstantial evidence at best."

Maggie interrupted me before I could say anything incriminating. "We're gonna get things cleared up."

Mom glared at all three of us, then turned around and let herself out the front door. I assumed she was going back to the mother-in-law cottage where she lived, but a second later I heard her car start and then pull away.

"Should we go after her?" I asked.

Tansy shook her head. "Just give her time to calm down." Maggie's interruption had been enough to distract Mom, but my oldest sister wasn't so easily fooled. "What's all this about getting Calvin off the hook? I thought we agreed we were going to leave this to the lawyers."

"That was before Calvin took off," I replied.

"When he skipped town, he put Sip & Spin in jeopardy. If he doesn't come back, we lose the shop," Maggie added. I sent her a silent thank-you. As the middle sister, Maggie was often the swing vote. When we worked together, we could convince Tansy of *almost* anything.

I got up and started another pot of coffee. I was going to need it. I felt like I'd woken up this morning in the Upside Down. Mom was acting like a sullen teenager. Beau had asked me out on a date. My uncle Calvin had been arrested and was now wanted by the police. And last night, I found a dead body in my shop. Maybe instead of brewing more coffee, I'd be better off going back to bed and pretending the last twenty-four hours had never happened.

No. This wasn't the time to bury my head in the sand. We had work to do. While I waited for the coffee, I turned back toward my sisters and leaned against the counter. "Beau says that him taking off like that makes him look bad. We've got to fix this before things get too far out of hand. Where do you think he'd go?"

"Beats me," Maggie said. "Vegas?"

"Somewhere closer to home, I think," Tansy said, getting into the spirit.

"Where's the closest track?" I asked. My sisters shrugged. We loved going to the rodeo as a family, but none of us had ever been to a horse-racing track.

"Maggie, you stay here and see if you can pull together a list of racetracks and OTBs in the area. You can use my laptop. It's in my bedroom. Juni, you're coming with me."

"Where are we going?" As usual, now that Tansy was on board she was taking over.

"Calvin's house. We'll tear the place apart if we have to, but we're gonna find out where he's gone, and then we're gonna drag him back to Cedar River, kicking and screaming, if that's what it takes," Tansy said.

I let out a sigh of relief. Finally, all three of the Jessup sisters were on the same page.

When we pulled up to his house, Calvin's old Bronco was still in his driveway. From the looks of the oil slick glistening under it, it hadn't moved in a few days. "Beau said Calvin ditched his ankle monitor in the street on his way home. I assumed he would come back here and pick up his truck, but it's still here," I mused aloud.

"We should have known something was up when he said he'd rather walk than get a ride." Tansy shook her head. "Uncle Calvin never walks anywhere. So how's he getting around?"

"Beats me," I admitted.

That's when I noticed Edie coming down the sidewalk. With her was the little beige dog she'd been walking this morning when the police came to arrest Calvin. "Gimme a sec," I told Tansy, and then hurried over to the older woman. "Good afternoon, Miss Edie. And who do we have here?" I knelt to pet the dog. She had short legs, a curly tail, and rolls of fat everywhere—in other words, a perfect little chonky puppy.

The dog stood on her hind legs and proceeded to try to bathe my entire face with her tongue. "This is Buffy," Edie said. "I think she likes you."

"Whatever gave you that impression?" I asked as the little dog wiggled in excitement.

"Don't let her fool you; she's a fine guard dog. Honorary member of the neighborhood watch and everything."

"I have no doubt about that." Little dogs weren't intimidating, but they would bark at the first sign of any movement, even if it was just a leaf. "Speaking of which, have you seen Calvin lately?" I wouldn't call Edie nosy, not to her face anyway, but she always knew what was going on, especially on her own block. She had a pair of binoculars by her front window, and it wasn't for bird-watching.

"Not since the police were here this morning, I haven't," she said. "Everything all right?"

Instead of answering her, I fished around in my bag until I found one of my new business cards and a pen. I wrote my cell phone number down on the back and handed it to her. "If you see him, will you give me a call?"

"Sure thing, sweetie," Edie said, tucking the card into one of the pockets of her dress.

"Thanks." I hurried back to where my sister was standing on the front porch, Calvin's key ring in her hand.

"Good thinking. Nothing happens on this block without Edie knowing about it. I assume she hasn't seen Uncle Calvin today?" she asked.

"Not since the arrest," I told her. "She promised she'd call if that changed."

"I can't believe him. I just can't," Tansy muttered to herself as she unlocked and opened the front door. "Hello? Anyone home?" No one answered, not that we'd expected any different. "How do you want to tackle this?"

The house wasn't large, but Calvin had lived here for

decades. He wasn't a hoarder, but looking around, it was obvious he wasn't a follower of the Marie Kondo method, either. Turning his place inside out was a good idea on paper, but now that we were here, it was overwhelming. Good thing I had nowhere better to be.

Three hours later, we were no closer to knowing where our uncle had disappeared to than when we'd started. There was a knock at the front door. Without waiting for an invitation, Beau breezed inside holding a large take-out bag from Whataburger in one hand and a cardboard tray with three large cups in the other. He put the food down on the long credenza in the foyer, the same one I'd caught him rifling through this morning. I hadn't found anything interesting in there and had moved on to the living room, where decorative baskets on the coffee table that had my mom's touch stamped all over them were filled with everything from water bills to a decade's worth of old *Reader's Digest* magazines.

"You brought dinner," I said, stating the obvious. I hadn't checked the time in a while, but my stomach grumbled at the mouthwatering smells. We didn't have Whataburgers in Oregon. We had In-N-Out Burger. Not the same. "And you knew we were here, how?"

I was starting to get paranoid that Beau had put us under surveillance. He wouldn't do that. Would he?

"I was on my way to your sister's house when I recognized Tansy's car in the driveway."

"And you thought you could bribe me with burgers?" I asked, still a bit suspicious.

"Not just any burger. Whataburger with cheese. Large fries. Spicy ketchup. Strawberry malted milkshake. Just the way you like it." He handed me the wrapped burger, fries, dipping sauce, and a straw from the bag.

Hearing a male voice, Tansy came out of our uncle's bedroom, where she had been searching. We were lucky that

Maggie wasn't here. She would have insisted on laundering everything and then reorganizing his sock drawer by color or something. I bet she had a spare drawer organizer or three lying around that she was dying to put to good use.

"We didn't invite you in," Tansy told him coldly.

Tansy didn't dislike Beau. As far as I could tell, she didn't dislike anyone. She had a generous heart and a sympathetic nature that even extended to welcoming both Mom and me to live with her indefinitely. However, she didn't have any forgiveness for the man who had broken my heart, no matter how long ago that was.

"Grilled chicken salad," he said in reply. "Diet Dr Pepper." He peeked into the bag and pulled out a small package. "Oh, my bad. They accidentally put a hot apple pie in here, too."

Tansy snatched the apple pie out of his hand. "I'll take that," she said, still glaring at him as she unwrapped the pie and took a bite.

"See, that's why I've always liked you, Tansy. You eat dessert first," Beau said with a grin.

"Wouldn't want it getting cold," she said between bites.

The front door opened again, and Maggie came inside. "Y'all are having a party and didn't invite me?" Without waiting for a response, or pausing to blink at the sight of Beau, she grabbed the final burger from the bag and unwrapped it. "A triple? Onion rings?" She tore the paper off a straw and stuck it in the final drink. "Unsweet tea? Beauregard Russell, it's like you don't know me at all."

"Um." He started to correct her, then thought better of it. I knew Beau's order as well as he knew mine. Triple with cheese. Large onion rings. Large unsweet. He had planned on bribing Tansy but hadn't counted on Maggie showing up when she did. I popped a fry in my mouth to keep from laughing out loud. "Well, you ladies enjoy your dinner, and call me if anything turns up."

"We'll be certain sure to do that," Tansy said, around a sip of Diet Dr Pepper.

"All sarcasm aside, we're on the same team, ladies. Does it look bad that Calvin ran? Sure does. Does that mean anything?" He took his cowboy hat off and scratched his head. "Well, that remains to be seen, doesn't it? But the longer he's out in the cold, the harder things are gonna be for him. So if you hear from him, you let me know, hear?"

"We hear," I said.

Beau let himself out.

It was a whole lot easier to stay mad at him when I wasn't sipping on a strawberry malted ice-cream shake he'd brought me.

Maggie swapped the onion rings for my fries, and the unsweet tea for Tansy's Diet Dr Pepper. We caught each other up while we ate. "I called around to all the OTBs I could find," she began. Growing up with an uncle like Calvin, I knew that the problem with offtrack betting was that there were plenty of places that weren't strictly legal and wouldn't come up in a Google search. "Everyone who answered the phone knew Uncle Calvin. Surprise, surprise. None of them have seen him today. A couple promised they'd call me if he showed up, but I'm not gonna hold my breath. You?"

"Nothing in the living room so far," I said, snatching back one of my fries and stretching to reach the spicy ketchup. "It's a wonder he can find anything in here." I pointed to a pile I'd made of anything that looked even slightly promising. "A phone number with no name scrawled on a piece of scrap paper, an expensive receipt for a steak house last week, and an invoice for a rental car he returned a few weeks ago."

"Maybe he was having car trouble? The Bronco has seen better days."

I agreed and moved on. "Also, we've got this." I pulled up the picture of the business card I'd taken on my phone, enlarged the numbers, and held it up next to one of the name-less phone numbers I'd found wadded up in the trash can next to his La-Z-Boy recliner. Recognizing someone's handwriting is a whole lot easier than recognizing their handwritten num-bers, but in my amateur opinion, they matched. "What do you think?" I passed it to Tansy.

She studied it and then handed it to Maggie. "Looks like Calvin's writing to me."

"I agree," Maggie said. "And it's his personal number on the card. Do we know who the other number belongs to?"

"No clue." I Googled it and got a dozen results promising that they had found the number and for a minimal fee and a credit card number they would be happy to provide the owner's full name, date of birth, Social Security number, and mother's maiden name. Thanks but no thanks.

Tansy typed the number into her phone. "It doesn't match anything in my contacts." That was a surprise. Tansy's contact list was at least as extensive as the old phone book that used to be delivered to our house twice a year. "What now?"

"We call it?" Maggie suggested, always the practical one.

Tansy pushed the button. The call did not go through. "Dis-connected," she announced as if we hadn't all heard the fa-miliar tones through the speakerphone. "Dead end."

I shrugged. "Maybe that's why the number was in the trash." It had been a long shot, but we didn't have a whole lot to go on.

"It's getting late, and I promised J.T. we would go to the movies tonight. We needed something to take our mind off . . . all of this." Maggie had only managed to eat half of the triple cheeseburger, but she'd polished off my fries. I'm glad her date night plans weren't for dinner, or she'd be too full to enjoy her-self.

After we cleaned up after ourselves and locked up, I rode home with Tansy. Mom's car was back in its usual spot. The curtains were drawn, but I could see lights on inside her cottage. "Should we check on her?" I asked.

"I'll do it," Tansy volunteered. She parked, and then headed for the cottage as I let myself in the main house. It was cool and dark and quiet inside. Even the few times in Oregon I had been between roommates, I didn't know that I was ever truly alone like this. I usually had every light on, even when I wasn't in the room, with the television on even if I wasn't watching. It was a good thing my apartment had been small; otherwise, my electric bill would have been outrageous.

But for once, I could appreciate the darkness and the solitude. It was a rare treat, which evaporated the second that Tansy came through the front door, flipping on the hall light. "What are you doing standing in the dark like a weirdo?" she asked. "Alexa, shuffle my playlist." Music drifted out of the speaker. "That's better."

Like me, Tansy had grown up in a household filled with the sounds of family and laughter. Even a moment's peace felt awkward and uncomfortable. Which was probably why we were so driven. Even before I owned my own business, I'd always worked long hours.

Tansy had never been very career minded. She tended to drift from job to job, usually in something people oriented like marketing or sales. She got bored easily, and was always up for trying something new. She was addicted to social events and would try anything, from skydiving to wine-and-ceramics, as long as she had a Groupon. She'd taken cooking classes, barrel-racing lessons, and even learned how to ice-skate—a skill that wasn't exactly practical in Texas. The only thing she seemed to stick with was long-distance solo sports, and she was always in training for her next event.

I crossed my fingers and hoped that she didn't tire of the record shop, because I was in it for the long haul.

"How's Mom?" I asked.

"Fine. Well, upset at her brother, but can you blame her? If you or Maggie ever pulled something like that, I'd be furious."

"But you're not mad at Uncle Calvin?"

Tansy thought about it for a minute. "Disappointed. Worried, even. But not mad. I'm sure he has a totally good reason for skipping town and he'll be back before we know it."

"What makes you so certain?" I asked.

"He left in a hurry. Didn't even pack a bag. His blood pressure meds are still in the bathroom, so he can't intend to stay away for long. His phone is on a charger next to his bed. I even found an envelope full of cash in his sock drawer."

"Wait a second, you found what?" I asked.

"Cash, and a lot of it. A few thousand at least. I was going to tell you while we were tossing his place, but then Beau showed up."

I didn't blame her for not wanting to talk in front of Beau, but I wished she'd brought up the money sooner. This changed everything. I was still assuming that Calvin had ditched the ankle monitor to hit up a racetrack for some fast cash to pay his tickets, but he was already flush. "He never intended to pay those fines, did he?" I asked.

"Only as a last resort," Tansy agreed. "He'd rather pay J.T. and Elroy the same amount to fight the tickets than to ever admit he was in the wrong."

"It doesn't make any sense. If he had the money, why did he run?"

"That's my point exactly. If he was planning something, he would have taken a suitcase at the very least. I don't think he's on the run. Speaking of which, I'm gonna go get a few miles in before it gets too late."

Tansy disappeared into her bedroom to change into her running clothes and shoes. In Texas, it was best to avoid doing anything outside during the heat of the day if you could help it, even in the spring and fall. It was common to see runners and bikers out on the street in the very early or very late hours, taking advantage of cooler temperatures.

"Are you sure that's a good idea?" I asked when she emerged. "It's awful late, and there's a murderer on the loose."

She was wearing a reflective shirt and fancy sneakers. Her short hair was tucked under a pink bandana. "Nothing to worry about. My phone's GPS tracker is turned on. I've got pepper spray." She patted the bag she wore around her waist like a tourist. "And I've taken every self-defense class between here and San Antonio. I'll be fine."

Tansy waved and let herself out the front door, leaving me alone in the house.

CHAPTER 7

I woke up early on Sunday morning. I couldn't remember the last time I'd slept in, since the lacy curtains in Tansy's guest room weren't exactly conducive for sleeping much past sunrise. Besides, ever since I'd come back to Texas, I'd had a list a mile long of things that had to be done so we could open the store on time.

Paint the walls. Mount the shelves. Order the industrial espresso machine. Get all the permits. Hire an inspector. Take the cat to the vet. Set up the website and e-store. Sort through arriving inventory. Tansy had a great ear for music and unsurprisingly knew almost every musician in Austin, so we spent our evenings listening to live music and gathering albums to sell on consignment. Sip & Spin was positioned to be the premier destination for local music lovers.

And now those plans were shot full of holes.

I sat up and stretched. I put on my glasses and checked my phone. One text message. For a second, I allowed myself to hope that it was Uncle Calvin. Instead, it was Beau, sent at 5:00 a.m. asking if I had any news.

What kind of person texts at 5:00 a.m. on a Sunday? The same kind of man who would break up with a girl he'd been dating for five years over text, I mused. I didn't text him back.

If I maintained radio silence long enough, he'd come find me. Maybe he'd bring a Sonic Rt 44 Cherry Limeade as a bribe. A girl could dream.

I opened the notepad app on my phone and made a list of what I wanted to accomplish today. It felt wrong, to be so focused on looking for my wayward uncle when I should be more concerned about the dead woman. I reassured myself that the police would figure out who murdered her. In the meantime, if I didn't find my uncle, we would lose the record shop.

Besides, who knew? Maybe Calvin knew something that would help find the killer. Buoyed by that possibility, I got up and started my day. A shower and two cups of coffee later, I borrowed my sister's car and headed out to tackle my list. First up was George's Auto Body, on the far side of town.

Tucked away by the train tracks was a crumbling industrial park. The long, low buildings that housed everything from shipping companies to sketchy telemarketing schemes were surrounded by cracked asphalt parking lots. George's Auto Body was at the far end, where the husks of car corpses long picked apart by vultures sat in crowded rows, waiting for repairs that never came. George Martín, the shop's namesake, had long since retired. His daughter Esméralda Martín-Brown ran things now.

I stepped inside the open garage door into a cavernous bay. Along the back were shelves lined with an assortment of common parts from windshield wipers to spark plugs. There was a rack of tires, and the scent of new rubber and old oil filled the air.

Most of the space was consumed by two hydraulic lifts. Both were centered over a shallow pit in the cement. Only the far station was occupied. Loud curses came from underneath a rusty, and apparently stubborn, Toyota Celica.

"Hello?" I called.

"Be right with you," a muffled voice replied. A Hispanic woman emerged from under the car. Esméralda had dark curly hair that was kept in check by a brightly colored oil-stained scarf. She wore a long-sleeved Henley under denim overalls.

It was mid-March, and the forecast called for highs in the low seventies, which was downright arctic to lifelong Texans. Even so, Esméralda was sweating. She removed her gloves and ran the back of her arm over her forehead. "How can I help you?" she asked, but she wasn't looking at me, instead staring past me to my sister's car. "Didn't I give you a tune-up last month? Everything okay?"

"The car's fine," I assured her.

She turned to me. I'd expected her to say something about me not being Tansy, but either she was more familiar with cars than people or my sister and I looked more alike than I realized. Sure, I was a few inches shorter, a dozen pounds heavier (on a good day), and seven years her junior. In contrast to my sister's year-round tan, I was still pale from my long stint in Oregon. My hair hung all the way down my back and I was wearing my favorite purple glasses, but there wasn't so much as a flash of hesitation on the mechanic's face. I was driving Tansy's car, and we bore a passing resemblance to each other. Therefore, I must be Tansy.

"I'm here for my uncle, Calvin Voigt," I said. Cedar River was a small enough town that even if I didn't actually know Esméralda Martín-Brown, I knew who she was. I just couldn't be sure she knew who Tansy and I were related to.

"Eighty-six Ford Bronco," she said.

"Yup," I confirmed. "Has he been in recently?"

She shook her head. "Your uncle is a do-it-yourselfer. Which explains why that old bucket of his never runs right for long. Last time he came in here was a year or so ago, looking for a tailgate. Got real disappointed when I didn't have any spare Broncos sitting around, so I directed him out to the junkyard in New Braunfels. Did he ever find the part he was looking for?"

I shrugged. "I have no idea. Well, thanks for your time."

"No problem. Needed a break anyway. Toss me that bottle, will ya?"

I glanced over and saw a reusable water bottle decorated with unicorn decals and pink flower stickers. I grinned at it. I adored unicorns. "Here," I said, walking the bottle over to her. "Love the unicorns."

She returned my smile. "Who doesn't?" She took a swig of water, set the bottle on the ground, and disappeared back into the pit under the car.

That wasn't a total waste of time, I told myself as I got behind the wheel and navigated the road weaving through the industrial park. At least once I could afford a car, I knew where I would take it if it ever needed work.

My next stop was the car rental agency on the other side of the complex. There were half a dozen shiny vehicles parked behind a fence, ranging from practical four-door sedans to full-size vans and a truck that looked like it could haul a house.

Behind the building was a long runway lined with hangars on one side. Cedar River Municipal Airport was most often used for hobby planes and the occasional helicopter. There were over seven hundred airports in the great state of Texas. The largest, like DFW International, were practically cities unto themselves. Ours was the wind-sock-on-a-stick variety common to rural areas.

Uncle Calvin used to house a plane here. I remember him taking me up in it when I was just a little thing. There is nothing in the world like the sensation of being in a tiny plane that wasn't much more than an engine and some fiberglass wings. The bank repo'd the plane when I was in junior high. I remembered thinking at the time how unfair that was, but looking back, I'm starting to think that anyone as irresponsible as my uncle was probably better off without a pilot's license, especially now that he was on the run.

I let myself into the rental car office. A friendly voice

greeted me. "Howdy! I'm Mickey. How can I help you today? We've got a special going on right now—rent four days for the price of three. That sound like something that interests you?"

I approached the counter and the eager, yellow polo shirt–clad employee. "Actually, I'm looking for some information. My uncle, Calvin Voigt, rented a car from you a few weeks ago."

They typed something into the computer before looking back up at me. "Yes, indeed. Was there anything wrong with the car?"

"No, no." I shook my head. "Not that I know of, at least. He returned it, right?"

"Certainly did," Mickey confirmed.

"And he hasn't been back to rent another car since then?"

"Nope," they said. "Just between you and me, if he did come back, we wouldn't rent to him because we found out his license was invalid."

Bless small towns. If I'd tried having this conversation in Austin or Portland, they wouldn't have talked to me at all without me providing two forms of ID and a warrant. They certainly wouldn't have volunteered that Calvin's license was invalid.

Then an idea sparked in the back of my brain. If his license was invalid, he'd have a hard time boarding a commercial flight, but he might have found another way out of town. "He didn't by any chance rent a plane, did he? Or maybe charter a flight?"

Mickey leaned over the keyboard again, hit a few keys, and looked back up at me. "Nope," they said again. "At least not through us. Most of the plane owners handle their own reservations and file their own flight plans. A few rent out their planes when they're not using them, but we haven't had anything come through here in a while."

But even though the rental agency was a dead end, it had given me plenty to think about. My uncle wasn't the most responsible person in the world. He had his own way of doing things, and his own moral code. Calvin would never kill someone, but if he knew something he might not volunteer that information to the cops. And if he was on the run because of, oh, I didn't know, a couple years' worth of unpaid traffic tickets finally coming to haunt him, he wouldn't be so foolish as to rent a car or hire a plane through a legit agency. Besides, he had enough friends that he could just as easily call in a favor or two and get all the help he needed to leave town and lie low until the heat was off.

Which would have been fine if he hadn't jumped bail and ditched his ankle monitor. A few days in jail and a fine was turning into a serious offense, and now my uncle's actions could cost us the record shop. Assuming, of course, that the cops cleared the murder scene and we were ever allowed to open. "What a mess," I muttered to myself.

"Excuse me?" the clerk asked. To be honest, I'd forgotten about them.

"Sorry, I wasn't talking to you. Thanks for your time. Have a great day."

"You too," Mickey said as I turned and walked away.

Back in my sister's car, I retraced my path back to Main Street and parked in the gravel lot behind United Steaks of America. Despite the name—which wasn't as punny as our only brewpub's, The Bitters End—United Steaks was the most upscale restaurant in town. That probably was everything there needed to be said about Cedar River.

Once I was inside, the maître d' greeted me with a scowl as he looked me up and down. I glanced down at my outfit. Fitted jeans. A Soundgarden T-shirt. Flip-flops. United Steaks had a dress code, and I didn't fit it.

The greeter was meticulously dressed in a crisp white shirt under a maroon blazer, with black shoes and black pants. He was clean-shaven with slicked-back hair and no jewelry. "Do you have a reservation, miss?"

It was a good thing I wasn't trying to get a table. I doubted they'd seat me dressed like this. I just needed to talk to the owner so I could ask him about the receipt I'd found at my uncle's house. Calvin had a talent for never picking up a tab. So why had he done so here last week? "I'm not here for lunch. I stopped by to see Rodger."

Rodger Mayhew had been our neighbor growing up. He was the youngest homeowner in the neighborhood, and the only single father. His daughter, Monica, was a sweet kid. I used to earn a few dollars babysitting her after school on occasion while Rodger was at the restaurant.

"I'm sorry. Mr. Mayhew isn't coming in today."

"Oh?" I hadn't known Rodger to ever miss a day of work, especially not on a busy weekend. "Is everything okay?"

"Not exactly." The maître d' looked around to verify no one was nearby. It was just after eleven in the morning. The restaurant had barely opened and the lunch rush had yet to start. I'd saved this stop for last for that very reason, hoping it would be the best time to talk to Rodger without bothering him. "I'm afraid Mr. Mayhew's daughter was murdered Friday night."

"What?" My brain felt like it was spinning. I grabbed the edge of the greeter's stand to steady myself. Unless Cedar River had gone very much downhill in recent years, the chances of two separate murders taking place in the same week, much less on the same night, were impossibly, infinitesimally small.

Focusing on Calvin's disappearance and the potential consequences to Sip & Spin had helped me if not forget, at least compartmentalize, that I had found a dead body in the supply closet of our record shop. I'd convinced myself that the police would solve the murder and my world would go back to normal. I'd taken solace in the fact that while it was tragic that someone had died in my shop, at least it was a stranger.

But the truth was that I'd known the victim. It was little Monica Mayhew.

CHAPTER 8

"I think I need to sit down for a sec," I said, my thoughts still swirling. I had to be wrong about Monica. I just had to be.

"Of course. Of course." The maître d' led me to the bar and watched as I climbed onto one of the high stools. Then he gestured at the bartender. "A glass of water for our guest, please?" He turned to me. "I have to get back. You'll be all right?"

"Yes. Thank you," I said.

The bartender approached. She was a petite white woman who looked to be around my mother's age. "You're pale as a sheet, hon. You sure you don't want something a little stronger than water?"

"It's eleven a.m. on a Sunday," I pointed out.

She shrugged. "And?"

"Water will do. Thanks."

She poured a glass and set it down in front of me on a paper doily. "You're a Jessup, ain't you?"

I nodded. "Juni Jessup," I said, offering my hand out of habit.

She took it and shook it heartily. She had a surprisingly strong grip. "Lana Lincoln. I haven't seen you around these parts before."

"I left town a few years back, and didn't visit as often as I ought to have," I admitted. "But I'm back now. My sisters and I just opened the record shop down the street."

She studied my face for a second. "Well, no wonder you look like you just seen a ghost. You're the one who found her, ain't you?"

I nodded and took a sip of the water. It was cool and refreshing. "Unfortunately. I didn't recognize her. I didn't know." I was babbling, and I knew it, but the bartender didn't seem to be put off by it. I guess in her profession she had to be used to all types. "I . . ." I took another sip. "Poor Rodger. I can't begin to imagine what he's going through right now."

Lana looked sympathetic as she topped off my glass. "People have been dropping by all weekend to pay their respects. I'm sure he appreciates it." Her eyes narrowed. "But you said you didn't know? You're not exactly dressed for the dining room and you're not one of my regulars, so what are you doing here, hon?"

"What?" It took me a second to remember why I'd dropped in on United Steaks in the first place. "Yeah, I uh, well, my uncle came in here a few nights ago and dropped a lot of money on dinner."

"Is that so?"

"It's just, that's not like Calvin. I mean, he likes his steak, but he usually gets it at the Winn-Dixie and grills it up at home. Says no one else can cook 'em as good as he can, and to be completely honest, he's much too cheap to pay for dinner at a fancy restaurant where he's expected to wear a tie and mind his manners."

"I know what you mean. I was pretty shocked to see him in here myself."

I lowered my glass of water. "You know Calvin Voight?"

"Hon, everyone in Cedar River knows Calvin. I didn't know the pretty lady he was in here with, though. Must have been pretty special for him to be springing for dinner. The few times he's been in here before, it's always been with a group and I ain't never before seen him reach for a wallet when the check comes."

That matched what I knew about him. "He was on a date?" I asked.

"Certainly looked that way."

"What was she like?"

"Drank white zin. Ordered the almond-crusted zucchini bites app, but sent 'em back. Good thing, too, because hardly nobody ever sends those back and I sure do hate seeing good food go to waste." She chuckled at me.

"What did she look like?" I asked.

"I only caught a glimpse of her. Pretty, though."

"White? Black? Tall? Short?"

Lana shrugged. "White? Hispanic maybe? Sorry, I wasn't paying that close of attention. She had on expensive shoes. Does that help?"

"Sure," I said. I would have preferred a high-definition photo with her full name, phone number, address, and license plate number, but I had more information now than I'd had a minute ago. "Thanks. It was real nice meeting you, Lana."

"Same, Juni," she said, picking up my glass.

"What do I owe you?"

She raised a single eyebrow. "For a glass of water? On the house. When that pretty lady with the expensive shoes comes to her senses and dumps Calvin, you tell him to stop by and say hello. Tell him there's a free whiskey waiting for him."

Now it was my turn to raise my eyebrows. I had no idea my uncle was so popular with the ladies, especially one who all but called him cheap. "Will do. And give Rodger my condolences, will you?"

She reached across the bar and patted my hand. "Of course I will, hon."

I waved at the maître d' on my way out of the restaurant,

but he was busy tending to customers and didn't notice me leaving. There were a few couples waiting in the lobby and more already seated. A trio of men around my age passed me on their way to the bar. I guess I'd come at a good time. The odors from the kitchen were tempting, but I wasn't dressed for the occasion, didn't have a reservation, and could hardly afford Froot Loops on my current budget, so I ignored them and went outside instead.

It took a second to adjust to the bright light outside after being inside the dark restaurant, but when I did I noticed a man in a cowboy hat was leaning against the driver's side door of my sister's car. I walked up to him. "Beau, we have got to stop meeting like this."

"You aren't answering your phone."

I pulled my phone out of my bag. There were two more texts and one call from Beau, a text from Maggie, a missed phone call from Mom, and a spam email offering to enhance my love life. "I've been busy."

"So I see." He nodded toward United Steaks. "Learn anything interesting?"

"Seriously, does this routine work on anyone? You should be out investigating a murder, not stalking me around town hoping that I'll do all your legwork for you."

His expression never changed. "You didn't answer my question."

I let out a huff in frustration. "Yeah? Well, you didn't tell me that the poor woman who was murdered in my shop was Monica Mayhew, so I guess we're even."

I scowled at him, and he grinned in return. He wasn't making it easy to stay annoyed at him. "I'm not permitted to talk about an open investigation. You understand. Besides, you found the body. I assumed you recognized her."

"The last time I saw Monica, she was yay high," I said, holding my hand level with my hip. "She was playing with

My Little Ponies and eating chicken nuggets shaped like dinosaurs."

"That's fair," he agreed. "You had lunch yet?"

I shook my head.

"Come on, then." He walked over to his truck and opened his passenger seat. "You coming?"

It was eerie, this grown-up version of the boy I used to know, pretending that we were besties or something. Acting like he'd never broken my heart. Making me miss him more than I had for years, even though he was right in front of me. Every minute we spent together stirred up confusing thoughts and feelings that I didn't have the time or energy to dissect right now.

The last thing I wanted was to agree to lunch, but if I got in his truck maybe he'd accidentally-on-purpose tell me more about the murder investigation. Or about his search for my uncle. I was at a dead end and grasping for straws. It couldn't hurt.

My stomach grumbled, which sealed the deal. I'd suffer through an awkward ride for the possibility of a new clue and free food. I gave a small harrumph to let him know this didn't mean all was forgiven before getting in the car. How bad could it be?

"Where are we going?" I asked after several minutes of driving in companionable silence. We had left Cedar River several miles ago and had merged onto the highway heading into Austin.

"You still like Thai food, right?"

I nodded. "You know me."

"Good. I just have a quick errand to run, and then we'll stop for lunch." He paused to pay attention to the road as we passed a long trailer hauling at least half a dozen horses, then went on. "I'm sorry you had to learn about Monica Mayhew the hard way. Seriously, Junebug, I thought you knew."

I let him get away with the old pet name this time, but only because he sounded contrite and he'd promised me Thai food. Beau knew perhaps better than anyone that the way to my heart was through my stomach. Cedar River had a great selection of restaurants, as long as you didn't mind choosing between steak, barbeque, and burgers. For pretty much anything else, Austin was just a drive away and once there, the possibilities were endless.

Beau kept driving. Traffic was light. The only noise in the cab of the truck was the monotonous sound of the wheels speeding down the highway.

When I couldn't stand the silence—or my own thoughts—any longer, I blurted out, "Uncle Calvin took a date to United Steaks a few days ago. I was hoping maybe I could find out who she was, and ask if she had any idea where he was hiding."

"Calvin Voigt has a special lady friend. That's helpful. Anyone we know?"

I shrugged and looked out the windshield as Austin loomed ahead of us. Austin might not be that impressive to someone from New York or L.A., but I'd grown up thinking of it as The Big City. It sprawled out as far as I could see with a few skyscrapers dotting the horizon, but from my vantage point it was mostly concrete and shopping malls. "Didn't get her name," I admitted.

"Have you asked your mom? She knows everything that goes on in Cedar River. If her brother was seeing someone, she'd know about it."

"That's a good idea."

"Why don't you call her?" he suggested.

"I'm sure I'll see her at home," I said, even though I was itching to pull out my phone and call her right now. But Beau would be listening, and I wasn't about to sic the cops on someone without even knowing who it was yet. My curiosity could wait.

Beau opened his mouth and I braced myself, half expecting him to pressure me into calling Mom right now. If he interrogated me, would he play good cop or bad cop? I couldn't picture him pulling out my fingernails with rusty pliers, but then again, he'd already ripped out my heart once. What would a couple of fingernails matter after that?

Instead of grilling me, he asked, "Remember prom?"

The sudden change in topic took me by surprise. "Of course I remember prom." The bigger high schools threw lavish parties in hotel ballrooms. Cedar River High had rented a pavilion in a park in downtown Austin, right on the banks of the river. The city lights reflected off the water as we slow danced to John Legend's "All of Me" under a full moon. Frankly, I felt sorry for those ballroom prom kids. Ours was a thousand times better.

"You wore that puffy pink dress," he continued.

The popular girls in our class all wore slinky sequined numbers. Even our high school mascot, an armadillo, showed up—in costume—wearing a corsage and an evening gown. I wore about a million yards of cotton-candy-colored tulle and felt like the belle of the ball, especially with Beau by my side. To this day, I had no idea how I—the shy, quiet nerd who would rather go to chess club than a pep rally—ended up at prom with the captain of the football team. But somehow, against all odds, we made one heck of a couple.

Until we didn't. One minute, we're touring apartments together. The next, I'm single. Thinking back on it, our breakup made about as much sense as our getting together in the first place—none. So why did spending time with Beau feel like I was picking at an old scab?

Beau exited the highway and took a side street without consulting his GPS. Trees arched over the road as we drove until we pulled into a parking lot. "You have got to be kidding me," I said, looking out the window. "We drove all this way to go to a bowling alley? You know we passed about a dozen on the way. What's wrong with them?"

"Nothing," he said, opening his door. "But this is the one that Calvin went to Friday night after your grand opening party."

I got out of the truck before he could reach my door. "Seriously?" I blinked at Beau. No wonder Calvin hadn't answered his door after the grand opening party. He'd been here.

"According to his credit card, he did."

Inside, the air conditioner was running full blast. The lights were bright, and the sounds of the arcade and heavy bowling balls striking pins echoed across the lanes. The air smelled like Axe body spray and feet. The old-school country music piped in through the overhead speakers was almost loud enough to drown out the rest of the din.

Twenty lanes stretched out across the length of the building, behind the requisite row of shelved loaner bowling balls. To the left were pinball, foosball, and air hockey games and tucked in behind that was the largest claw machine I'd ever seen in my life. Some of the prizes inside were three feet tall, but of course those were buried under the rubble of cheap rubber balls and knockoff Bart Simpsons.

To our right was the shoe rental station and from beyond that wafted the mingling odors of chili cheese fries, pizza, and beer. My stomach rumbled.

"I know what you're thinking, but trust me, you do *not* want those nachos," he said.

"You don't know me as well as you think you do," I lied. I was hungry, and the nacho cheese smelled amazing.

"Uh-huh," he said, clearly unconvinced. "This should just take a second."

He got the attention of the woman dutifully spraying sanitizer into the rental shoes lined up along the counter. I thought about what Lana the bartender had said about Uncle Calvin's date's taste in shoes. Did people who wore expensive footwear rent bowling shoes?

"Need to speak to the manager," Beau told the shoe attendant once she sauntered in our direction.

"Sure thing," she said, leaning onto the counter, which made the neck of her tight blouse dip precariously low. She flashed Beau a smile that showed off a diamond on one of her front teeth. "Marv's right over there." She pointed to a booth overlooking the lanes.

"Thanks," Beau said, tipping his hat at her before leading us in the direction she had indicated. A large man sprawled out across the seat, taking up half the booth by himself. He was wearing black-and-white cow print pants with a silver lamé shirt unbuttoned halfway to his navel. Thick hair covered his chest where the shirt did not, which was a stark contrast to his shiny bald head.

"Marv? Detective Beauregard Russell." He held his badge up at waist level, where Marv could see it, but the family working on their last frames at the nearest lane could not. "Mind if we have a word?"

To his credit, Marv didn't seem fazed. Gold rings flashed on his hand as he patted the red vinyl seat next to him. "Help yourself." He gave me the full head-to-toe once-over before returning his attention to Beau. "Get you anything? Beer? Popcorn?"

"We're good," he answered for us as we slid into the booth.

I used to think his habit of ordering for both of us was charming, especially since he always seemed to know exactly what I wanted, but now I found it presumptuous. However, at this point, I was starting to regret all the water I'd had at United Steaks. While this place looked relatively clean, bowling alleys tended to cater to kids and beer drinkers. Neither group was, in my limited experience, exceptionally diligent in the restroom. I'd wait until we got someplace cleaner. Like a Waffle House at 2:00 a.m.

"How can I help you, Detective?" Marv asked.

"What's your full name, Marv?"

"Marvin Knickleback. No relation to the band." He chuckled at his own joke. The way his lamé shirt jiggled when he laughed was mesmerizing. That, or my hunger was making me light-headed.

"I'm looking for a customer," Beau said. He pulled a sheet of paper out of his back pocket, smoothed it against the table, and slid it to the manager. "Name's Calvin Voigt. He was in here last Friday night. Settled up around two, according to his credit card."

Marv glanced at the picture before saying, "We get a lot of folks, especially Friday nights."

"You'd remember this one," I said. "Big guy. Boisterous. Life of the party. Will talk your ear off if you give him half a chance."

"Sweetheart." He gestured toward the lanes. "You just described half my customers. But yeah, I think maybe I recognize this guy. He's in one of the pickup leagues."

"Pickup leagues?" I asked.

"Folks that can't commit to a team. They show up some nights, shake hands, rent a couple lanes, and throw the ball around and drink beer for a few hours."

"At two in the morning?" Beau asked.

"We're open late on weekends. It's mostly teenagers and night owls after ten or so, but as long as they're pumping quarters into the arcade or rolling, I'll keep the lights on for them."

"And Calvin Voigt is one of these night owls?" Beau asked.

"Can't be certain, but he maybe looks familiar. I don't work the late shift that often myself, you see, but last Friday the kid I hired called out sick. More likely he got a hot date. Anyway,

I ended up here until closing and I remember a pickup league making a racket over there on thirteen."

"You remember what lane they were on but not whether or not you saw this man?" Beau asked, tapping the printout of Calvin's picture.

Marv shrugged. "What can I say? I'm more concerned with my lanes than who's using 'em."

We stood. "Appreciate your cooperation, Mr. Knickleback."

"Always happy to help the boys in blue," Marv said. "Y'all come back anytime."

"That was a spectacular waste of time," I told Beau as we headed out into the sunshine.

"Was it, though? Calvin's credit card receipt puts him here after the party Friday night. In fact, it puts him here pretty much two or three weekends a month. I've no doubt that Marv Knickleback knows all his regulars."

"He lied to us?"

"He lied to us," Beau said with a nod. "I don't want to shock you or nothing, but lots of folks lie to the police. Especially if they think they're helping a friend."

"So what was the point?"

"Was he nervous? Scared?"

I didn't know if he really wanted my opinion or was just quizzing me. Either way, I thought about it. "No," I said. "Pretty relaxed, actually."

"Surprised to see us?"

I glanced back at the bowling alley. "I don't know. Maybe? A little?"

"If your uncle had been hiding out in the back room, how do you think Marv would have reacted?" Beau asked.

"Nervous. Scared. Not at all surprised to see us."

"Bingo." He opened the passenger door for me before getting in the other side.

"But why'd you bring me along?"

"I told you. I had to run an errand." He started the truck and pulled out of the parking lot. "Beside, a guy like Marv isn't gonna let his guard down with a cop, but I knew a pretty girl would distract him enough that I could get a good read on him."

"You used me?" I asked.

We stopped at a red light and he turned to look at me. "Did I? Or did I give you a whole lot of insight into your uncle's whereabouts that you didn't have ten minutes ago? Insight that I might add if you'd asked me about directly, I wouldn't be allowed to tell you. Ongoing investigation, remember?" The light turned green and we moved forward.

"I could have gotten the same information off his credit card statement," I pointed out.

"You certainly could have. But did you?"

I thought about it. I'd combed through my uncle's receipts last night, but I'd missed the recurring bowling charges. If I'd had access to his current bill, I might have questioned a charge after the grand opening party, but that bill wasn't due in the mail for a few weeks still.

A thought occurred to me. "You know what this means, don't you?"

"Enlighten me."

"This pretty much exonerates my uncle."

"How do you figure?" he asked.

"If you killed a girl, at your family shop, during a party, would you immediately jump in your car and head to a bowling alley?" Although, to be fair, Calvin might have been at the bowling alley, but his Bronco was still parked in his driveway. I had no idea how he was getting around.

"I can't rightly tell you what I would do in that particular hypothetical, because I wouldn't ever put myself in that situation," Beau said. He waited a few beats. "But I'll admit, you got a point. If Calvin had skipped town Friday night, it would be another story. It won't hold up in court, but him going out to toss a bowling ball around doesn't exactly scream guilty to me."

I thought about that. "Wait a second. That's why you were so suspicious of Calvin. You thought he was at home with the doors locked and the shades drawn, as if that was an admission of guilt."

"It did look bad," he agreed. "But I've been honest with you all along. I only wanted to talk to Calvin because of the business card. The fact that he was dodging me threw up a few red flags I hadn't been expecting."

"Except he wasn't dodging you. He was bowling. Does that mean my uncle's not a suspect anymore?"

Beau maneuvered into a parking lot in front of a strip mall. In the center was a discount clothing store, flanked by an optometrist on one side and a cell phone provider on the other. We got out of the truck and walked toward a Thai restaurant on the far end. Just when I thought the silence was going to go on forever, he finally answered my question. "Normally, yes. But he ran, Juniper. Innocent men don't run."

I stopped midstride and stared at him. I didn't remember the last time Beau had called me Juniper. That was a sure sign that he was dead serious. Which could only mean one thing.

Detective Beauregard Russell, and, by extension, the Cedar River Police Department, thought that my uncle was a murderer.

CHAPTER 9

"I've lost my appetite," I said, stopping in the middle of the parking lot. "Can you drive me back to Cedar River?"

Beau looked at me and then looked at the Thai restaurant in front of us. "I'm telling you, this place has the best Shrimp Pad Thai in Texas."

I blinked at him. He was acting as if he hadn't just accused my favorite uncle of murder. Sure, Calvin hung out at bowling alleys at two o'clock in the morning, didn't pay his traffic tickets, and occasionally left my sisters and me out to dry. But he didn't mean anything by it. If he had any idea how much trouble he was causing, he would have come back in a heartbeat and turned himself in. I believed that with my whole heart.

But Beau didn't seem to care about any of that.

"Come on, I know it doesn't look like much, but trust me. You'll love it," he said, as if I would still have an appetite after the bomb he'd just dropped.

"I want to go home." I pulled out my phone. "I can call an Uber." And just like that, I had an idea how Calvin was getting around. He had to be using ride share apps, which was good news because they were traceable. Not that I was going to share my flash of inspiration with Beau.

"Fine. I'll take you home. No biggie."

The ride back to Cedar River was tense. There was no joking around this time. No reminiscing about prom. I was tempted to turn on the radio just to break the silence, but in the end, I decided that this way was better. Maybe Beau would get the picture and stop turning up around every corner, pretending to be my friend when he really was using me to find my uncle so he could arrest him.

He pulled up behind Tansy's car in the United Steaks parking lot, which was now full, with overflow taking up every available spot on the street. He put his truck in park but didn't walk around and open my door like usual. Instead, he busied himself with his phone.

I unclipped the seat belt, opened the door, and stepped one foot outside the truck when he finally spoke. "Oh, and by the way, we're releasing the crime scene. You should be good to open tomorrow morning."

"Gee, thanks," I said. It was hard to stay mad at him after he told me such good news, but I managed by focusing on the fact that he'd dangled this little tidbit in front of me like a carrot on a stick. He could have told me at any time today, but he'd waited until now.

As if reading my thoughts, he tapped the screen of his phone, where it was mounted to his dashboard. "Look. I just got the notification a minute ago. I'm not holding out on you." He let out a sigh. "Can I call you later, after you've calmed down?"

When would men learn that telling women to calm down never helped? "Better if you didn't." I got out of his truck and closed the door behind me. He waited until I was strapped into the passenger seat of Tansy's car before he left. I pulled out of the spot, much to the glee of a car circling the lot, and headed home.

That night at family dinner, I felt guilty not telling my sisters about Beau's suspicions, but I didn't want them to feel as hopeless as I now did. Instead, I concentrated on eating and hoped that no one would notice that I wasn't talking. Which lasted about fifteen seconds.

"Everything okay, Juni?" my mother asked. "You're even quieter than usual."

"Just worried about Calvin," I admitted.

"Well, stop that. Your uncle will come home when he's good and ready, and not a second sooner. Y'all should be focusing on the shop."

"Bea, these greens are delicious," J.T. said. "And for the record, I agree with you. Elroy and I will sort out this business with Calvin. You ladies have your hands full already."

Maggie patted her husband's hand. "I know you will, honey."

I envied their easy relationship. From the moment they met, they only had eyes for each other. They got married soon after and seemed blissfully happy ever since. My sister had found her soul mate in J.T. and I couldn't be happier for her.

Hashtag relationship goals.

"And how was your date with Beau?" Mom asked.

"It wasn't a date," I said firmly. I didn't need to ask her how she knew I'd spent the afternoon with him. Half a dozen people had seen me get out of his truck. Any one of them would have called my mother immediately.

"You know, you really shouldn't be talking to him at all without myself or Elroy present," my brother-in-law reminded me. "At least not about Sip & Spin, the murdered woman, or your uncle."

I nodded. "I know, J.T." In a way, it was a relief. If I couldn't talk to Beau about any of those things, I wouldn't have any reason to see him at all. That was probably for the best. "Speaking of which, the murdered woman was Monica Mayhew." There was silence around the table as my family stared at me. "You know, Rodger Mayhew's daughter?"

"Well, of course it was, darling," my mother said, breaking the silence. I didn't know why I was surprised. My mother had a hardwired connection into the Cedar River rumor mill. If there was gossip going around, she'd either heard it or started it. If people in town were dropping by United Steaks to offer their condolences to Rodger Mayhew, of course my mom was in the know.

"I assumed you knew," Maggie said. That, too, made sense. J.T. was tight-lipped. I guess you'd have to be in his profession, especially considering his mother-in-law was the head of the scuttlebutt squad. But I'm sure he told his wife all sorts of things he would never dream about telling the rest of us. Then she corrected my assumption by asking, "Didn't you recognize her?"

"I haven't seen her since she was a kid," I explained.

"It's public knowledge by now," Tansy added. Unlike our mother, my oldest sister didn't chase after every tidbit of juicy gossip, but she always seemed to be in the know anyway. She was easy to talk to and had a magnetic personality that made people want to be around her. I didn't need to tell her to keep her ear to the ground, but I might have to remind her to share if she heard anything interesting. Apparently, my family had forgotten that I'd been away long enough that I was no longer in the inner Cedar River circle. "I'm surprised Beau didn't tell you sooner," she continued.

"Can we please not talk about Beau?" I asked. My sisters exchanged meaningful glances and I rolled my eyes. Having sisters was great. It was like having built-in best friends from birth. Until they ganged up on me. But their insistence on digging into my personal life sparked a thought. "Was Monica dating anyone?"

"Not to my knowledge," Maggie said.

"She'd been seeing some guy in Killeen, but he got orders to Germany a while back," Tansy corrected her. The nearby

Army base in Killeen had a constantly revolving population of soldiers. "We were in the same ceramics class a few months ago. She was bummed about him leaving, but I got the impression that they weren't all that serious."

I might not be a forensics expert, but I watched enough reruns of *Cold Case Files* on Netflix to know that when something bad happened the best suspect was the significant other. If Monica was single, there went that possibility.

Just to be certain, I pulled my phone out of my pocket and logged into Facebook. Monica's profile was surprisingly public and we had several friends in common. I doubted she used the platform much—she was generation TikTok—but like myself, she had an account to appease her relatives. Her relationship status was single, and her wall was filled with expressions of sympathy. I guess I was the last person in town to find out she was dead, even though I was the one who found her.

"She was too young to settle down," Maggie said, despite the fact that she hadn't been much older than Monica when she met her husband. She stood. "Anyone else need a refill? Sweet tea? Water?" Even though everyone said we were good, she returned from the kitchen with a pitcher of each and thankfully changed the subject. "Juni, you said we could get back in the shop tomorrow?"

I nodded. "The cops released the scene this afternoon. We can open tomorrow morning," I confirmed.

♪ ♫ ♪

A long, restless night's sleep later and the day we'd all been working so hard for finally arrived. I didn't remember ever being excited for a Monday morning before, but the day dawned bright and early and I was up before my alarm had a chance to rudely jolt me out of my sleep. Despite my long hair, I was in and out of the shower in a flash—a remnant of growing up sharing a bathroom with two older sisters—before jumping on my trike and heading to the shop.

I assumed that I would be the first one there since we didn't open until ten, but I was wrong.

Maggie's Lexus was already parked out front, and through the windows I could see her running a vacuum over the floor. I waved at my sister as I parked my tricycle. I opened the front door and went inside while she was working her way toward the back of the shop. When she turned around, she jumped and picked up the vacuum cleaner, still running, and brandished it like a baseball bat.

"Whoa, it's just me," I said, raising my hands in surrender.

Maggie put down the vacuum and switched it off. It was a lightweight upright model. If it had been the big Kirby we'd had growing up, she probably would have thrown her back out lifting it like that. "Never *ever* sneak up on someone vacuuming," she said, visibly out of breath.

"I'm so sorry. I thought you saw me."

She nodded. "I guess I'm a little on edge. Because of the . . ." She glanced behind her at the storage closet. The door was closed. The tote full of cleaning supplies on the checkout counter was filled with her personal cleaners she'd brought from home. I knew that because my sister has a favorite brand of every type of cleaner imaginable and it wasn't the stuff we bought in bulk from Sam's Club for the shop.

Yes, my sister has favorite cleaning supplies. It's one of the many things I love about her.

" . . well, you know." As she finally finished her sentence, she rubbed her arms as if she was cold, although the air in the shop was pleasant.

"Yeah, I know." I turned and locked the main entrance. "So no one else disturbs us until it's officially opening time."

"I'm surprised to see you here so early," Maggie said.

"I wanted to get a jump on things." I looked around the

shop. I'd expected to find the shop in shambles. Partially empty Solo cups and crumpled taco wrappers from the party. Dirty footprints and fingerprint powder from the investigation. But instead, every surface gleamed, especially the espresso machine at the barista station, which was calling my name. I was *not* an early bird. "But I see you already beat me to it."

Lured in by the siren song of caffeine, I drifted over to the elaborate coffeemaker and started preparing a drink. "Want anything?"

"What's the special of the day?"

"Friends in Mocha Places," I told her, after checking the chart we'd created. It was espresso, steamed soy milk, chocolate syrup, and a dash of non-alcoholic Amaretto, topped with whipped cream. If the customers liked it half as much as my sisters and I did, it would be a best seller. "Or, if someone is looking for something cold, we have Vanilla Ice Iced Coffee." It was one of my favorites, medium roast coffee served over ice with a splash of vanilla flavoring and a dollop of cold milk.

A few months ago, I'd barely known the difference between a macchiato, a latte, and a frappe and had no idea how to make any of them. It had taken a week of reading the complicated instructions and watching YouTube videos to figure out our fancy new barista station, and I'm certain there were still at least a few functions we hadn't yet discovered.

I mixed up two of the drink specials. It was good practice, and delicious to boot. I took a sip and let myself enjoy it before continuing the conversation.

"I thought I was early enough to get the jump on cleaning before customers started arriving, but I should have known better," I told her. Daffy peeked his head around the corner and seeing that the vacuum cleaner, the bane of his existence, was quiet, sauntered into the shop. He wove between my legs. "Morning, Daffodil," I said, scratching him on the head. He purred in response.

"I've already fed him," Maggie told me. "Don't believe him if he says otherwise."

"Noted. Is there anything else left to do?"

"You can help me set up the center displays. Even on wheels, they're a little much for one person."

"Sure thing," I said. We'd squeezed them into the back, along with the café tables and chairs, to make room for the party. Together, we maneuvered the unwieldy displays into the middle of the shop and set up the tables in the corner. Once everything was in place, the store was filled with new and gently used records looking for a forever home. Freshly roasted coffee scented the air. "I think we're ready."

"I think you're right," Maggie agreed. "Since you're already here, mind taking the morning shift? I've got some errands to run."

"Fine with me." We'd worked up a schedule so we were all working roughly the same amount of hours, but we'd all agreed to be flexible and cover for each other as much as possible. For now, we planned on opening at ten and closing at seven, but we might end up adjusting that after we'd been in business for a while, depending on foot traffic.

"Rolling Stones or Vampire Weekend?" I asked, holding up two albums. We planned on having music playing whenever possible. Even if Sip & Spin was open twenty-four hours a day, we had a large enough selection to choose from that we would never have to replay a single song. Which, come to think of it, probably accounted for my eclectic taste in music. Growing up in a record shop, there was always something new to hear.

Maggie looked at them. "I think we should start with one of Grandma Rose's favorites," she suggested.

"Diana Ross and the Supremes it is then," I agreed. I put the record on the player connected to the sound system, flipped the sign to Open, and unlocked the door. "Sip & Spin is officially open for business."

A few minutes after Maggie dragged her vacuum and cleaners to her car and drove away, we had our first customer. The morning crowd was more interested in coffee than records and made themselves at home in the high-backed stools at our café tables as they sipped their drinks and took advantage of our free Wi-Fi. More than one customer commented on our lack of pastries, and I noted it as a possible addition. The bakery across the street served the most delicious array of donuts, muffins, and scones but only offered basic drip coffee. We had the fancy espresso machine, but no snacks. Maybe we could work out a mutually beneficial arrangement.

In the morning, everyone browsed the records upstairs and down, but most of the sales were for coffee. On the plus side, Friends in Mocha Places was a hit. As the day wore on and the temperature rose outside, Vanilla Ice Iced Coffee gained in popularity.

Business would pick up, I told myself. We'd done the hard part already. The shop looked fantastic. We'd cultivated an eclectic collection of rare, popular, and local albums. We'd designed a fun menu of delicious coffees with clever, music-themed names. We'd gotten the word out to the community that we were open for business. And, if there were any locals who hadn't known about Sip & Spin before the grand opening party, they'd all heard of us now thanks to the dead body in the supply closet. We had our thirty seconds of fame on news stations around the state even before we made our first sale.

To be honest, I could have done without the notoriety, but all publicity was good publicity, right?

Then again, we could sell every record we had in stock today and it wouldn't make a lick of difference if Calvin didn't show up for court and we lost the shop. It was frustrating, being helpless. I didn't know where my uncle was hiding. And I had no idea who had killed Monica Mayhew, or why. Or why they'd chosen our shop to do it in.

I glanced up at the clock mounted above the register. It was handcrafted by a local artist—made from an old vinyl record with the Sip & Spin logo cut out of it. According to the clock, it was late afternoon, and there was only one customer in the store. They were nursing a cappuccino and listening to a local punk band on one of the turntables. They glanced up and nodded as if to indicate they didn't need any help, so I left them to enjoy the music while I logged onto the shop's computer.

The computer was vital for processing internet orders, doing research, and helping locate rare albums for our customers. It was also directly connected to the security feed. We'd already turned over the hard drives from the night of the party, but everything was backed up in the cloud, just in case. Granted, when I'd set up the system, I'd been worried that someone might break in and take the security footage to cover their tracks, not that our tapes would become evidence in a murder investigation. But at least we still had a copy.

I pulled up the footage and my hopes fell. We had three cameras inside. One in the far corner covered the first floor and one focused on the cash register. The one pointed at the register was covered by our grand opening banner. The other one was obscured by a clump of helium balloons that had gotten trapped under the balcony overhang. I fast-forwarded, but the view never got any better. The balloons shifted throughout the night, but there were so many of them that one was almost always directly in front of the camera. The third camera was upstairs. It hadn't recorded anything at all, even though I could swear it had been working earlier.

I climbed the stairs to the loft and headed for the camera, which was mounted high up on the wall. There was no indicator light that I could see. Using the nearest shelf as a makeshift ladder, I could reach the camera if I stretched. I pushed the reset button. A few seconds later, the light blinked a few times and then started glowing solid red. I went back downstairs, checked the feed, and verified that it was working now. Better late than never, I guess.

The customer brought the album they'd been listening to up to the register. "I've never heard of this band before, but I really like their sound."

"They're pretty good," I agreed. "We have another album of theirs, if you're interested. It's a live one."

"Yeah, I'll take that, too."

I rang it up and watched them leave with a satisfied smile. Finally, I'd made a real sale. And I'd hooked a customer on a new band, to boot. This day was looking up.

Once they were gone, I went back to the security footage. An outside camera covered the main entrance and part of the sidewalk out front. This one was more useful because I could see who came and went, but I couldn't tell what they were doing once they got inside. Considering that we'd had a few hundred people circulate through the shop during the grand opening party, it only served to confirm my suspicion that almost everyone from Cedar River and a good deal of the Austin music scene had come by that night.

Rather than try to identify every person on the video, I decided to leave the grunt work to the cops. Even if I recognized every face, I couldn't exactly call them all up and ask them if they'd murdered a woman in my shop last Friday.

Well, I could. I just didn't know how much good that would do.

As a last-ditch effort, I flipped to the final feed. The camera covering the back door showed little action. A few teenagers cut though the alley on their skateboards and tossed something in our dumpster. An unfamiliar dog wandered past, only to get chased away by another stray. Daffy appeared several times, triggering the motion sensor each time, before settling in for a long grooming session.

And then a man walked into the frame. He was tall and narrow shouldered. He wore a large cowboy hat that obscured his face. He could have been literally anyone.

Daffy paused his grooming to watch as the man opened the back door and walked into the record shop, disappearing out of frame.

CHAPTER 10

I picked up my phone and selected my brother-in-law's contact. He answered on the second ring. "Juni?" he asked.

"Hey. When you get a minute, can you swing by the shop? It's business."

"Sure thing. Be there in fifteen?"

"Great." While I waited, I busied myself around the shop. Maggie had done almost too good of a job cleaning—not that I would expect anything less from her—which left me with little to do. I checked our online orders and saw several waiting for me. I pulled the requested stock and set it aside to mail out after I verified the payments and printed the labels.

One of the orders had come through email instead of the website. It was from a local artist inquiring about buying a few dozen junk records. I replied that we could easily accommodate them, advising them to swing by anytime.

Very loosely speaking, I mentally categorized records as either collectables, playables, or junk. Junks were the records we picked up at garage sales and thrift stores for practically nothing. They were scratched, warped, or missing labels. We'd pick through them and make sure nothing of value was hiding in plain sight and then sell them to upcyclers.

Back in my grandparents' day, if a record got scratched it

would get tossed in a landfill. Now they were in high demand by artisans who used them for everything from wallpaper to creating unique artwork like the vinyl clock on our wall. It certainly beat tossing old albums in the trash.

The front door opened and J.T. stepped inside. He took off his cowboy hat and ran a hand over his hair. "You needed something?" he asked.

My brother-in-law was what I consider the quintessential Texan. Brash. Loud. Always ready with a friendly smile and a helping hand that was true to his personal life but belied his killer instinct as a lawyer. His scruffy beard was cultivated to put clients and juries at ease. "Look at me!" it screamed. "I'm just like you!" He was an absolute snake in the courtroom, one I was glad to have in my corner.

"I wanted to show you something and get your opinion."

"Sure thing," he said. He came around the counter and stood behind me, hovering over my shoulder. He ruffled the hair on top of my head like he'd done for as long as I'd known him. There was a significant age difference between me and my sisters—five years between me and Maggie, and another two between Maggie and Tansy. I was an awkward fifteen-year-old when J.T. entered the picture, and like the rest of my family, he still treated me like a kid, even though I was all grown-up now.

"You see this guy?" I asked, playing the footage for him.

"Yup. Any idea who it might be?"

I shook my head. "None. I was hoping you might know. To be honest, I didn't recognize half of the guests, and that's when I could see their faces. All we've got here is the top of some dude's hat."

"The angle's all wrong. I can see cars driving past the alley, but we wouldn't see who's walking in the back door unless they paused and looked up at the camera. Want me to help you adjust it?"

"I wouldn't turn it down." J.T. had helped us hang all the cameras initially because he was good with a power screwdriver and wasn't afraid to stand on the top rung of a ladder. But he was no cinematographer. I propped open the back door as he dragged the ladder out of the supply closet. I ran back and forth from the computer monitor a few times, until the angle was better.

"Thanks, you're an absolute lifesaver," I told him as he brought the ladder back in and propped it against the wall.

He swiped his forearm over his forehead. "Was the back door locked during the party?"

"I doubt it," I said. "We were pushing pretty hard to make sure everything was ready for the grand opening, and we were in and out the back door so much we weren't terribly vigilant about locking it." I stopped and tried to think back to Friday night. "When we were cleaning up after the party, I took the trash out and the door wasn't locked then."

"So anybody could have come in the back door," he stated.

"Yeah," I agreed. "Pretty much. Do you think this will help exonerate Uncle Calvin?"

He glanced back at the computer monitor, where the image was frozen on the mystery man. "I'm sorry, but there's not much to go on with this footage. For all we know, it's just a customer who stepped out to take a phone call or sneak a smoke."

"Yes, but then we would see him walking out, and we don't."

"Parking was crazy that night. He could have been taking a shortcut."

"But it casts reasonable doubt, don't you think?"

He put his hands on my shoulders. "Juni, I know how much you care about your uncle. And this store. And your sisters. We all do. But leave this to the pros, okay? Don't go sniffing around and causing more problems for your uncle. And don't you dare go talking to Beau about anything without me present, hear?"

"I don't think that's gonna be a problem," I told him. To be fair, I was referring specifically to his moratorium on hanging out with Beau. I couldn't make any promises about the snooping bit. Not with as much as was on the line.

"Good deal," he said, taking one last glance at the monitor before heading to the front door. "You know how to reach me if you need anything." Then he settled his hat on his head and let himself out.

I stared at the screen after he left, more as a distraction than anything else. Did the man in the video look familiar or had I just been looking at it too long? I couldn't be sure. At least half the men at the party had been wearing cowboy hats. Some, like Beau, took them off as soon as they got inside. Others left them on. I might recognize the hat or its shiny silver band if I saw it again, but no matter how hard I squinted, I didn't recognize the man wearing it.

A customer walked into the shop. I minimized the security footage and turned to greet him. "Hi, how can I help you?" I asked in my most pleasant customer service voice. "You looking for music or coffee? Our special of the day is . . ."

The man interrupted me. "Need to talk to Calvin." The rancher had a weathered look about him that could have been a very well-preserved seventy, a hard fifty, or anything in-between.

"Sorry, but he's not here," I told him. I wasn't about to give this stranger any additional information. If my uncle's possible connection to the murder and his sudden disappearance hadn't made its way to the grapevine yet, I wasn't going to be the one to spill the tea. Mentally, I pantomimed locking my lips and throwing away the key. "Can I take your name and number?"

"Name's Jed. And my number is five thousand. As in dollars. That's how much Calvin Voigt owes me." He slapped a piece of paper down on the counter. Near as I could tell, it was covered in nonsense, written in my uncle's scrawl. "You have him call me. Sooner, rather than later, you hear?"

I nodded. "I'll pass him the message."

The man turned and stormed out, all but colliding with Tansy.

"Excuse me!" she exclaimed, hopping out of his way.

He grunted at her and barreled through the door.

"What was that all about?" she asked as she approached the counter. "Was he upset because we don't have pumpkin spice? I know it's only March, but I really do think we should keep it in stock because it's so popular."

As soon as the angry rancher was gone, Daffy appeared, right on cue. He batted at the sheet of paper on the counter, and I rescued it from him. "He wasn't upset about our coffee flavors," I told her. I held the page up to the light, as if maybe it would make more sense when viewed from a different angle. It did not. "Or at least I don't think he was. He said that Uncle Calvin owed him five thousand dollars, and left this."

"Well, he can get in line," Tansy said. She poured herself a latte and added a flourish in the foam. I could make a lopsided heart with the foam, but that was the extent of my skills so far. Tansy, always the overachiever, had quite the knack for it already. I was getting pretty good at mixing drinks, but I *really* needed to practice my latte art.

Tansy had always been the artistic one in the family. Drawing, painting, ceramics, you name it and she was good at it. Maggie outshone us both in math, which is why she kept all the books for Sip & Spin, as well as Taggart and McGibbons, J.T.'s law firm. Me? I was a whiz with languages; whether it was coming in first place at the spelling bee or learning a new programming language, that was my jam. Which may have been why I was so fascinated with the paper Jed had left.

"What's that?" Tansy asked, noticing the page for the first time.

"Beats me." It wasn't simple mirror writing. I'd mastered that in fourth grade. There was no sign of stains that might have indicated the presence of invisible ink, and there were obvious breaks between words and sentences instead of one long string of text. "A code of some sort."

I opened Google Translate and typed the first few lines into the search box. A language suggestion popped up— Croatian—but the result was nonsensical. "'Wrote it along the way to a friend dropped his own letter himself.' Does that mean anything to you?" I asked my sister.

"That makes no sense," she said. Daffy, bored now that I'd taken his new toy away from him, jumped off the counter and meowed up at my sister, demanding her full attention.

"I agree. Besides, when did Uncle Calvin start sending out IOUs in Croatian?"

The door opened with a pleasant jingle, and the cat was off like a shot before Teddy even stepped inside. I slid the odd note under the computer's keyboard as he called out, "Juni! Tansy! Lovely day, isn't it?"

"It is," Tansy agreed. "Got anything for us today?"

Teddy stepped around one of the big central record displays to approach the counter. That's when I noticed his outfit. He wore sensible black shoes instead of his usual cowboy boots, with white socks, long dark blue shorts with a pinstripe running down the side that showed off well-defined calf muscles, and a light blue polo shirt with the United States Postal Service logo above the pocket.

"You're a mailman?" I asked, surprised that I didn't know this.

"Postal worker," he corrected me. "And yeah. It's a sweet job. I work outside, get plenty of exercise, and talk to everyone. It's pretty much ideal. Plus, there's a union and a government retirement package."

"That does sound sweet," I agreed. My last job had a 401(k), but it evaporated, along with my employment, when the company closed without warning and the owners disappeared. And now owning a small business meant my future—not to mention my present—was entirely in my own hands. It was a lot of pressure, but it was exciting, too. "Can I get you a coffee? On the house, of course. Friends in Mocha Places is getting rave reviews."

"Thanks, but can I get a plain black?"

"One Got My Mind Set on Brew, coming right up." That was an order I could handle with ease. It was simple drip coffee, no foam art required.

While I prepared his drink, Teddy put a package on the counter, along with a small stack of mail all rubber banded together. "Got anything going out today?" he asked.

I glanced over at the stack of records I'd pulled but hadn't had a chance to do anything with yet. "I'll have some for you tomorrow." I made a mental note that from now on I'd process internet orders early in my shift so they'd be ready when Teddy came by. "Who's the package from?"

"Return to sender," Teddy said.

I looked at Tansy. "We haven't sent out any packages yet."

Teddy shrugged and took the offered coffee. "Don't know what to tell you. Hey, when did you get a cat?"

"You saw Daffy?" If the skittish cat was curious enough to stick his head out with a stranger in the shop, I hoped that he would eventually learn to accept, and maybe even like, our customers.

"I saw a flash of orange-and-white tail just now. Daffy? As in Duck?"

"As in Daffodil," I clarified.

Teddy chuckled. "You Jessups and your flowery names. Is it too late to name this place Flower Records?"

I shook my head. "I tried. Maggie and Tansy outvoted me.

But I'm glad they did. 'Sip & Spin' has a nice ring to it, don't you think?"

"Sure does. Well, I gotta get going, but thanks for the coffee. How about I pay you back by taking you out to dinner sometime this week?"

"You bought me pizza Friday," I reminded him.

"Pizza isn't dinner."

"So what is it?" I asked.

"It's pizza. See you around," Teddy said before he left.

"I think Teddy Garza just asked you on a date," Tansy said as soon as the door closed behind him.

"Don't be silly. He's Teddy. One of my oldest and dearest friends."

"Uh-huh," my sister said skeptically. "Hey, what's the ladder doing in the hallway?"

"J.T. came by here earlier to adjust the security camera by the back door," I explained. "He mounted it too high last time. I'll take care of it."

I moved down the hall, then hesitated with my hand on the doorknob of the supply closet. I *really* didn't want to open the door. Last time, it hadn't been pleasant

"Want me to do it?" Tansy asked.

"Nah, I'm good." I couldn't avoid the supply closet forever. What if I was the only one working and the bathroom ran out of toilet paper or we needed more coffee cups? I gathered my courage and opened the door.

The supply closet was empty. Well, not *empty* empty. The shelves were neatly arranged and logically ordered with supplies—or at least to Maggie's logic. But there was no dead body. Good thing, too. I didn't think I'd be able to handle finding more than one murder victim in a week. Or a lifetime.

The light flickered and I reached up to tap the bulb out of habit. The space we were leasing had gone through a lot of updates over the years. Back when my grandparents, and later my parents, ran the record shop, we didn't even have central AC. We just propped open the front and back doors and set up fans in the corners on hot days. The building was well maintained, but some things never changed, I supposed. Like the shoddy wiring inside the supply closet.

When I was little, I spent untold hours in this shop. Before I was old enough to go to school, I would go to work with my parents. After I started school, the bus dropped me off here instead of at home. I could still picture me and my sisters sitting on high stools pulled up to the checkout counter, doing our homework between customers.

I knew every inch of this place. Every tile. Every crack in the sidewalk out front. I couldn't have been much older than four or five when I discovered the loose panel in the fake-wood siding of the storage closet walls. If I pushed on it just right, it slid aside, revealing a small, dark cubbyhole.

All that had been inside was a cheap wooden box with a flimsy lock. But in my head, I'd discovered a lost pirate chest. I tried for days to pick the lock with no luck. Eventually, I gave up but brought one of my favorite Beanie Babies from home—Scorch the dragon, with shiny red wings and a row of green felt scales down his back—and left him in the cubby to guard the treasure.

I wondered if Scorch was still there after all these decades. Surely, by now someone else would have discovered the hidey-hole, but curiosity got the best of me. I pushed on the panel, and it moved. I knelt in front of it and slid it open. When I was a kid, I would have stuck my hand inside without hesitation, but I was older and more cautious now. I pulled out my phone, turned on the flashlight app, and shone it into the hole.

Scorch was still there, covered in cobwebs. His tail had been ravaged by tiny rodent teeth. His shiny wings were intact and caught the light of my phone.

But the box he was supposed to be guarding was gone.

In its place was a perfect rectangle etched into decades of dust. I ran my finger over the empty space where my pirate treasure should have been and it came away clean. Whoever had removed the wooden chest had done so recently.

CHAPTER 11

"What's taking you so long?" Tansy called, jolting me back to the present.

I slid the loose panel back into place and scooted the mop bucket over in front of it for good measure. "Nothing!" I called back. I maneuvered the ladder back into the space where it belonged. "Weird question," I asked when I returned to the front, "did you ever know of any hiding places in the shop?"

"Like for hide-and-seek? Aren't you a little old for that?"

"Of course," I said, not wanting to explain myself. I should have known that Tansy hadn't been the one to remove the treasure chest. I tried to imagine her down on her hands and knees in white pants and a pastel yellow twinset feeling along the bottom of the supply closet, and failed.

"Got any ideas for lunch?" I asked, changing the subject.

"Actually, I do. I've been asking around, and Monica Mayhew worked for some big-shot Austin lawyer. We can drop by, ask her a few questions, and grab some barbeque at a stand I like on the way back. How does that sound?"

"What kind of questions?" I asked.

"You know, the usual. Was Monica acting weird before her death? Did she have any enemies? Do you know who killed her? You know, that sort of thing."

I couldn't tell if she was joking or not. "If we prove Uncle Calvin wasn't involved with Monica's death, he'll poke his head out and then we can convince him to turn himself in," I said, ignoring the flippant comments my sister had just made to focus on the big picture. I was glad that Tansy had come around. "Monica's employer sounds like a great place to start." I thought back to my earlier conversation with our brother-in-law. "When J.T. was here this morning, he was pretty adamant that we don't get involved. Said our snooping around could make things worse for Calvin."

"What J.T. doesn't know won't hurt him," Tansy said. She looked over the empty store. "We'll put a sign up that we'll be back in an hour."

"Okay," I agreed. We turned out the lights, taped up a sign, and locked the doors—front and back—on our way out. "Tell me about this big-shot Austin lawyer."

"Her name is Jocelyn Reyes," Tansy said as she headed for the highway. "Her commercials are everywhere. I called her office this morning, and scheduled a consultation."

"You what? We don't need another lawyer, not when we already have J.T. and Elroy," I said.

"We're just using Calvin's case to get our foot in the door. Otherwise, how could we get a busy lawyer like Reyes to meet with us?"

"Good thinking," I admitted. I wished I'd thought of that myself. "I'm glad you brought me along."

"Of course! The only thing better than one of the Jessup sisters is *two* of the Jessup sisters," Tansy said with a smile. She navigated her way through Austin and found parking in an underground garage of an office building. Downtown Austin was an amalgamation of the very old and the very new, woven together in a delicate truce. At the heart of Austin was the state capitol, a late-1800s behemoth constructed from pink granite modeled after the Capitol Building in Washington. It was surrounded by museums, office buildings, and the famous stretch of bars along Sixth Street.

What served as the center of the government during the day was the beating heart of the vibrant music scene at night, but at all times it embodied the unofficial motto of Keep Austin Weird. From colorful murals to a larger-than-life statue of Willie Nelson, Austin was simultaneously a living art exhibit and a thriving business center. Even the building the law firm inhabited was a fusion of contemporary architecture on the outside with an art deco–inspired lobby.

We took the elevator up to the top floor. An assistant whisked us inside, where Jocelyn Reyes rose from behind a sleek glass desk to greet us. She was a petite Hispanic woman who radiated confidence. She wore a purple lace V-necked dress that accented her curvy figure and matched her bright purple lipstick. Her warm brown hair had subtle red highlights and big, bouncy curls that looked effortless but probably took an hour to perfect in the morning.

She extended a hand. Her nails were painted the same shade of purple as her lips and dress, and they were a perfect, uniform length. "Have a seat, ladies. How can I help y'all today?" She spoke with a classic Texas drawl.

After introducing ourselves and shaking hands, we sat. Tansy folded her hands in her lap. "We're here because our uncle's in a spot of trouble."

"Uh-huh," Reyes said, taking notes on a legal pad. "And your uncle isn't joining us today, because?"

"He's lying low," I said.

Reyes turned her gaze toward me, and despite her wide, friendly smile and straight, white teeth I felt myself squirm in my seat as she looked right through me. I imagined she would be very intimidating in a courtroom. "Lying low, you say. And what's your uncle being accused of?"

"Officially, unpaid traffic tickets," I replied.

"And unofficially?" she asked. She was sharp.

Instead of answering, Tansy asked, "Do you know Monica Mayhew?"

"I might." Reyes didn't even blink.

"She works here?" Tansy pressed.

"What's this all about?"

"So she does work here?" I asked.

Reyes rose from her chair. "Ladies, I'm a busy woman. If you have questions about any current or former employees, feel free to contact my Human Resources administrator. In the meantime, if you don't want to play straight with me, I must insist that you leave my office."

I glanced at Tansy, who shrugged. We might as well lay our cards out on the table before Reyes kicked us out. "Monica Mayhew is dead. And the police think our uncle might be involved."

Reyes sat back down. She looked stunned. "Monica is dead? When did this happen?"

"Last Friday," Tansy said. "But I'm surprised you didn't realize something was up when she didn't show up for work today."

"Monica hasn't worked here for a while, a few months at least. You can ask my new assistant how long ago that was on your way out. She was her replacement. No, she was her replacement's replacement. I go through a lot of assistants."

I raised my eyebrows. An assistant at a respectable law firm wasn't typically a revolving-door position, unless something else was going on. Like if the boss was a barracuda. "Why'd she quit?" I asked.

"Oh, she didn't quit. I had to let her go." Reyes drew herself up straighter in her chair. Clearly, she'd already recovered from the news about Monica. "Nice girl. A bit of a Goody Two-shoes, if you know what I mean. Very competent, when she was at work. But she lived out in the sticks. Oak Creek? Piney Lake?"

"Cedar River," Tansy and I said, simultaneously.

"Yes, that's the place. Always had some excuse for being late. Traffic was a nightmare. Her car broke down. Yadda, yadda, yadda. I told her she'd be better off getting an apartment downtown and then she wouldn't have to worry about that, but she helped out at her mom's deli or something in the evenings."

"Her father's steak house," I corrected her. "She was raised by a single dad."

"Who didn't believe in watches?" Reyes asked, shaking her head. Meeting her made me doubly glad to be a part of the family business. She flapped a hand in a dismissive gesture. "Which is neither here nor there. I'm sorry to hear that Monica is dead. I'll have my new assistant send flowers to the family. But I still don't understand what your uncle has to do with any of this. Start from the beginning. Who exactly is your uncle, and what was the nature of his relationship with Monica?"

"His name is Calvin Voigt," I said. "And right now, he's the police's only suspect."

I didn't know what kind of reaction I'd expected. Dollar signs to flash in her eyes maybe. But I wasn't prepared for her to say, in an eerily calm voice, "I think it's time you ladies left."

"Excuse me?" Tansy asked.

"You heard me. I've got a full schedule already. A murder case takes dedicated resources. I think y'all would be better off finding a lawyer who doesn't have a personal connection with the victim."

I wouldn't exactly have described her connection with Monica as personal. Based on what she'd told us, it was barely even professional.

But Reyes wasn't done yet. "You might be better off looking for someone who does pro bono work. A public defender, maybe," she added, looking pointedly at my outfit.

Where she saw a thirty-year-old T-shirt, I saw a vintage Tori Amos concert tee. My jeans were also a classic. I'd rescued the bell-bottoms with hand-embroidered daisies along the sides out of the back of my mom's closet when I was still in high school and only wore them on special occasions, like my first full day at Sip & Spin. My boots, well I didn't have an excuse for my well-worn Doc Martens other than they were comfortable and complemented my throwback outfit with style.

Tansy started to come to my defense, but I lightly touched her elbow and rose from my chair. "Thanks for your time. And the recommendation. I assume you validate parking?"

"We do not," she said with an aggrieved glare.

"Come on, Tansy, we've wasted enough of our time today," I said, urging my sister to follow me out of the room.

"Wow, that woman was a piece of work," Tansy said. Her voice was loud enough to have carried back through the open door, and I had no doubt that she had intended it that way.

"Tell me about it," the assistant at the front desk said in an undertone. "And by the way, we totally validate." She held out her hand. Tansy passed her the garage ticket. "Sorry to hear about Monica. I overheard Dragon Lady complaining about her, but usually all I get is complaints that I'm not as good as her."

"Overheard?" I asked, glancing back at the thick wooden door that separated us from the lawyer.

She pointed toward the multiline phone on her desk. "Sometimes I forget to turn off the speaker. Yet another reason why I'm not as good as the perfect Monica Mayhew. She really bent over backward to keep the boss happy, and then she was fired just for being late twice." The assistant shook her head. "Seriously. Know anyone who's hiring?"

"Not right now," I told her. "But we run a record shop in Cedar River." I handed her my business card. "Once things pick up, we might need some help."

She grinned. "I'll give you guys a call in a few weeks. I'm Ella." She handed Tansy back the validated ticket.

"Thanks, Ella. I look forward to your call," Tansy said.

"Thanks," I echoed, and followed her out of the office and into the elevator. "What did you think?"

"I think that woman makes me glad I'm in business for myself."

"I was thinking the same thing," I admitted. "I've had some difficult bosses before, but nothing like her." I paused, thinking. "I wonder if Monica ever accidentally overheard something she wasn't supposed to."

"Like what?" We located Tansy's car in the garage, and she beeped the doors unlocked.

"Who knows," I said as I sat and adjusted my seat belt. "Maybe it's unfair of me, but I assume not all of Reyes's clients are one hundred percent aboveboard. Who knows what someone might have admitted in the privacy of their lawyer's office."

"Even if we had access to a list of her clients, it would be next to impossible to connect those dots," Tansy pointed out.

As usual, my eldest sister was right, but it seemed like a possible murder motive to me. Flimsy? Sure. But it was still better than accusing my uncle just because Monica had his business card in her hand.

"You still up for barbeque?" Tansy asked.

"When am I not?" The Pacific Northwest had an awful lot to offer, but it didn't have honest-to-goodness Texas barbeque.

We stopped and picked up lunch, making sure to get enough for all three of us in the event that Maggie was hungry. I was tempted to sample lunch in the car, but barbeque is notoriously messy and the shop wasn't far away, so I resisted.

While Tansy drove, I let my mind wander. Reyes had called Monica a Goody Two-shoes. That much hadn't changed since she was a kid. Competent. Well-mannered. Helping her dad out at the restaurant in the evenings after a full day of dealing with Jocelyn Reyes. Poor Monica didn't deserve to have her life cut short, not that anyone did.

As if reading my mind, Tansy said, "We need to figure out who killed her."

"We do," I agreed. And not just for Calvin. We needed to do it for Monica.

CHAPTER 12

"Where have y'all been?" Maggie asked as soon as we walked into the shop.

I set the bag of takeout on one of the café tables. "Picking up lunch," I told her. "Want me to make you a plate?"

Her eyes got wide and I swear she started to drool. She decided to let it slide that Tansy and I had locked up the store and taken off in the middle of our first day. Then again, that was bound to happen on occasion. Even with all three of us rotating shifts, there would be times that we didn't have enough coverage. "Get any potato salad? Corn bread?"

"Of course," Tansy said. "What do we look like, amateurs?" We spread out the to-go containers on the coffee counter as Maggie checked out a customer. "Been busy?"

"I wish," she said as the customer waved on their way out. "That was the only customer I've had in the last hour. He was interested in a rocksteady band he'd heard on Sixth Street, and I also introduced him to some classic ska." It would have been nice to open Sip & Spin Records on Sixth Street in downtown Austin to be closer to the music scene, but the rent was way too expensive.

Besides, this was home. There was something magical

about being in the same space that was originally our grandparents' record shop, and the thought of fighting traffic into and
out of Austin every day made me cringe. I didn't know how
Monica had done it. There were plenty of good jobs right here
in Cedar River, but I guess she had her reasons. Maybe working for Reyes had come with hazard pay.

"Seriously, where have you two been?" Maggie asked
around a mouthful of barbeque.

Tansy looked at me as if to ask whether or not we should
tell her. "Might as well," I said, answering her silent question.
"There aren't any secrets between us. Besides, Maggie and I
were talking earlier and she agrees. We're more motivated than
anyone to figure out who killed Monica Mayhew and bring
Uncle Calvin home."

"We went to see Monica's former boss," Tansy said, "a
lawyer named Jocelyn Reyes."

"I've heard of her," Maggie interrupted. "J.T. is always complaining about her."

"Oh really?" I leaned in closer. "What does he say? She
a bad lawyer?" She struck me as highly competent, but how
much could I know about a person after a single conversation?

"Just the opposite. She's good, real good. And her prices
are competitive. J.T. lost a client to her recently. Was awful
mad about it, too, but she's since referred two clients and an intern, so I guess they're even. You say Monica worked for her?"

"She fired Monica recently," I clarified.

The front door opened and our mother breezed inside. "Is
that barbeque I smell?" she asked, making a beeline to the
makeshift buffet and helping herself to a plate. "This isn't
from Betty-B-Que." Cedar River's only dedicated barbeque
restaurant, a tiny tucked-away storefront, was famous for its
macaroni and okra side that was admittedly good enough to
serve as a main course.

"Nope," Tansy said. She glanced at us, but she didn't need to say what we were all thinking. If Mom didn't want us investigating, she might put her foot down and order us to stop. Sure, we weren't kids anymore, but when Bea Jessup laid down the law we were best off obeying. But if we *didn't* tell her and she heard about it from anyone else, she would be livid.

Mom didn't seem to notice the silent conversation and subsequent agreement going over her head. "This isn't from one of those food trucks, is it? I don't trust those trucks. How can you know that they're clean? If they have a complaint, they just move a block over and no one's ever the wiser."

"Actually, food trucks are highly regulated and very competitive," I corrected her. "They rely on repeat customers and word of mouth, and they can't survive without a good Yelp rating. You didn't complain about the truck we had for the grand opening."

"Our guests did seem to like it," she admitted. "But I was too busy entertaining to get a sample."

"Me too," I said. I still regretted that. I'd have to track them down and try their tacos as soon as I had free time. "But no, this wasn't from a truck." I turned the bag around, showing the logo, a smiling pig with a bib around its neck. "Picked it up in Austin."

"You went all the way to Austin to get barbeque? This better be worth it." She took a bite, chewed, and swallowed. "This is good."

"Try the beans," Tansy suggested. "They're slow cooked in maple syrup and Texas bourbon. And no, we didn't go all the way downtown for barbeque. We wanted a word with Monica Mayhew's former employer, Jocelyn Reyes."

"Wait a second," Mom interjected. "You girls aren't thinking about doing anything foolish now, are you? Calvin will come back on his own time. No need to go making things more complicated than they have to be."

Uh-oh. Maybe we should have kept our mouths shut. "We just wanted to chat with her old boss about Monica, that's all. Calvin doesn't have anything to do with it," I corrected her.

"Actually, that's not entirely true," Mom said, wiping her lips delicately with a paper napkin. Only my fastidious mother could make eating messy barbeque look neat. "Jocelyn Reyes, you say? Didn't she and Calvin date back in the day?"

"What?" I asked. At the same time, Tansy said, "Excuse me?" Maggie was too busy eating a miniature loaf of honey-drizzled jalapeño corn bread to contribute, but her eyes got wide and I could tell she was just as surprised as we were.

"When was this?" Tansy asked. "I can't remember the last time Uncle Calvin was serious about anyone, and I certainly would recall if he'd brought that lawyer around. She was not someone I'd forget easily."

"Oh, this was long before your time." Mom flapped a dismissive hand at us. "Gosh, that must have been what, eighty-five? Eighty-six? They broke up right around the time your dad and me started getting serious."

"Wait up. You're telling me that you can remember the name of someone your brother dated nearly forty years ago?"

Mom took another helping of beans and added a smoked sausage to her plate. "Jocelyn was not very forgettable. Besides"—she rested her fork on her plate to free up a hand before tapping her temple—"mind like a steel trap. Ask me anything. My kindergarten teacher was Mrs. Gilripple. I wore a little yellow dress to my first day at school and cried when I spilled grape juice on it. Need more?"

"No, Ma, we're good," Tansy admitted. "Your memory is uncanny. Why'd they break up?"

"Who knows? I was eighteen and had more important things to worry about than my annoying older brother and his girlfriend. You girls have no idea how good you have it. Calvin and I didn't get along half as well as y'all did growing up. I love my brother to pieces, but, well, you know how he is."

My sisters and I exchanged knowing looks. We hadn't always gotten along. There were a few times I thought we might spark World War III. But at the end of the day, we were sisters. We might not have always seen eye to eye, but we'd always have each other's backs.

Uncle Calvin on the other hand, he meant well, but he wasn't exactly reliable. Just look at him now. When we needed him most, he was nowhere to be found. But at the end of the day, he was family.

"Girls, thanks for lunch, but I've got mah-jongg to get to, and you know how vicious those ladies can be if you're late or take too long to call a tile." Mom belonged to every club in Cedar River. She was a joiner. She folded her plate and slid it into the trash can and gave us all hugs before she left.

"I wonder why Jocelyn didn't mention that she used to date Calvin," I said to Tansy after she was gone.

"She probably didn't put two and two together. We have Dad's last name, and it's been a long time."

"But she knew we were from Cedar River," I pointed out. "And we said we were there on behalf of Calvin Voigt. Come to think about it, as soon as we said his name she tossed us out of her office." I tried to recall the details of the meeting. She had gotten squirrely the second we mentioned our uncle. Now I understood why.

If forty years from now, Beau's nieces came to me asking for my help clearing him of murder charges, I'd probably act the same way. Good thing Beau was an only child.

"Guys, we need to be careful. J.T. said we shouldn't get involved," Maggie said.

"And he's got a point," I admitted. "But J.T. doesn't have anything to lose. If Calvin doesn't come back in time for his hearing, J.T. and Elroy still have their law firm, but we default on Sip

& Spin. And he didn't grow up down the street from Monica and her dad. This is business for him. For us, it's family."

"J.T. *is* family," Maggie insisted.

"Sure he is," Tansy agreed. "Which is why he wants this mess solved just as much as we do. But while he's concentrating on the legal side of things, what does it hurt if we ask a few questions?"

"Nothing, I guess" Maggie said cautiously, adding, "as long as he doesn't find out."

"Exactly," I said. "Which is why we won't tell him. What do you say tomorrow you and I go over to talk to Calvin's old business partner and see if he knows anything useful."

"Samuel?" Maggie asked. "Don't you think that the cops would have already talked to him? Everyone in Cedar River knows that Samuel Davis and Calvin are as thick as thieves."

"Juni's right. He might tell us something that he forgot"— she put air quotes around "forgot"—"to tell the cops." Tansy nodded at me with a look of respect on her face. I'm sure she would have come up with the idea to talk to our uncle's best friend and former business partner eventually, but she was proud I'd thought of it first.

"What if J.T. asks me what I'm doing tomorrow?"

"Tell him you're spending quality time with your sisters," Tansy said, draping her arm around her shoulder. "Which is true."

"I just don't feel right keeping secrets from my husband."

"If anything comes of it, we'll tell him right away," I promised.

She bit her bottom lip. "Fine. But while we're gone, Tansy has to watch the shop. We can't keep closing in the middle of the day all willy-nilly."

"Agreed," Tansy and I said.

"Okay, I'm in. Don't either of you have somewhere to be? I can cover the shop for a few hours."

Tansy nodded. "I've got library books I need to return. And it's a lovely day, not too hot. I could get a run in."

"Juni?" Maggie asked me.

As much as I hated to admit it, I didn't have any plans. I was used to working long days and having little to no social life. "Actually, I'm free if you have things to do."

"I was thinking about making lasagna tonight. But I'd have to go shopping first."

"Go ahead, Maggie. I've got this," I assured her.

"You certain?"

"Yup."

Maggie cleaned up the empty takeout containers and left with Tansy. Alone now, I selected a record at random from the local bands display and put it on the record player. A few customers wandered in and spent some time perusing the records upstairs and down. One bought three albums, but the others ended up only ordering afternoon coffee.

In between customers, I checked the internet orders. We had no new requests since this morning, so I packaged up the albums I'd pulled earlier and printed out labels for them. I set them aside for Teddy's pickup tomorrow and noticed the returned package I'd forgotten about.

It was packaged the same as the outgoing records. Our LP mailers were generic sturdy envelopes we had purchased in bulk that we stamped with our logo before mailing out. I flipped over the package. There was no logo, but "Sip & Spin" was on the return address. I didn't recognize the name of the intended recipient. The address was two towns over. Between the packaging and the postage, even at media rate, it would have cost less in gas to drop the album off than to send it through the mail, assuming it had come from us.

There was only one way to tell what was inside. I pulled the tab to open the package and reached inside to pull out a record in a plain white sleeve. That was weird. We only sold records that came with a dust jacket. It was part of the appeal of vinyl. Depending on how elaborate it was, some collectors were more interested in the dust jacket than the music on the album.

But the blank sleeve wasn't the only thing weird about the package. I pulled out the record. The label was worn away so badly I could only guess what the contents were. I could put it on the player and find out, but the surface was so badly scratched I doubted it would play. It was a junk album. The cost of postage alone was much more than the record was worth.

I started back to the storeroom to put the now-empty sleeve on the shelf with the others and toss the record in the junk bin when I realized that the sleeve wasn't actually empty. Through the center hole, I saw a sheet of paper.

After fishing the paper out, I laid it on the counter next to the cash register and stared uncomprehending at the unreadable words written on it in my uncle's handwriting. I pulled out the page that the angry customer had brought in earlier this morning and compared them side by side.

Both were written on standard letter-size paper, the same plain color and generic weight as what we had in our printer. Both were covered in my uncle's familiar scribble in black ink. One was slightly lighter than the other, as if the pen was running out.

That was where the similarities ended. While both looked like gibberish to me, it was obvious that they didn't say the same thing.

I opened the translator on the search engine and typed in a few lines. I expected Croatian to be detected again, but this time it came up as Estonian. A few of the words came back as scrambled nonsensical letters, but in the center were the words "Baby Shark" duplicated several times.

"Huh," I said aloud. I had no idea what either of these letters meant, or what my uncle had gotten himself into, but I was going to find out.

CHAPTER 13

Traffic at Sip & Spin picked up later in the day. The earlier hours had seen mostly walk-ins who browsed for a few minutes before leaving with a specialty coffee. The evening customers wanted to talk music and listened to several albums before purchasing a stack of records and maybe grabbing a coffee as an afterthought.

It got so busy at one point that I had to call Tansy in for backup. My big sister was unsurprisingly music savvy. As the oldest, she'd spent more time than Maggie or I ever did in the shop back when my grandparents had owned it, but it was more than that. She was a full-on aficionado, especially when it came to the local music scene.

Looking for an all-Hispanic punk band? A lesbian jazz trio? Boot-scooting rap? Austin had it, and Tansy could recommend the best without hesitation.

In one of our rare breaks between customers that evening— Sip & Spin wasn't empty, as it had been much of the morning, but everyone was occupied at the turntables, listening to records—I decided to put her to the test. "If I was in the mood for local bagpipe music, what would you recommend?"

Tansy gave me a sly smile, walked over to the racks, and came back with three albums. "Austin doesn't have much in the way of resident pipers, but both TRF and Scarby have faire favorites." The Texas Renaissance Festival over by Houston and Scarborough Faire up near Dallas—known as TRF and Scarby to the locals—were great places to dress up in medieval costume and eat giant turkey legs while watching a live jousting match and listening to bagpipes play in the background. She tapped each record in succession. "Are you in the mood for high-energy drumbeats, traditional Scottish tunes with lyrical vocals, or marching-band-style bagpipes?"

"You are good," I told her.

"I know." She winked at me and returned the albums to the rack, stopping to check on the customers at the record players to make sure everyone was all set. While she was occupied with them, the front door opened. A woman entered the store and headed directly to the counter.

"Officer Jayden Holt," I greeted her. Even out of uniform, she carried herself with unmistakable authority. Her hair was pulled back in a tight ponytail. She wore dark indigo jeans and a tank top under an unbuttoned oversize shirt. She had on neither cowboy boots nor a cowboy hat but made up for it with a necklace with a small silver pendant in the shape of Texas dangling from it. An inlaid diamond glittered from the approximate location of Austin.

"Juniper Jessup," she said, returning my greeting.

"'Juni' is fine," I reminded her. "How can I help you?" Part of me was suspicious. Cedar River was a small town and Sip & Spin was open to the public, but it seemed a little too coincidental that a cop would drop in while my family was under scrutiny. Maybe I was just being paranoid.

"I missed the grand opening party, and wanted to drop by and see if you carry any Esther Phillips."

I breathed a sigh of relief. Jayden really was here to shop, not to interrogate us.

"Ahh, the golden age of R and B," Tansy said, joining our

conversation. "We certainly do. Did you know that she was a native Texan?"

"I had no idea," Jayden said.

"Yup, born in Galveston. If you like Esther Phillips, you might also want to check out a few local Austin jazz groups." She led the officer upstairs to the R&B section in the loft as my phone rang.

I didn't recognize the number, but it had an Austin area code, so I picked up. "Hello?"

"Juni, I didn't catch you at a bad time, did I?" a familiar voice asked.

"Miss Edie?" I clutched my phone tighter. "Is it my uncle? Is he home?"

"No, sweetie. But I was wondering if you could do me a little favor?"

"Sure thing," I offered. It was only fair, seeing as how I'd asked her to keep an eye on Calvin's house for me. Besides, in these parts, we all helped each other out when we could. "What can I do for you?"

"It's my dog. I ran out of Buffy's medicine. I already called in a refill at the vet. Is there any way you could pick it up for me?"

"Of course I will. Do you need it right away?"

"The vet closes soon, but I don't need the pills until bed-time."

"No problem. I'll go pick up the meds now and drop them off on my way home if that's okay," I told her.

"Oh, that would be perfectly lovely of you."

"No problem. I'll see you in a few hours." I disconnected the call as another customer came up to check out with their selections.

"Find everything you were looking for?" I asked automatically. My high school customer service experience had come back as easily as if I'd never left. Once I started programming, I'd sworn against ever going back to a retail position, but this was different. This was my own shop. These customers were my neighbors. And I was surrounded all day by good music and delicious coffee options. It was a far cry from running a cash register at a generic chain store at a mall for minimum wage.

"Yup. Great selection," he said. He was closer to my mom's age than my own and had the deeply tanned skin of someone who'd spent a lifetime outdoors. His only jewelry was a thick silver bracelet with turquoise inlay, and while he didn't have a cowboy hat on right now, there was a visible ring around his thinning hair that clearly demonstrated that he wore one often.

I scanned in his records. He'd picked out a few of the old cowboy spirituals along with a modern popular country group. "If you like these guys, we have a similar local artist," I told him, recalling what Tansy had told a customer who had come in earlier.

"I don't know; this is for my granddaughter. I'm trying to get her interested in vinyl, but you know kids these days."

"Sure do," I agreed with him. "But vinyl is making a serious comeback as the younger generation is rediscovering the superior sound. I love to see families connecting over music. This is a family business, you know." I waved my hand toward the racks of records. "My grandparents started a record store here in the sixties. My parents ran it for years after my grandparents retired, and now my sisters and I are reviving the tradition."

"Well, isn't that nice?" he asked. "You know, I think I will take that album you recommended."

I hurried around the counter and snagged the last copy of it off the rack. For the local bands, we only had room to carry a few albums, but if we sold out of someone, especially on our first day of business, we would certainly be reordering from them. I added the record to the stack, rang them up, and put everything into a bag. "I hope you'll come back with your granddaughter sometime."

"I will," he assured me. He picked up his bag, then paused for a second before asking, "You said family business?"

"Yup. Me and my sisters."

"You any relation to Calvin Voigt?"

"He's my uncle."

"I heard he's in a bit of a kerfuffle right now," he said.

"Something like that," I confirmed. I didn't feel comfortable talking about our personal troubles with a stranger, but at the same time maybe he knew something about my uncle's whereabouts that I didn't. "You hear from him recently?"

He shook his head. "Not since last weekend. I was wondering if you girls were gonna keep the game going, or if I had to wait until Calvin got back in town."

"Game?" I asked. "What game?"

"Never mind," he said. "Forget I said anything. Thanks again for the suggestions." He hurried out of the store, almost bowling over Jayden in his haste.

"What was that about?" she asked me.

"Beats me," I told her honestly. My uncle was certainly into *something* shady, but what it was I had no idea. If I did, I wouldn't be sharing that information with a police officer, even an off-duty one. I turned my attention to the albums in her arms. "Looks like you found some good ones."

"Do y'all sell needles, too? I can't remember the last time I blew the dust off my old player and who knows what shape the needle's in."

"Sure do." I grabbed one of the most common ones and added it to her stack of albums. "If this doesn't fit your player, just bring it back and we'll swap it out."

As I rang up her purchases, Tansy brought over a to-go cup of coffee. "Vanilla Ice Iced Coffee. On the house."

Jayden looked up at her. "I love iced coffee. Thank you." She paid, took her records and drink, and left.

"I'm gonna walk over to the vet and pick up a prescription for Miss Edie's dog," I told Tansy. "Need anything while I'm out?"

"I'm good," she assured me.

The evening was warm. Couples and families were wandering the sidewalks, running errands, or heading to dinner. A car with the Roadrunners logo plastered to their back window double-parked in front of the bakery. Roadrunners was a local delivery service, like Uber Eats but just for Cedar River. Today traffic on Main Street was light and cars had no problem getting around it. I got to the vet just as they were locking up. They let me in and gave me a small paper bag. Inside was a bottle of pills and a dog biscuit in the shape of a bone.

"Thanks!" I told them before retracing my steps back to the shop, where my sister was helping customers.

As the evening wore down, I was pleased with our sales, especially for a weekday. I knew part of it was the excitement of having something new in town and that this level of interest wasn't sustainable. But it was a start. If every person who came in tonight told a friend and then they told a friend, we could make it.

That is, of course, unless Uncle Calvin failed to appear in court and we forfeited the shop to the bail bonds people.

Thinking about my uncle made me wonder what the customer who'd come in earlier had meant about the game. What game? Unlike my sister Maggie, Calvin wasn't much for team sports.

Maybe it was a game they'd planned on attending together. Uncle Calvin liked baseball, but the season hadn't started yet. Local football was for him, like many Texans, his real passion, but that was more of a fall and winter sport. It was the end of hockey season, but my uncle knew about as much about hockey as I did, which is to say it was played on ice.

Of the major sports, that only left basketball. It wasn't a sport that was terribly popular in my family. For some unfathomable reason, Texans seemed to lean toward outdoor sports that required layers of sunscreen and buckets of Gatorade to watch. I guess we really were gluttons for punishment.

But March Madness, at least in these parts, was more about the play-off brackets than the basketball game. And brackets usually involved betting. Was Uncle Calvin betting on sports as well as horse racing? It fit his M.O., but something still felt off.

What had the customer said again? Something about keeping the game going, I thought. We used to do March Madness brackets at my office in Oregon. Buy-in was ten dollars, winner take all, but you had to pick your teams before the play-offs ever started. It wouldn't make sense that they needed to keep the game going halfway through play-offs.

I wish I'd thought to ask the right questions while he was in front of me. He'd paid cash, so I didn't even have his name on a credit card receipt. I had no idea who he was, but I'd probably recognize him if I saw him again. Yes, Cedar River was a small town, but not so small that everyone knew everyone. Besides, I'd been gone long enough that he could have moved to town after I'd left and our paths would never have crossed.

A flash of inspiration struck me and I rewound the security footage from the evening. I found the customer and took a screenshot. I studied him for a second. He was average height with slumped shoulders. I couldn't swear before a judge that he wasn't the same man as I'd seen on the back door security footage from the night of the party, but even without a cowboy hat on, I was 95 percent certain they weren't the same person. The man in that footage had been taller and narrower and had better posture.

"Hey, Tansy." I waved my sister over.

She was busy cleaning up the barista station and making sure it would be ready for tomorrow. "What's up?"

"Come take a look at this man." I swiveled the screen so she could see it. "Look familiar to you?"

She studied the screen. "Vaguely. I've probably seen him around town. Why? What's up?"

I shook my head. "I don't know. Just a feeling."

Her brow furrowed. "Did he bother you or something?"

"No, nothing like that. He just asked if we were going to keep up with Calvin's game. Do you have any idea what he was talking about?"

She shrugged. "Are you sure he said game and not league? Because you know how much Calvin loves to bowl."

"Fairly certain." Especially since, if Marv Knickleback was correct, my uncle wasn't in a bowling league. Instead, he preferred pickup games where the only score that counted at the end of the night was how many beers had been consumed. Maybe that was the game the customer was talking about?

"Sorry then, I've got nothing. Toss me my keys, will ya?" She took the keys, locked the front door, and turned over the Open sign. "So, how did we do?"

"Not bad." I clicked the button on the computer screen to display the day's receipts. The old-fashioned cash register on the counter was mostly for show. Inventory and credit card sales would be a total nightmare if we tried to rely on an analog cash register for tracking sales. I pulled out the money drawer and slipped it into the floor safe for the night. We didn't have a lot of customers who still used cash, but we had a few, like our customer who'd inquired about Uncle Calvin's game. "Not bad at all."

"Good. Well, how about I give you a ride home, and then we start all over again tomorrow?"

"Actually, I rode my trike in today, and I need to swing by

Miss Edie's. Besides, I might as well put some miles on the tricycle before it's too hot to enjoy it." I'd ridden pretty much everywhere in Oregon unless I had to go downtown for work or something. It was fun, and it was good exercise. Now that I was home and surrounded by all the food I loved, it didn't hurt to ride whenever I had a chance.

"Well, okay then." She didn't look convinced. "But keep your phone on and call me if you need me."

"Will do," I promised. Like I said, my sister could be a wee bit overprotective at times, but I loved her for it. It felt nice, knowing someone was looking out for me. "See you at home in a bit."

We let ourselves out. Tansy took her sweet time leaving. I think she was giving me enough time to change my mind if I wanted to. Instead, I fastened my helmet and took off toward home. A minute later, Tansy gave me a cheerful toot on her horn as she passed me.

The ride home was quiet, a good way to unwind after a long day. I wouldn't always be the first one in and the last one to leave; that would be unfair. But in my excitement of the first day, I had hardly noticed. Now as I pedaled, I realized that my legs were sore from standing on my feet for hours. It was going to take me a while to get used to that again, after several years of sitting behind a computer all day.

I rode down Main Street, past the Cedar Spines Bookstore and the beauty salon. I pedaled past the Sweet Shoppe. I slowed at the last intersection, across from the municipal parking lot, and noticed a truck parked on the cross street. As I watched, the engine sprang to life as the truck pulled out of its parking spot and headed straight for me.

CHAPTER 14

The truck pulled up alongside me. Once I got a good look at it, I recognized it as Beau's truck and relaxed. Even if I hadn't been riding around in it just yesterday, I would always know his truck.

This one was nearly a spitting image of the one he'd driven when I first met him. It was full-size. American made. Dark blue, bordering on black, with a splash of dried mud around the tires. It was a truck that could haul a four-wheeler out of a bog or go on date night to the drive-through movie theater one town over. It was practical but flashy. Dependable but a little dangerous at the same time. It was very Beau.

There had never been a doubt that Beau would go into law enforcement, just like his father and his father before him. I was impressed that he'd risen through the ranks to make detective at his age, but not necessarily surprised. He'd always done anything he had his mind set on, which made the fact that he was currently pursuing my own uncle positively nerve-racking.

He pulled over to the curb in front of me and rolled down his window. "Beauregard Russell, you just about scared the pants off me. What do you want?" I asked when I pulled up alongside him.

He got out of the truck. "Need a lift? Your tricycle should fit in the back."

"I'm good."

"I know you are, but"—he glanced over his shoulder as if to see if the boogieman was sneaking up on us—"look, Juni, you've been gone a long time. The streets of Cedar River aren't as safe as they used to be."

"You're telling me. I found a dead body in my record shop just the other day, remember?"

He shook his head. "That's not funny."

"Never said it was. What do you want, Beau?"

"To talk."

"We *are* talking," I pointed out.

He sighed and sat down on the curb. He took his hat off and laid it across his knees. "Is this the way it's gonna be with us now?"

I thought about it. "I don't know. Maybe. Probably. Whatever we used to have, used to be, has been over for a long time. And I still don't know why."

"I was young. And dumb." He paused. "And scared."

"Gee, that clears things up," I said, fighting the urge to roll my eyes. I'd waited six years for an explanation, and that's the best he could do?

"Would you have taken that internship if we hadn't broken up?" he asked.

I thought about that for a second. Then I shrugged. "Guess we'll never know, since you made the decision for both of us. And now you're hunting my uncle like you would a rabid coyote. So you'll have to excuse me if I'm not dying to rekindle our . . ." I tried to come up with the right word. "Friendship"? That wasn't right. "Relationship"? Even worse: "Us."

"I'm not hunting him, Junebug. I just want to find out who killed Monica Mayhew and see your uncle safe at home where he belongs. Isn't that what we both want?" He patted the curb next to him.

I got off my trike and sat down next to him. The curb was warm, and the grass was damp. In a few months, the pavement would be so hot I could fry an egg on the sidewalk—I've done it—and the grass would turn brown and wither away, but springtime in Texas was pleasant. Not like Oregon springs, which were just a long, rainy extension of winter until summer finally broke free and then it was glorious.

But I was several thousand miles from Oregon now, and the longer I was away, the more it faded from my mind, like an odd, half-forgotten dream.

Texas, specifically Cedar River, had never done that. Memories of my hometown were as sharp on the day I came back as they'd been on the day I left. Maybe that was because my family was here. To be completely honest, Beau had a part in that, too. In any event, I could live anywhere in the country, anywhere in the world, maybe, and this, right here, would always be my home.

Well, maybe not *right here* right here. Not on this specific curb. But close enough.

"You have a fun day?" he asked.

I blinked at him. How could he possibly have known that my sister and I had gone to Austin to interrogate Monica's old boss? "What do you mean by that?"

He looked confused at my defensiveness. "The shop? Opening day? How did it go?"

Relief washed over me. "Oh, the shop. Yeah, it was good. Lots of customers. A few sales."

"What did you think I meant?" he asked, studying my face.

"Um, nothing?"

"Spill it, Juniper."

"Nothing to spill," I said.

"You're lying."

I changed the subject. "That officer you work with, Jayden Holt, came in today to look at some records. She seems nice."

He nodded. "She is. And smart to boot. Mentioned she was gonna drop in on her lunch break and browse your selection. Said she went by and you were closed. In the middle of the day. Thought that was odd."

My heart raced as I tried to figure out exactly how much Beau already knew. It wouldn't do anyone any good to give him more information than I had to. "Tansy and I went out to get lunch. Barbeque. Business was slow, so we stepped out together."

"Betty's?" he asked.

I had no idea he'd become such an effective interrogator. If I told Beau we'd gone to Austin, he'd know for certain that something was up. If I said we'd gone to Betty-B-Que and he found out later that I was lying, I'd be in a heap of trouble. So I changed the subject. Again. "New truck?"

"Not really. You hear from your uncle today?"

"Nope." At least we were back on steady ground. This was one thing I didn't have to lie about. "If I knew where he was, I would tell you. Pinkie swear."

"Pinkie swear?" He chuckled. "What are we, twelve?" He stood and put his hat back on before holding out his hand. "Come on, Juni, let me give you a ride home."

I took his hand and let him help me up. "Thanks, but I'm good."

"You sure?"

I nodded. "Certain sure."

"You'll call me if you hear from Calvin." It wasn't a question.

"I will," I agreed.

He took off and I got back on my trike and started pedaling. The breeze picked up, probably coming from the river, just

a few blocks away. I was tempted to take a detour, maybe sit
by the riverbank for a while and let my troubles fall away,
but Tansy was waiting for me. Stopping to talk to Beau had
already made me later than expected, and I still needed to stop
by Edie's to drop off her dog's medicine.

I sped up, hoping to make up for lost time. The road
curved gently and the houses on either side of me were quiet.
I pulled into Miss Edie's driveway, walked up to the front
door, and knocked. Inside, there was a flurry of barking. She
was right about Buffy making a good guard dog. Although,
I wasn't certain that a burglar would knock before making
entry.

Edie opened the door wearing a housecoat. Buffy ran in
circles around my legs, yipping in excitement. I bent down to
scratch her just above her looped-over tail. Then I straightened
and handed the bag I'd picked up from the vet to the older
woman. "Here you go. Hope it's not too late for her pill."

"Not at all. Would you like to come inside? I have that fruit
punch you kids always liked so much. Or an open bottle of
wine, if that's more your speed now that you're all grown-up."
She winked at me.

"Thanks, but maybe another time. I never drink and trike."

She laughed and patted my arm. "Such a good girl. I'm
sorry for asking you to pick up Buffy's prescription for me.
Monica Mayhew always helped me with things like that, and
with her gone, I had no idea who to call."

"You can always call me," I assured her. "It's the least I can
do. So, you knew Monica pretty well, I guess?"

"Of course I did. I don't think there's a single kid in Cedar River I haven't babysat a dozen times, but Rodger always
needed a little extra help, being a single dad and all. I can't even
begin to imagine what he's going through now," Edie's usually
merry face creased with concern and sadness.

I nodded. "I know. It's just awful." It occurred to me that

I knew almost nothing about grown-up Monica. Maybe Edie could fill in some of the blanks. "Who did Monica hang around with?"

"She was always popular, but most of the kids she went to school with have moved on. You know how it is. They go off to college or move away to the city. She had a boyfriend for a while. Roy, I think? Real handsome fellow. But he got deployed a few months back."

"Was she seeing anyone lately?" I asked.

"I don't think she dated anyone after Roy, at least not that she talked about. Well, I hate to be rude, but I need to give Buffy her pill before it gets too late. Thanks again for helping me out."

"Anytime," I told her. She ushered the dog inside and closed the door. As I walked back to my tricycle, I glanced next door at my uncle's house. His old Bronco still sat in the driveway, reminding me that I had one lead I hadn't yet followed up on. If Calvin wasn't driving his own truck, he had to be getting around somehow. Cedar River may be in the sticks, but it wasn't impossible to get an Uber here.

Tansy had said that his phone was on the charger in his bedroom. I knew where he hid his spare key—in one of those fake rock hide-a-keys in the front yard. I was already here. I could let myself in and check his recent apps for myself. His phone would be a snap to unlock. His favorite PIN, as long as I'd known him, was 4–3–2–1. I might not learn where he was now, but with any luck, I could figure out where he'd been recently.

I walked my trike over to Calvin's driveway. It only took a few seconds of looking around to locate the fake rock by his front porch. I shook it, but nothing rattled around inside. It was empty, which didn't make any sense. Whoever last used the key should have returned it when they were done.

The easiest, and wisest, thing to do would be to go home

and return in the morning with his key ring, which was still at Tansy's house. But I was already here. I rattled the doorknob, and to my surprise, it was unlocked. The door swung open and I stepped inside.

It felt like I was doing something wrong, which was just plain silly. I was always welcome in my uncle's house, whether he was home or not. In my family, we didn't knock when we came over; we just let ourselves in. So why did I feel like an intruder?

There was a pile of mail just inside the door, underneath the mail slot. I picked it up and shoved in it my bag. Who was paying Calvin's bills while he was away? I made a mental note to ask my mom later what she wanted to do. It was too much to hope for Calvin to have set up automatic bill pay when he couldn't even set the clock on the microwave.

The curtains were closed, and it was dark inside. I reached for the hall light, then hesitated before switching it on. There was no reason to *not* turn on the light, but I was only going to be here for a minute. I felt my way down the hallway. As my eyes adjusted, I realized it wasn't totally dark. There was a soft glow from the kitchen appliance clocks off to my right and a night-light in the bathroom on my left. Down the hall, I could make out the shape of the doorway to my uncle's bedroom.

Wait, that wasn't right.

Uncle Calvin was a heavy sleeper, but he didn't always keep conventional hours. He was a fan of late-night poker games, and according to Mary Knickleback, midnight bowling leagues. As a result, he'd long ago installed blackout drapes over every window. He said it was to cut down on his summer cooling bills, but I assumed it was his way of sleeping in—or sleeping it off—without getting awakened by something as thoughtless as the morning sun.

Come to think about it, I could benefit from replacing

the lacy sheers in my bedroom with blackout drapes. Tansy wouldn't mind.

A flicker of light in front of me brought my wandering attention span back to the task at hand. The setting sun cast enough light through the bedroom windows that I could almost make out the shape of his dresser, which meant the blackout curtains were open.

Uncle Calvin liked his privacy. He never opened his drapes. Never.

But they were open now.

I paused, one hand still resting on the wall. I held my breath and tried to make as little noise as possible, and almost let out a shaky laugh as a result. If no one was in the dark house with me, I was being silly. If there *was* someone in the bedroom, they'd already heard me enter the house and it didn't matter how quiet I was being now.

I tried to calm myself thinking things through logically. The house was empty, or at least it should have been. I couldn't hold my breath forever. I let it out slowly, but to my ears, it sounded like a freight train blowing its whistle as it approached the crossroads. I listened as hard as I could. Was that creak a footstep on a loose floorboard or the normal sounds of a house settling at night? Was that murmur someone breathing or the whisper of a ceiling fan?

I was tempted to shout out "Hello?" and get it over with. If there *was* someone else in the house, they would know that the game was up. If I was alone, only I'd know how foolish I was being.

Then the shadows moved.

I yelped, unable to stop myself. I heard running footsteps. The open doorway to my uncle's bedroom was filled with the tall, narrow-shouldered silhouette of a man in a cowboy hat. He paused. I took a stumbling step backward before he barreled down the hallway toward me.

The intruder slammed his elbow into me, knocking me into the wall.

He sprinted the rest of the way down the hall, flung open the front door, and raced outside. Finally, my wits kicked in and I ran after him. I got to the front stoop and frantically scanned the neighborhood around me. There were no shadowy figures lurking around the corners of houses. I didn't see anyone dashing across lawns or running down the sidewalk.

A car engine started up and I swiveled my head, trying to locate the source of the sound. Nothing moved on the block. The car peeled off. The noise came from a parallel street. The intruder had been smart enough to park a block away.

I considered going after the intruder but decided against it. I couldn't catch him, not on a trike. I probably couldn't have caught him in a car with the head start he had. Instead, I did the sensible thing, for once. I pulled out my phone and called Beau.

CHAPTER 15

"Tell me again exactly what happened," Beau said. I was seated on the porch swing. He stood beside me. For once, he wasn't smiling.

Behind me, I could hear uniformed officers talking as they searched Calvin's house. Again. "I already told you everything twice," I protested. I wished I'd taken Tansy's offer of a ride home. Or Beau's. I'd texted Tansy so she wouldn't worry, but of course she was worried, and now her car was parked at the curb. She was leaning against it, waiting for Beau to finish with me so we could leave.

"Then tell me a third time. This man, did you recognize him?"

"If I had, don't you think I would have said something by now?" I said, a little more snappish than I'd intended. I blamed that on the late hour, my waning adrenaline, and my general annoyance with Beauregard Russell. "It was dark inside. I didn't see his face. Didn't see much more than a shadow." I thought about it for a minute. "He was tall and skinny, like the dude on the security footage, from the party. The guy at the back door?"

He nodded. "I know who you're talking about. And you're sure you didn't get a good look at him?"

"Certain sure. But I'm pretty sure he got a look at me. He

was backlit, and his eyes had longer to adjust to the darkness. When he saw me, he hesitated for a second. Maybe he was as shocked to see me as I was to see him."

"You'd tell me if it was Calvin, right?" Beau asked.

Aha. So that's where this was going. Beau really did have a one-track mind. It was a good thing that my sisters and I were looking into the alternatives. "I tell you that I got assaulted in the act of interrupting an intruder, and your first thought is that my uncle did it? You've spent one too many summers out in the Texas heat and fried something up here." I tapped my temple. Beau scowled. "Calvin would never hurt me." On purpose, I added to myself. His disappearing act wasn't exactly making my life easier.

Officer Jayden Holt and a uniformed white man I didn't know came to the door. I stood up, letting the swing come to a rest on the backs of my knees. My shoulder and elbow were sore from where I'd slammed into the wall, but all things considered, I was lucky.

"There are signs of an intruder." Jayden cast her eyes to me before returning her attention to Beau. "Couple of drawers open, but nothing was tossed. Either they knew exactly what they wanted, or they were interrupted before they could get started."

"His phone?" I asked. "It was on the nightstand. Plugged in."

"Not anymore," she replied. "Charger's there, but no phone."

"There was an envelope filled with cash," I told them. I tried to remember what Tansy had said about it. "In the sock drawer of his dresser."

"Not now, there isn't. What was he doing with an envelope of cash?"

"Beats me. He probably won it at the track." Which didn't make sense. My uncle lost a lot more on the ponies than he ever got back. Why was he keeping cash in his bedroom instead of a checking account?

"How did you know about it?"

I shrugged. "Tansy found it the other day."

"And exactly why was your sister going through his drawers?" Beau asked.

"We were trying to figure out where he went," I said. "After he left the courthouse, he went poof into thin air and his devoted nieces were worried about him."

"No one just goes poof," Beau said.

"Uncle Calvin did. As soon as he was bailed out, he walked out of the courthouse and hasn't been seen since. His car's in the driveway. His phone *was* plugged in. As far as we can tell, he's on foot with nothing but the clothes on his back. Look, I get it. My uncle's got a reputation. The black sheep of Cedar River. He's never met a multilevel marketing scheme or riverboat casino that he didn't like, but he's not a criminal."

Jayden tried to get the conversation back on track. "You've explained how you knew the cash was there, but how did the intruder know?"

I blinked at her. "I have no idea," I said.

"Or Calvin snuck back earlier for the cash and his phone. Everyone in town knows that Calvin is missing and his house is standing empty. Your uncle's got a big mouth, Juni. If he had a pile of cash sitting around, he would have bragged about it. Anyone could have broken in looking for it," Beau suggested.

He had a point, but how many people could have come and gone without anyone noticing? My shoulder hurt. My elbow hurt. And now, trying to untangle all the possibilities, my head was starting to hurt. I was ready to go home.

"If you'll excuse me, I'm done," I announced. Without waiting for permission, I thumb locked the front door and pulled it shut behind me. One of us could come back tomorrow with the keys to lock the dead bolt. I stepped off the porch and walked my tricycle down to the curb, where Tansy was waiting in her car.

As I pushed the trike, I noticed that in spite of the late hour, my uncle's neighbors were milling around on their lawns. Some were in clumps, speculating together as they watched the show. Others, like Miss Edie, sat on their porches. I waved at her. Her little dog, Buffy, replied with a bark. I couldn't blame the lookie-loos. Between Calvin's arrest and the break-in tonight, this was the most excitement this block had seen in decades.

I just wish Buffy had barked when the intruder entered the house, and then Edie might have called the cops to investigate before I went inside.

I veered around a police cruiser and arrived at Tansy's car. I looked at it, and then at my tricycle. I was tired and didn't want to pedal home, even though it was only a few blocks. But there was no way my trike would fit in her trunk unless we disassembled it, and that would take more time and energy than I had left.

Beau had escorted me down the driveway. "If you want to catch a lift home with your sister, I can drop your tricycle off later."

I almost declined the offer, out of sheer stubbornness. But then I reminded myself that turning down assistance when I needed it was silly. "I would very much appreciate that," I told him.

He looked surprised, as if he'd expected me to put up a fight. He took the handles of my trike and rolled it toward his truck. "Drive safe," he told us before heading to his truck.

"Jump off a cliff," Tansy responded to his retreating back.

As she got back into the driver's seat, I got into the passenger side and buckled the belt. On the ride to her house, I said, "I really appreciate you sticking up for me, but Beau's not the enemy."

"He broke my baby sister's heart."

"I think in some twisted macho way, he thought he was

doing me a favor." Breaking up with Beau had been rough, but if I'd never left Cedar River I'd always wonder what I was missing out on. That didn't give him the right to make that kind of decision for me, but what was done was done.

"Men are dumb," Tansy said.

"You'll get no argument from me." I leaned back in the seat and fought the urge to close my eyes. I wasn't eight years old anymore. If I fell asleep in the car, no one was going to carry me inside and tuck me into bed. Talking kept me awake long enough to get home.

Tansy pulled into her driveway before turning to me. "He's still dead to me." We got out of the car.

"That was a long time ago," I reminded her as she unlocked the front door. "We're friends now." I thought back over all the little interactions we'd had since I'd moved back home. They had a familiarity that should surprise nobody considering how well we used to know each other, but the more I thought about it, the more I realized we'd only interacted when it pertained to my uncle. Was I just part of a case to him? And if so, why was he sharing information? "Kinda. Maybe."

"I can't tell you what to do, but I'd think twice before letting him get too close again."

"You're right." I waited a beat before adding, "You can't tell me what to do." I grinned at her to make sure she knew I was joking and then added a spontaneous hug. "Night, big sis."

"Night, little sis," she replied.

We went our separate ways, she to her room and me to mine.

♪ ♫ ♪

The next day I was up with the sun, and not by choice. I dragged myself into the kitchen and started coffee. While it brewed, I dug through the junk drawer until I found a measuring tape. Coffee in hand, I returned to my bedroom and measured the windows. I went online, and a few clicks later blackout curtains were ordered.

Seriously, how did we survive before the internet?

I showered and dressed. It was a Britney Spears concert tee kind of day, which would complement today's coffee special—Oops! . . . I Did It Americano Blend.

My trike was waiting for me outside, as promised. It looked suspiciously shiny. I checked the tires. No mud. Someone had washed it, and I had a feeling that someone was the local detective.

Even though my elbow was sore from colliding with the wall the night before, biking to the shop this morning on my newly cleaned tricycle was pleasant. I detoured by Lucy's Market to buy cat food for Daffy and still managed to make it to Sip & Spin before either of my sisters. The cat materialized like magic as soon as I opened a can and spooned the food into his bowl. While he ate, I got everything ready for the day.

The barista station was prepped. The outgoing mail was neatly stacked. I filled one new internet order. I was just about to flip the sign to Open when Maggie rapped on the front door.

"I thought it was my turn to open," she said as I let her inside.

"It was. It is. I just figured since I was up anyway, I might as well come in and lend a hand. Hey, isn't that the same dress as you wore yesterday?" My sister's wardrobe was consistent, but I was surprised to see her wear the same exact dress two days in a row.

"Not hardly," she said, smoothing the knee-length skirt. Her dress had a high, square neck and three-quarter-length sleeves. It was pretty, conservative, and feminine. It looked exactly like what the wife of a lawyer might wear to a community picnic. "This one is lilac with blue and white flowers. The one I wore yesterday was white with blue and lilac flowers."

"You can see how I might be confused."

She shook her head affably. "There's a distinct difference. I'm sure the concert T-shirt you wore yesterday, the concert T-shirt you're wearing today, and the one you'll wear tomorrow will be nothing alike."

"Don't listen to her, Britney," I said in a stage whisper to my shirt. "She's just jealous."

Maggie laughed. "That must be it. Sorry I'm late." She held up a canvas shopping bag and pulled out a can of cat food. "We were low, so I stopped by the pet store on the way to work." Daffy purred loudly as he wound figure eights around her ankles. "Poor Daffy, you must be starving."

"Believe it or not, I already fed him. And stocked up on cat food. Great minds think alike."

Maggie laughed. "It's a good thing you told me, or I would have fed him twice."

"He certainly wouldn't have stopped you. Hey, since you're here, you don't need me, right?" My sister nodded. "I was thinking about heading over to UT today to see if someone in the language department can help me translate those notes we keep finding." I hadn't been back to the University of Texas since graduation, and I was happy to have even a flimsy excuse to visit.

"Sounds good. But first, Billie Holiday or Billie Eilish this morning?"

"Eilish," I said.

"Good call," Maggie said. As she flipped through the records looking for the right one, she asked, "Are you okay? Last night must have been terrifying."

"I'm okay," I assured her. Though Tansy was the only one I'd called, I assumed she'd texted Maggie. Who had probably called Mom. "You didn't tell Mom, did you?"

Maggie raised one eyebrow. "Of course I did. You didn't want her hearing from someone else, would you?"

Honestly, I was surprised that Mom hadn't been camped

outside my bedroom door this morning to check on me. Come to think of it, I didn't remember seeing her car this morning. She'd always been something of an early riser. I'm sure she had something important to do like volunteering for the mobile pet spay and neuter van or organizing a fundraiser for widows and orphans.

My mother didn't know how to be idle. But no matter how important the cause, I was surprised she hadn't ambushed me yet. I patted my pockets. No phone. I knew I'd had it this morning when I was ordering blackout curtains online. Had I left it at home? No, that wasn't possible. I'd used it to pay for the cat food.

"What's wrong?" Maggie asked.

"I can't find my phone. Be right back." I checked the cash register area. No phone. I checked the storeroom, where I'd stacked the cat food. No phone. I checked my bag. No phone. "I'm gonna retrace my steps," I announced. I picked up the two nonsensical letters, gave Duffy one more scratch under his chin, and headed for the front door. "Oh, when Teddy drops by, those packages by the register need to go out."

"Don't worry about me, baby sis. I've got everything covered."

"Thanks," I said. Maggie liked to remind me often that I was five years younger than her. The age difference meant a lot more when I was eight than it did at twenty-eight. Although, to be fair, she and J.T. had been happily married for over a decade. They owned a house and leased two nice cars, while I was still single and crashing in Tansy's guest room. I would always be the baby of the family, and it didn't help that both of my sisters seemed so much better at adulting.

If I'd stayed in Oregon, I would have gotten another job. Eventually. I would have put a down payment on a house, something small and near the ocean. Maybe I would have even met an attractive neighbor while out in my garden planting vegetables and we'd be on our way to our third date by now. It wasn't a bad plan, but it had one glaring drawback. I wouldn't see my sisters every day. Coming home was the right choice, even if I was biking slowly down Main Street, keeping one eye on the pavement for signs of my phone.

Luckily, there were no shattered remnants of my phone in the street, but I still had no idea where it was. I reached Lucy's Market and parked my trike. Another nice thing about living in a small town was that I didn't have to bother locking my tricycle whenever I left it somewhere. It wasn't like Cedar River had zero crime exactly—I'd discovered a dead body *and* gotten attacked by an intruder in the course of a week—but if someone decided to take my lime green adult tricycle with a giant basket on the back, it was unique enough that it would likely get recovered within hours because everyone would have heard through the grapevine that it had been stolen.

One of the checkout clerks waved me down as soon as I entered the grocery store. I made a beeline for her register. "I'm so glad you came back," she said. She was an older white woman with silver hair and green-framed reading glasses that hung from a turquoise bead chain around her neck. I'll admit I envied her glasses—I didn't have a green pair. She wore the standard grocery smock over a shapeless dress that looked like the quintessential grandma gown, or at least what I supposed other grandmas wore. My own grandma had been less conventional. She was still wearing tie-dye shirts with bell-bottoms until her final days. "You left your phone," the clerk said, reaching into her smock and producing my phone.

"Oh, thank goodness," I said. I took my phone and hugged it to my chest. "What can I do to repay you?" I didn't have a lot of money and none of it was cash, but she deserved a reward. I certainly couldn't afford to replace my phone right now.

"Just doing my job, sweetie. Wait a second, you're Rose Voigt's daughter, aren't you?"

"Granddaughter, actually," I corrected her.

"Maggie?" She tilted her head sideways to get a better look at me.

In spite of the age difference, my sisters and I really did look alike. Tansy was the tallest and leanest and I had the longest hair and wore glasses, but if I ever dressed in one of Tansy's coordinating twinsets or one of Maggie's floral dresses, I could probably pass for one of them enough to fool anyone other than Mom, J.T., and Uncle Calvin.

"I'm Juni."

"Oh, that's nice. I'd heard that you were back. Welcome home, sweetie."

That this stranger recognized me from my familial appearance was no surprise. I was used to that. It was the first time I'd been confused with my mom, but I like to think that was a compliment, because my mother was quite the looker back in the day. The fact that the clerk knew I'd just moved back to Cedar River should have been disconcerting, but part of everyone looking out for each other—and their bikes—was knowing everybody's business. "Thanks. Glad to be home."

I started to walk away, but she put her tiny hand on my arm. "Wait a second. You're the one who found her, right?"

There was no need to ask her who she meant. Monica Mayhew. "Yes, ma'am. Did you know her?"

"Saw her practically every day. She was one of those Roadrunners."

The Roadrunners would deliver anything from groceries to fast food, or pick up prescriptions at the pharmacy, dry cleaning, or pretty much anything anyone could imagine, as long as it was in Cedar River. I'd hired them to pass out flyers with their deliveries for the Sip & Spin grand opening.

"I'd heard that she was working for Jocelyn Reyes, until she got fired. I didn't know where she was working now," I said. Unlike my mother and my oldest sister, I generally avoided gossip, but any information I could glean about Monica that might help exonerate my uncle was means that justified the ends.

"Such an industrious young woman. A real shame. She worked for her daddy, out at United Steaks, when it got busy, of course. She did Roadrunners deliveries and always refused tips from seniors. Such a jewel. Plus, she was taking law classes at UT. I guess she caught the bug working for that big-city lawyer."

"Wow. That's a lot to have on one plate. I didn't know she was studying to be a lawyer." I'd worked odd jobs in high school and had a part-time work-study job in college, but I didn't think that I could have juggled multiple jobs along with a full load of classes. On top of that, law school was notoriously difficult and time-consuming.

The more I learned about Monica, the more tragic her death seemed, and the more driven I was to find out who killed her.

"She was interning with your brother-in-law, wasn't she? So you had to have known about the law school."

I blinked at her. I hadn't known that, probably for the same reason everyone in my family assumed I knew who she was as soon as she was identified. Everyone assumed I was in the loop when, in many ways, I was an outsider now. I snuck a glance at the clerk's name tag so I would at least know one thing. Her name was Agnes. "She worked for J.T.?"

Now it was her turn to look confused. "Well, I certainly thought so, but maybe I got mixed up? Happens sometimes. Last night I made scrambled eggs, bacon, and griddle toast for dinner. Ira thought I'd lost my dang mind."

"Personally, I love scrambled eggs for dinner, especially after a long day," I told her. "In fact, I might have waffles for brinner tonight. You tell Ira that for me."

Agnes laughed. "I think I might just do that, sweetheart." While we were talking, a patron had arrived and had unloaded a grocery cart onto the belt. He was so involved in something on his phone that he hadn't noticed the lack of attention yet, but he would soon. "Nice chatting with you, but I better be getting back to it. Don't go leaving your phone everywhere, now you hear?"

"Yes, ma'am. Thanks again." I gave her my brightest smile.

I glanced down at my phone as I headed out of the store. I had five missed calls and six texts from my mom. Instead of calling her back, I sent her a quick text assuring her I was fine and promising I would tell her everything over dinner tonight. Daughterly duty done, I stepped back into the sunshine ready to restart my day.

CHAPTER 16

As soon as I got outside, I pulled up the Uber app and scheduled a ride. I was grateful that we had access to ride-sharing
services in Cedar River. Despite our nearness to Austin, it
mostly felt like we lived out in the middle of nowhere. The
nearest available car was ten minutes away, so I changed the
pickup point for Sip & Spin and pedaled back to the shop.

I was just parking my trike when the Uber showed up. I
waved at my sister through the window before getting in the
backseat of the car.

"I've heard good things about that place," the driver said,
gesturing toward our record shop before doing a U-turn on
Main Street.

"Glad to hear it," I told her. "I own the place, along with
my sisters. You should drop by sometime."

"Oh, I don't even have a record player."

"That's okay. We sell those, too." Maggie had thought that
it was a waste of space and money to stock record players
when anyone could order one online for next day delivery,
but Tansy and I talked her into it. Now that might be about
to pay off.

She nodded. "I'll swing by sometime. You heading to UT?"
the driver asked.

"Yup."

"That's my alma mater," she told me.

"Mine too!"

"Criminology major. You?" she asked.

"Information systems."

"Isn't it funny? I drop a small fortune in tuition for a degree, then end up driving for Uber full-time to try to pay off my student loans. The amount of information I have in my head about criminology is, well, just about criminal, but I can't get a job in the field. And you're here with a computer degree working at a record store."

"A record shop that I co-own," I said, slightly defensively. "And up until a few weeks ago, I did work in IT."

"Oh," she replied. "I guess there goes that theory."

"What theory?"

"That no one ever goes into the same field as their degree. So, why are you heading to campus this morning? You enrolling in business classes or something?"

That wasn't a bad idea. It wouldn't hurt to know a little more about the ins and outs of running a business, now that I was an honest-to-goodness small business owner. And I was looking for something to occupy my time outside of the shop. I could take classes on campus or online and could study between customers. There was just one problem. I was broke.

"Or something," I finally answered, and we lapsed into silence.

When the driver dropped me off on campus, not gonna lie, it felt like coming home. I'd spent four years here studying, working, and partying. I'd never lived on campus—my parents' house was too close to justify the expense—but I'd spent most of my time here. When I wasn't in class or the computer lab, I was at my work-study job, or in one of my study groups in the library. I stayed late for football games and plays and art exhibits. I came in early for student fundraisers and once for a twenty-four-hour public reading of the *Iliad* and the *Odyssey*, in Greek.

I lost track of how many karaoke nights at the non-alcoholic student pub or art openings I'd gone to over the years, usually without Beau. He'd skipped college in lieu of going to the police academy immediately after high school. While I was in English Lit, he was a rookie. By the time I graduated, he had his own beat. He was so tired at night he'd often fall asleep in the seat next to me at football games or improv shows, on the rare occasions that he could get away.

Looking back, I realized that Beau had been an enormous part of my high school experience but was only a footnote to my college years. I was a full-time student with a part-time job. He worked long, odd hours. Would we have stayed together if I hadn't gotten a job offer out of state? I guess I'd never know.

As I wandered the huge campus, I remembered the time that someone filled the fountain with dish soap and the bubbles covered the South Mall. I fondly recalled going to a sit-in at the dining hall to convince the administration to add a new footbridge over a busy road that ran through campus. And of course, there were all the football games—which might as well be the official pastime of Texas.

But there were also nights I stayed up studying so late I crashed in my car instead of driving home. I would wake up sore and sweaty, then grab a quick shower at the gym before going to my first class. I had hated those early-morning classes, but they freed up my afternoons for computer lab and work-study.

As I wandered the huge campus reminiscing, a stream of students passed me. Some were in a hurry, clearly late for class. Junior year I had two classes in opposite corners of the campus. Even when my first class let out on time, I couldn't get to the second before it started. After the third time the professor yelled at me for being a tardy, sweaty mess from sprinting across campus, I dropped that class. Best decision of my college career. Well, that and never dating a frat boy.

I found the language arts building easily. I'd taken my English classes here, as well as a sampling of other languages just for fun. I loved being exposed to new cultures and words, even if I couldn't hope to become fluent after a single semester. My grasp of geography had never come as easily to me as languages, though. All I knew about Croatia and Estonia I'd had to Google. They were on opposite sides of Europe. Estonia was up in the north, near Finland and Russia. Croatia was in the south, closer to Italy and the Balkans. As far as I knew, there was no Croatian Studies department, so I checked the directory and headed toward a professor who taught both Greek and Italian.

The name on the door was Professor Kyrkos, and a plaque above the name read: "It's all Greek to me." I knocked and a male voice told me to come in.

The room was stuffed with crowded bookshelves and filing cabinets with folders piled on top of them. So much for the paperless office of the future we were promised. A man about my age, maybe a little older, sat behind a desk, typing frantically on a laptop. His hair was the color of carrots and looked about eighteen months overdue for a haircut.

"Sup?" he asked, without bothering to glance in my direction.

"I was wondering if you could point me to someone who could translate these." The search engine had identified likely languages, but considering the results of the translations, I didn't trust it much. I was much happier to talk to an expert, even if he looked young enough to have gone to school with me.

He held out his hand, while still clicking away with his mouse with the other. I handed him the pages. He glanced at them. "These aren't Greek." He finally looked up. "And you're not a student."

"An alum," I told him. "To be honest, I'm not sure exactly what language these are in, Professor Kyrkos."

"Oh, I'm not Professor K," he said dismissively. "I'm her grad student." He studied the pages closer. He tapped the first one. "What is this, Russian? I don't read Russian."

"Google Translate said one might be Croatian and the other is probably Estonian."

"We have a Serbian and Croatian professor, but they only teach in the fall and summer semesters. They spend the rest of the year back home in Belgrade, and never check their email." The grad student frowned at the other page. "Professor Fedorov in the math department might be able to translate the Estonian one, if he's in a good mood. Wait a second, this is one of his pranks, isn't it?"

"I assure you, I don't know any Professor Fedorov and, as far as I know, this isn't a joke," I answered. I couldn't 100 percent assure him it wasn't a prank because, knowing my uncle, it very well could be. But if it was, I couldn't see the end game.

He started typing into his laptop. "Seriously?" He turned the laptop around. He'd used a different translation program than I had, but the results were similar. "These are the lyrics to 'Baby Shark.' Get out of my office."

"But . . ."

"I said get lost." He shoved the letters across the desk. "Tell Fedorov I'm not falling for it this time. And close the door after you." I hurried out of the office.

Well, that was a bust.

I was half tempted to seek out this Professor Fedorov, but I hadn't had much luck in math when I was a student. I didn't think it'd be much better now. Besides, both myself and the grad student had come up with the same results, more or less. Even worse, now I had the old campfire song "Baby Shark" stuck in my head.

Do do, do-do do do.

Instead of trying to track down Professor Fedorov, I headed to the admin building. While most of my memories of college were centered around the computer sciences department, a lot of my time on campus was spent here. Every week, I'd rotate between the various admin jobs that they trusted to the part-timers and interns—answering the phones, any kind of data entry that didn't include student information, and other assignments that no one wanted. Trust me, you've never really lived until you proofread a one-thousand-page course catalog.

I found the registrar's office without a problem. The woman standing behind the desk could have easily been me back in my college days. I'd certainly drawn front desk duty my share of times. She was dressed in a UT burnt orange hoodie. Her hair was piled on top of her head and held in place with a colorful rubber band. She wore no makeup and had an angry-looking zit between her eyebrows. Even though she was sipping from a twenty-four-ounce reusable coffee mug, she looked like she was about to fall asleep on her feet.

She blinked at me as she slowly removed her earbuds. "Can I help you?"

In my experience, there were two kinds of people in customer service. The first loves interacting with people and makes it their mission in life to help everyone they come into contact with, even when most of their requests could have been answered if they'd just check the website first. The second were normal.

This woman was clearly the second type. It was obvious she disliked her job, but everyone's got bills—or, more likely in her case, student loans—to pay. I couldn't help the fact that she was stuck in a job where she was likely underpaid, underappreciated, and overworked, but at least I could try to make our interaction as painless as possible.

"Hi! My name's Juniper Jessup. I actually used to do your job, back when I was a student here. Do they still make you swipe your key card just to get into the break room?"

"Yup," she said.

"It still break every other week?"

"Yup," she said.

"That's the worst. Especially when your lunch is in the fridge."

"Yup," she repeated.

Okay, I wasn't going to get anywhere with her by establishing a rapport. Maybe it was time to get to the point. "I'm trying to confirm that a student here recently enrolled in a specific class."

"I can't help you because of FERPA," she said. "Come on, if you used to work here you would know that."

FERPA, or the Family Educational Rights and Privacy Act, was the academic equivalent of HIPAA. It protected students' personal information from nosy people like me. I nodded. "Yup, I get it. Only thing, though, the student is, unfortunately, deceased."

"FERPA," she repeated.

"Hey, yeah, I understand completely. You can't tell me anything. I already know she's enrolled. I just need to verify what classes she was enrolled in."

"Do you have a warrant, or a death certificate and proof of power of attorney?"

"Not exactly, but . . ."

She interrupted me. "FERPA." She took another long sip of coffee without breaking eye contact and then continued to hold my gaze without blinking. Either she was in training for the staring world championships or she'd fallen asleep with her eyes open.

"Well then, thanks for your time." I was tempted to storm off in frustration but then remembered that the woman was just doing her job. "There's a trick to it. The break room. Mind if I show you?"

"You're not allowed back here."

I shrugged. "It will just take a second."

"Fine. Why not?"

Before she could change her mind, I hurried around the counter and headed for the break room. Mounted on the wall next to the break room was a message board that had been ancient even back when I worked there. Ghosts of previous messages, never fully erased, were still visible behind today's announcement of "Whoever poured Dr Pepper in my Bonsai can go to A&M."

Some things never changed.

A&M, our rival school, was about two hours down the road. To be honest, it was a good school, but I'd grown up hearing Aggie jokes, so when it was my time to pick a college A&M had never even been on my radar.

"Ouch," I said, looking at the sign.

"Waste of a perfectly good Dr Pepper if you ask me."

The bottom third of the message board was made of cork, with a variety of pushpins that were used to hold up notices and flyers. But what I was interested in was the jagged chunk of magnet at the top that was strong enough to support a large manila envelope. I pried the magnet off the board and slid it down the door near the card reader.

The break-room door popped open.

Inside were two small tables and an assortment of unmatched chairs. There were two upright machines—one offered a variety of sodas and the other was filled with chips and candy bars. They'd been upgraded since my time and now were equipped with credit card readers and tap-to-pay. The prices had gone up as well. There was a wall of windows overlooking a green lawn and in the corner was a refrigerator that was older than I was.

"Easy as pecan pie," I said, handing her the magnet.

"Thanks," she said.

"Any chance I could change your mind? Maybe just get a quick peek at that record?" I asked.

"FERPA," she said. "And you shouldn't be back here."

I shrugged. "I had to try. Good luck with the break room, and with everything."

"Thanks. But I'm still not giving you that information."

I grinned at her. That last time, I hadn't even been trying. I'd just been being nice. I left back the way I'd come. It had been a long shot. I knew as well as anybody that they shouldn't give me any information about Monica, but I'd hoped for a less diligent admin. Not that it mattered. Even if Monica had been enrolled in law school, it wasn't exactly a motive for murder.

But it made me wonder what was.

CHAPTER 17

"Why would you kill somebody?" I asked Maggie, once I'd returned to the record shop.

"Huh?" she replied.

We only had one customer in Sip & Spin, and she glanced over at me in surprise. She was sitting at one of the café tables and humming along to the ABBA album playing over the speakers as she waited for her coffee. She'd ordered an Oops! . . . I Did It Americano Blend. It was a delicious mixture of medium and dark roast beans brewed as a double shot espresso and then diluted with hot water and topped with a sprinkle of nutmeg. It had approximately twice the kick of a regular drip coffee, with a rich, bold flavor.

If I could figure out a way to mainline it, I would.

"She's just joking," Maggie assured her. "You're joking, right?"

"Of course I'm joking," I replied. I wasn't, but it was probably best to not discuss murder in front of customers.

As Maggie finished assisting her, I busied myself with checking for internet orders, answering emails, and verifying that our website was working correctly. We'd had a couple of hiccups at first, but I swapped out some sloppily coded free plug-ins with ones I wrote myself, and we'd had smooth sailing ever since. "Got an email from Roadrunners. They want to know if we want to sign up for delivery service."

Maggie shook her head. "It's a bad idea."

"Why? What if someone's stuck at home with a broken leg and Mariah Carey on vinyl is the only thing that could take their mind off their troubles? We could literally save their day by delivering a new record to them."

"Sure, sure, but the problem with online shopping is that no one browses anymore. There's no connection between customer and proprietor. No relationship."

"No upsell," I added.

"Exactly. Someone comes in here looking for a particular album, and we show them that we also have the European remix of all of that artist's B sides. Instead of spending twenty bucks, now they've spent fifty, and leave with new music they might have never heard before. Win-win."

"What about that theoretical customer with the broken leg?" I asked.

"Obviously we would help them, too. They can call, email, or fill out the form on the website just like they would do for Roadrunners, and one of us could drop it off on the way home. Same service, but no delivery fee and we don't have to give Roadrunners a cut."

I nodded. "Makes sense. I'll let them know that we're not interested, but I still have every intention of using their service. Not having a car isn't so bad when I can still get anything that won't fit in the basket on my trike delivered to my doorstep. Besides, I like supporting local businesses."

"Exactly. Now what were you talking about earlier? Asking why I would murder someone?"

The door jingled and Teddy stepped inside. He was wearing his postal worker uniform, with a bulging mail sack slung across his body. "Ladies," he said, flashing a charming smile as he approached the counter.

I glanced over at where I'd left the outgoing packages. They were gone. In their place was a bundle of mail gathered up with a thick rubber band. Most of it appeared to be junk mail for the previous store owners, or the store owners before them. "Forget something?" I asked.

"Nope, but when I came by earlier you weren't here."

"I was over at UT," I explained.

"Going back to school?"

"Just visiting."

"Ah." He leaned one elbow on the counter. "So I was thinking about that dinner. You got plans tonight?"

"You in the mood for waffles?" I asked, recalling my conversation with Agnes the grocery clerk from earlier.

"For supper? Why not? The diner has pecan waffles. Might have to sweet-talk them into making them in the evening, but it's worth a shot. What do you say?"

I hesitated. When did Teddy-the-friend become Teddy-the-hot-confident-guy? And which Teddy would I rather spend time with? Waffles for dinner sounded more like two old friends hanging out than a date. "Sounds fun. Tansy's closing tonight, so I could meet you whenever."

"I'll swing back by here around six thirty. Sound good?" He straightened up and readjusted his mailbag.

"Sure thing," I agreed.

"Before you go," Maggie asked, "would you ever murder anyone?"

"That depends. Is this conversation being recorded?" he asked with a grin.

I pointed at the video camera over my head. "Yup."

"Well, in that case, for the record, I'd never kill anyone. Of course not."

"Off-the-record?" I prompted.

"I mean, I guess anyone's capable of anything, in the right situation."

"But if you *were* fixing to murder someone, how would you do it?" Maggie asked.

"Geez, what are you two ladies planning?" he asked, raising one eyebrow suggestively.

"Nothing," I said. At the same time, Maggie said, "Murder, obviously."

"Well, in that case, I hope you know what you're doing."

"We do," Maggie said as I said, "We most certainly do not."

"Glad to see y'all are at least on the same page. Gotta run." He patted the mailbag. "The mail waits for no one. See you at six thirty, Juni. And you two try not to murder anyone today, okay?"

"No promises," Maggie said.

I said, "See you tonight."

He left.

"Not a date, right?" I asked my sister.

"Depends." She looked me up and down, taking in my faded Britney concert T-shirt, mom-waist jeans, and skull-and-crossbones-patterned Chucks. "Are you going home to change first?"

"Nope." Although now that she mentioned it, maybe I should. I'd been so busy getting Sip & Spin ready for customers, I'd neglected my nails and my hair had split ends. I wore makeup for the grand opening but hadn't bothered since. I could stand a full makeover before a night out, but on the other hand, I didn't want to try too hard and give Teddy the wrong impression.

"Then it's definitely not a date."

By the time that Tansy came to relieve us, it was midafternoon. "Maggie and I had salad for lunch," I told her. "No leftovers, but I think there are some cookies from the bakery across the street that somehow ended up on top of the minifridge in back." They had been on the counter for a while, but that had turned out to be a bad idea, since neither of us could stop snacking on them.

"I already ate." She made shooing motions at us. "You two scram. Don't you have plans? Besides, you won't be doing anyone any good if you burn out the first week we're open."

I didn't admit it out loud to my sisters, but I wasn't exactly worried about burning out. I was used to working long hours and I liked working at the shop. I got to listen to any album I wanted and there was a never-ending supply of coffee. I got to chat with customers about music and album art all day, and when I was alone, Daffy kept me company.

"You ready to interrogate Samuel Davis?" Maggie asked as we settled into her car. Before Calvin cut ties with Prankenstein and subsequently invested in Sip & Spin, he and Samuel had been business partners. They were also best friends going way back. If anyone knew what our uncle was up to, it was Samuel.

"First, can we swing by your husband's office?"

"What for?"

"Just have a quick question I want to ask him." Yes, I could call, but since we were out and about anyway, it wouldn't hurt to stop by and talk in person. In my experience, people tended to be more open when they were standing right in front of you.

"Suit yourself," Maggie said.

J.T.'s office was on the edge of town. Ironically, the building had once been a jail. It had been converted to office space when the new sheriff's station was built across the street. The bars had been removed from the redbrick window frames, but if I looked close enough I could still make out where the holes had been filled in with tinted concrete.

There were several other offices in the building—a dentist, a therapist, and even a spa. Personally, the building didn't scream relaxation and pampering to me, but I caught a glimpse through the open door, and the interior of the spa changed my mind with its bright white walls, lush greenery everywhere, and a gurgling fountain near the reception desk. When the record shop started to turn a profit, the first thing I would do was come back here and splurge on a massage.

We took the stairs up to the second floor. The sign above the door advertising Taggart and McGibbons looked new. Then I remembered that J.T. and Elroy mentioned that they had recently bought out a third partner, so it made sense that they needed a new sign to reflect their new name.

We went inside and were greeted by a young man sitting behind a reception desk. On the wall behind him was an enormous framed portrait of J.T. and Elroy, both wearing black cowboy hats with shiny silver bands, crisp black button-down shirts, and bolo ties with a silver clasp in the shape of the state of Texas. In my personal opinion, they looked more like funeral directors than lawyers, but it gave the overall impression of two serious good old boys who could get the job done. Not a bad image to project to potential clients.

"Mrs. Taggart, I'm sorry, but your husband's in court today. Was he expecting you?"

"Sorry, Gary, I completely forgot." Maggie turned to me. "To be honest, he's so busy, I can never keep track of his schedule."

"No biggie." I guess I'd have to call him after all.

"Anything I can help you pretty ladies with?" Elroy asked, emerging from his office. "Come on back. Have a seat."

We followed him into his office. Unlike the spa downstairs, he'd left the original cinder-block walls of the old jail exposed. Hanging behind his desk was an enormous, nearly life-size oil painting of a longhorn steer. Above it was one of the largest mounted pair of longhorn horns I'd ever seen, but neither the painting nor the horns were as impressive as the view out of the massive window overlooking the river. His chair was upholstered in brown-and-white cowhide and his desk appeared to be made of reclaimed barnwood. Toss in a roll of barbed wire and a saddle and I would have sworn we were on a ranch instead of in a law office, if it weren't so clean.

"This about Calvin? Unfortunately, I don't have any updates. The court's pressuring me and J.T. to produce our client, but there's not much we can do until he pops his head out of whatever hidey-hole he's hunkered down in. Y'all haven't heard from him, have you?"

"Nope," Maggie said. "I don't get it. This isn't like him to just up and leave without telling anyone."

"The man's facing some pretty serious charges."

"He's innocent," I protested. I still had no idea who killed Monica or why, but I knew in my heart that my uncle wasn't involved.

"Why, of course he is," Elroy said in the same soothing voice he'd use on a jury. "You just keep telling yourself that. Juni, I heard you were poking around Calvin's house late last night and bumped into an uninvited guest. You all right? Nothing too serious, I presume."

"Just scrapes and bruises," I told him.

"Good, good. Maybe, just until this is all settled, you take it easy. I don't want to hear that you girls decided to go playing Nancy Drew and got yourselves hurt."

"Thanks, but there's no need to worry about us," I said. It was bad enough that Beau and J.T. thought they could boss me around, and now Elroy was getting on the bandwagon, too? I'm sure he meant well, but I was getting tired of the men in town telling me what to do. "While we're here, I have a question about Monica Mayhew. She worked here as an intern, right?"

He nodded. "A short while, yes. What a shame. Such a bright young lady."

"That's what everyone says," I said. "I remember her as a precocious little kid, but even back then she always got straight A's and all her teachers loved her. Not a surprise that she wanted to go to law school."

"She was a smart one, all right. I told her that defense was where the money's at, but she had her mind set on being a prosecutor," he said. "Wanted to be one of the good guys."

That aligned with what Jocelyn Reyes had told us. What had she called Monica? A Goody Two-shoes. "How were her classes going?" I prompted.

He scratched his temple. "I don't think she'd started yet. She was talking about enrolling in the fall semester."

"How long did she work here?"

He shook his head. "Not more than a few weeks. We had a big tort case, and needed someone to help sort through evidentiary discovery. She had experience. We ended up settling out of court and didn't need her help anymore, so we let her go. I'd heard that your uncle was hiring, and recommended that she give him a call." He paused. "With all that's happened, I think maybe I shouldn't have done that."

"Wait a second," Maggie interrupted. "Monica worked for Calvin? Why hasn't anyone mentioned this before now?"

Elroy shrugged. "I don't know that she ever got the job. I get the feeling Prankenstein isn't doing so well. Not long after I recommended her, Samuel Davis and your uncle came to me to draw up papers dissolving their partnership."

I glanced at my sister. As if she knew what I was thinking, she nodded. It was a good thing we were headed to see Samuel next. Maybe he could clear some of this up for us.

"Uncle Calvin tell you why he walked away from the business?" Maggie asked.

Elroy shook his head. "Said it was personal. You know how your uncle can be. Stubborn as a mule and only half as useful."

I shrugged and rose from my chair. I agreed with the first half of that statement. "Thanks for your time, but we need to get going."

"Don't worry, I'll add it to the bill," he replied. Then he saw the look on my face. "Just kidding!"

"You better be," Maggie grumbled. She stood with me and picked up a picture from the desk and turned it around to look at it. In it, a smiling Elroy in a gray-and-blue-checkered shirt, a cowboy hat, and dark jeans posed with one arm around a pretty brunette a head shorter than him. She had on a white sundress with pink cowboy boots. Behind them was a rustic split-rail fence and behind that was a field of bluebonnets that stretched to the horizon. "How's Mina? I haven't seen her around recently."

"Oh, you know Mina. She's like your mom, always got her hands full with her causes. The town is trying to raise funds to pave the old rail bridge over the river, make it part of a bike path. If y'all are interested in volunteering, I'm sure she could use a hand or four."

"Thanks. I might do that," I said. Mina was a bundle of energy with a heart made out of gold. A bike—or, in my case, trike—trail did sound promising, and working on the project might be a good way to do something nice for the town.

"You give her our love," Maggie added.

"Will do." Elroy walked us to the door. "Now you remember what I said. Don't go sticking your nose where it don't belong. One close call was enough."

I nodded politely. "I heard ya." As we took the stairs down, I asked Maggie, "Is he always aggressively overprotective like that?" I was used to it from my sisters, but I didn't know Elroy enough for him to be bossing me around, even if it *was* for my own good.

"That's just Elroy being Elroy. He means well. He's just looking out for us."

"You think he's got a point?" I wanted to know what had happened to Monica, especially if we could use that information to clear our uncle's name. But my run-in with the intruder at Uncle Calvin's house had scared me more than I'd like to admit.

"I think that family sticks together," Maggie said. "And right now, our family needs us."

"You're right. We'll keep digging. But maybe I won't be going into any dark houses alone anymore."

"I think that's about the most sensible thing my baby sister's ever said," Maggie said.

In response, I stuck my tongue out at her. She had a point. Not about my sensibility, but about family. If we didn't look out for our uncle, who would?

CHAPTER 18

Maggie backtracked through town, past a large field where lumbering oil derricks and longhorn cattle coexisted in peace, and finally arrived at the industrial park that dead-ended in the tiny Cedar River airport.

"I was here just the other day," I said.

"Why were you all the way out here?" Maggie asked. She pulled up in front of a warehouse and parked in a spot marked as "Prankenstein Customers Only."

"I thought since his old Bronco was still at the house, maybe Uncle Calvin had rented a car. If that was the case, the rental agency could have turned on the GPS and we could have located him in a heartbeat. But no luck, obviously. That's why I went back to his house after work yesterday, to check his cell phone and see if he'd been using any of the ride-sharing apps to get around and, if so, see where he'd been going before he disappeared."

"Like where?"

"I don't know. That's why I wanted to look at his app. But without his phone, we're pretty much stuck asking Beau to get a warrant, knowing if he found anything he wouldn't share it with us, or trying to figure out his password and log into his account with my phone."

"That shouldn't be hard," Maggie said. "He uses the same password for everything."

"That's what I thought, but I might have accidentally locked his account out on my way back from UT trying too many combinations of four–three–two–one," I admitted, thinking back on my attempts to break into my uncle's account on my Uber ride back to Cedar River.

"He doesn't use that password anymore," Maggie said.

"What? Since when?"

"Since his old phone got stolen a while back. We convinced him to use a new PIN and password, but you know Uncle Calvin. Can't teach an old dog new tricks."

"So what does he use now?" I was fascinated. To say that my uncle wasn't tech savvy was an understatement.

She rummaged around in her glove box until she found an old envelope and wrote down the password and PIN that he used now. I recognized the password. It was the same one we used for all the shop accounts, one we could all easily remember. "No matter how many times we tell him, he keeps forgetting."

"Does he forget the new phone PIN, too?" I asked.

Maggie nodded. "All the time. But we set up fingerprint recognition so he doesn't have to remember it anymore."

That was good and bad news. If a stranger had stolen his phone last night, it would be harder to break into. But if one of Calvin's friends was bringing it to him, he wouldn't need to reach out to one of us to remind him of his PIN to unlock it. I folded the envelope and stuck it into my bag.

We headed toward the Prankenstein warehouse. It was low-slung with corrugated metal on the storefront in lieu of siding. It had been bright yellow once upon a time, but the Texas sun had faded it to beige. There was no sign over the door, just the suite number. I tried the door. It was locked. There was a small window next to the door, but it was plastered over with newspaper from the inside. "I don't think they get a lot of visitors," I said.

A rough male voice came out of nowhere, crackling with static. "What do y'all want?"

I glanced around and located a small camera tucked up under the sun-bleached awning. I waved at it. "Here to talk."

"Is that you, Tansy?" he asked.

I put my hands on my hips. Samuel's security system either was junk or he was messing with us. My sisters and I didn't look *that* much alike, not to people who knew us well. "It's Juni."

"And Maggie," my sister added.

"What do you girls want?"

"Can we talk?" I asked. "Face-to-face?"

I heard the sound of a bolt being thrown. The door opened a crack. "You two alone?"

"Yes, sir," Maggie said.

The door opened wider and an older Black man appeared in the doorway. Samuel Davis and my uncle Calvin had started the business together, but now Samuel ran it all by himself. I wondered if they'd had some kind of falling-out, which was weird because they'd been best friends since disco was popular. Pretty much anytime one of them got into trouble, the other was by his side. Samuel was an honorary uncle to us and always had a seat at the Thanksgiving table. Not a Christmas dinner or Fourth of July picnic passed without him.

I'd known him my entire life. Now his thick hair and closely trimmed goatee were almost completely white. He wore thin-framed bifocals, the kind that you can see the line on a mile away, and laugh lines were etched deeply into his face. "Well?" he asked. "To what do I owe the pleasure?"

"Have you seen . . ."

"Nope," he interrupted me. "Police already came by, asking the same question. Y'all got nothing better to do than harass an old Black man, huh?"

"Now, Uncle Samuel," Maggie said.

"Don't start Uncle Samueling me, girl. You only call me that when you want something, little Maggie."

Maggie rolled her eyes. "We didn't come here to argue with you."

"Then why *did* you come?"

Here's the thing about Samuel. He and Calvin both are jokers. Comedians. Samuel still offers me a can of peanuts almost every time he sees me, even though the can is almost as old as he is and everyone knows it's loaded with fake snakes on a spring.

When he and my uncle wanted to start a business together, no one who knew them was surprised they opened a joke store. At first, Prankenstein sold cheap magic tricks, whoopie cushions, and those annoying buzzer rings. They imported them in bulk from overseas and sold them to local dollar stores. There wasn't much profit to be made in wholesale, so in a stroke of genius they pivoted to a new business model, and now Prankenstein shipped gag gifts anonymously through the mail. Their best seller was a glitter bomb that they guaranteed would stay in the intended victim's—I mean recipient's—carpet for months.

Calvin and Samuel did their best to prank each other constantly, but after nearly five decades of friendship it was hard to get one over on each other. Anyone in the family was fair game for their tricks. Personally, I'd learned to never open any package indoors from a Texas zip code, even if I'd verified the sender. Just in case.

I'd known Samuel to be grumpy on occasion—he said that it was his sacred right and if I ever got to his age I'd be grumpy, too. Only he'd used that line since he was in his midforties. But this wasn't grumpy Samuel. Or joking Samuel. This was defensive Samuel, which was a new one for me

"Please. We're worried about him," I said. I was thinking

about what Beau had said after we visited Marv Knickleback at the bowling alley. Samuel was guilty. Of what? I wasn't sure. But he knew more than he was telling us.

He nodded gravely. "You're right. Wait right here. He left something for you in case he had to take off in a hurry." He closed the door.

"He's hiding something," Maggie said.

"Obviously," I agreed.

Samuel returned and handed me a plain white envelope. "He said this would explain everything."

I ripped open the envelope and a puff of sticky glitter exploded in my face. It stuck to my glasses, my hair, and even my lips. "What the . . . ?"

But the door was already shut. I heard the lock being thrown.

I took off my glasses and resisted the urge to wipe the glue and glitter mixture off. The last thing I needed was to scratch the lenses. "I don't think Samuel wants to talk to us."

"You think?" Maggie asked, giggling. As far as I could tell, she was glitter-free.

"Real funny. You got water in your car?"

"Of course."

We rinsed off my glasses as best we could, but the sticky residue was stubborn. "I guess I'll be getting a shower before dinner after all," I said, looking down at myself. My shirt, my pants, my arms, and even my shoes were covered in shiny flakes of glitter. "Mind giving me a lift home?"

"You think you're getting in my car like that?" Maggie asked. "It's a lease!"

"You want me to walk all the way home? It's like ten miles, and I'm supposed to meet Teddy at six thirty."

"Then you better get a move on."

"Maggie . . . ," I said in my best attempt to sound intimidating. But I doubt even Dave Bautista could look intimidating covered in glitter.

"Fine. Let me see what we've got in here." She popped the trunk and rummaged around for a minute. She came up holding an oversize beach towel and three plastic grocery sacks.

"What exactly do you expect me to do with the bags?"

She handed me two. "These are for your shoes."

"Fine." I bent over, stepped into each sack, and tied them around my ankles to form noisy booties. "And the other one?"

"Um, it's for your head."

I blinked at my sister. "You want me to put a plastic bag over my head?"

"Not your whole head. Just your hair."

"Sure. Fine. Whatever you say." It wasn't like I could be humiliated any more than I already was. I loved having long hair, even if it did take forever to dry. But the thought of how long it would take to get all this glitter out of it made me cringe. Maybe it was time for a change? A buzz cut maybe?

"I know that look, Juni. Don't go doing anything drastic. I'll help you wash your hair."

"And what about Samuel?" I asked, looking back over my shoulder. No doubt he was watching us through the video camera. "I'm thinking we could fill his car with fire ants." I glanced around the lot. Samuel's car was nowhere in sight. Smart move.

"Do you really want to start a prank war with Samuel Davis?"

"I don't know. Maybe." I sighed. "You're right; it would end badly."

"When am I not?" she asked in a singsong voice. She spread the beach towel over the seat. "Please, pretty please, try to keep all the glitter on the towel."

"I'll do my best," I promised. It beat walking home.

As soon as we got in the car, my phone rang. I looked down at the caller ID. It was Beau.

"You gonna get that?" my sister asked.

"I'm thinking," I said. I thought about it long enough for the call to go to voicemail. Then the phone started ringing again. This time I answered. "Yeah?"

"We just got a report of a disturbance out at the Prankenstein warehouse. You wouldn't know anything about that, would you?"

I picked at the glitter stuck to my shirt. "Nope."

"Nothing?" he pressed.

I turned in my seat and surveyed the mostly empty parking lot behind us as we wound our way back to the main road. A small airplane was coming in for a landing, its engines noisy even with our windows rolled up. A semitruck was unloading at one of the docks a few doors down from Prankenstein. As far as I could tell, there was no one around to report our conversation with Samuel. "Sorry," I told him. "Gotta go." I disconnected the phone.

It took over an hour to brush all the glitter out of my hair, and another hour in the shower scrubbing my skin raw. The towel was in the trash. My clothes were soaking in the deep sink in the laundry room. Maggie begged me to put them out of their misery, but I refused. A vintage Britney Spears concert T-shirt was bad enough, but discontinued Chucks? I'd sooner part with my toe.

I slapped some moisturizer on my face, and it stung. I bit my lip. Maggie was right. I could not win a prank war with Samuel, but I wasn't forgiving this anytime soon. There wasn't enough time to dry my hair, so I braided it while it was still wet. My hair kept getting snagged on tiny flecks of glitter we'd missed.

While I was showering, Maggie had been going through my clothes. I emerged from the bathroom wrapped in a towel. She was standing in my bedroom looking confused. "Do you not own one single dress?"

I shook my head. "Nope. Where would I wear one?"

"Oh, I don't know, on a date?"

"It's not a date."

"Maybe Tansy's got something in her closet that would work."

"I appreciate the effort, but in case you haven't noticed, Tansy's skinnier than I am."

"I'll run home and get you one of mine," she said.

"No time for that." I appreciated the offer, but floral dresses weren't my style. I grabbed the top item on her handful of clothes. It turned out to be a polo shirt with my previous company's name and slogan—"Coding the good code!"—stitched above the breast pocket. "This will work."

She shook her head. "Are we certain we're related?"

I laughed. "Pretty certain. Now get out of here and let me get dressed. I'll just be a minute."

She grumbled something under her breath. If I had to bet, Maggie had never gotten dressed in less than half an hour. It would take even longer if she had to iron her outfit first.

True to my word, I was dressed and ready to go in the time it would have taken her to tie her shoes, not that she would ever wear tennis shoes unless she was playing volleyball or softball. "Thanks for sticking around and driving me back to the shop. It wouldn't be so bad, except my trike is still at Sip & Spin."

"No problem." Then Maggie slapped herself on the forehead. "I'm such a loser!"

"What? What did I miss?"

"I forgot to take a picture of you before we got all the glitter off. Would you mind terribly if we went back to Samuel's and re-created it with another glitter bomb so I can post it on Instagram?"

I pursed my lips. "What do you think?"

Maggie shrugged. "Had to ask."

She dropped me off in front of the shop. "Tell J.T. I said hi," I said.

"I will."

She drove away. I was about to go into the store when I heard a sharp whistle. I turned and saw Teddy coming up the sidewalk. He'd changed out of his postal worker uniform and into his cowboy uniform—tight jeans, a checkered shirt, and a large cowboy hat. I had to admit it was a good look on him. "How's that for timing?"

"Perfection," I agreed.

"I see you dressed up for the occasion," he said.

I glanced down at myself. Polo shirt from a company that no longer existed, check. Comfortable jeans that were fraying around the hems, check. Green Doc Marten boots, check. For the record, I had cowboy boots. Several pairs. They might take away my Texan card if I ever admitted this out loud, but my Docs were more comfortable.

Altogether, it was a very comfortable outfit. A typical Juni outfit. But not exactly a dressy one. Before I could ask him what he meant, he rubbed his thumb over my cheek, and when he pulled it back it sparkled with glitter I'd missed.

"Oh, that. Yeah, I can explain."

"No explanation necessary. It's cute. Come on, I'm starving, and those pecan waffles aren't going to eat themselves."

I nodded. The salad I'd had for lunch seemed like a very long time ago, and I was looking forward to spending time with him, even if I still wasn't sure whether or not it was a date. "Let's do this."

CHAPTER 19

"So, what'd you do today?" Teddy asked.

I told him all about the weird letters that prompted my trip to UT, our stop at Taggart and McGibbons, and the encounter with Samuel at Prankenstein. When I described the sticky glitter bomb, Teddy laughed so hard that the other diners turned to stare at us.

"Juni, Juni, Juni," he said, wheezing as he struggled to catch his breath. "That's why you had glitter stuck to your face."

I shrugged. "Yup."

"I should have known. Samuel and Calvin are a postal employee's worst nightmare. One of their 'special deliveries' exploded in my mailbag once and I just about called the ATF on them. Now anything they want to mail has to be delivered in person to the central post office in Austin, where it gets scanned in the X-ray machine." He grinned. "I had to get a new mailbag. Everyone on my route complained for weeks that there was glitter on their Social Security checks and grocery store flyers."

"That must have been awful," I said.

"It was, but it was kinda funny, too."

"I'm sure I'll feel the same way," I said, gingerly touching my cheek. It felt like I'd been out in the sun all day without any SPF. "Once my skin grows back, that is."

"Mind if I take a look at those strange pages you mentioned?" That was the Teddy I remembered so fondly. He'd always loved a good puzzle.

I took them out of the bag and slid them across the table to him right as our pecan waffles arrived. The server reminded me of one of my cousins on my dad's side of the family—short, curvy, and cheerful, despite our odd dinner request. "Careful. I don't want you getting syrup on them," I told Teddy.

He picked up the syrup and pretended like he was going to pour it over the letters. I reached for the papers, almost causing him to drop the syrup. "Hey!" Teddy said, snatching them up with his free hand and holding them off the table. "You're gonna make me spill for real."

"Please, just be careful," I pleaded.

"Aye, aye." He stacked the letters neatly and slid them to the side of the booth closest to the window, where the other syrups were lined up next to a bottle of ketchup, salt and pepper shakers, and a pop-up napkin dispenser. They could wait there safely until the syrup was put away.

I slathered my waffle with butter, and once Teddy made careful concentric circles of syrup on his waffle I drowned mine. I took a bite. It was hot, sweet, and packed with flavorful pecans. "You were right," I told him. "These are delicious."

"Told ya. And just think, if Samuel Davis had met you at the door with a gun instead of a glitter bomb, you would have missed this."

"Nice change of subject. Subtle. But Uncle Samuel wouldn't hurt me or Maggie. Not ever."

"You say that, Juni, but you go sticking your nose in other people's business, and it might get bitten off."

"Can we talk about something else for a while?"

"Of course we can. Like what?"

"Um . . ." He'd stumped me. I needed a hobby. While I was in Oregon, I picked up crocheting from a neighbor. I ended up making a few scarves and hats, a hooded sweater, and an enormous blanket—all things that were totally useless in Texas. Maybe I could learn how to crochet those adorable amigurumi instead. I could crochet little stuffed coffee cups or Koozie sleeves for the takeaway cups, and sell them at Sip & Spin. "Tell me about your job."

"I deliver the mail," he said.

"And?"

"And packages."

Our table fell silent again.

"Okay then, *why* do you deliver mail? You were always so gung ho about working for a think tank, using that big brain of yours to solve all the world's problems or something."

He shrugged. "Turns out I didn't much like it. I took a job with a company with promise, but they were more interested in their bonuses than fixing the environment. I got too jaded too fast. After we got sold to a fracking company, of all things, I quit. It was right around Christmas this past year, and the post office was hiring. I realized that walking my route and talking to my neighbors—bringing them checks and presents and helping them mail out cards and whatnot—was more fulfilling than sitting around a conference room all day throwing out ideas that no one listened to."

"For what it's worth, Cedar River is lucky to have you."

"Eh, I'm lucky to have Cedar River. Hey, did you hear about the new principal over at the new high school? He's all . . ."

I interrupted, "Wait a second. If Calvin and Samuel were on some kind of postmaster's watch list, how were they making their deliveries?"

"Huh?"

I tapped the letters. "One of these was dropped off by a local rancher. The other came back as returned mail, but I didn't send out the package." I grabbed my phone and opened the internet browser. I logged into a website and scrolled through the results. "See?" I turned the phone toward Teddy.

"What am I looking at?"

"Packages mailed out from Sip & Spin."

Teddy let out a low whistle. "There are dozens of packages here. I had no idea you were doing this much business."

"That's just it. We're not. We've had maybe a handful of internet orders so far. And look at these dates. They're all from before we opened."

"What exactly are you saying?"

"I'm saying that someone has been sending packages out from the Sip & Spin postal account and it wasn't me."

"Tansy? Maggie?"

I shook my head. "Maggie's responsible for inventory and bills. Tansy's the event organizer and the connection to the local music scene. I'm responsible for the website and online orders. If this many orders had come through the online store, I would have noticed."

"Maybe someone hacked your USPS account?" Teddy suggested. "How many people know the password?"

"Just me, my sisters, Mom, and Calvin." We used the same shared password for everything at the record shop. It was the same password Maggie had written down earlier, the one that everyone in the family knew. There was no reason for a stranger to hack our account and mail out junk records to strangers around Texas. It had been my uncle. But why?

"You know, depending on who was sending things out from your shop, and what they were sending, they might be in a whole heap of trouble."

"Wait. Before you go jumping to conclusions, it's not what you think."

"And how do you know what I'm thinking, Juni?" Teddy asked.

"Because I was thinking the same thing for a minute. My

uncle wasn't exactly going to get nominated for the most law-abiding citizen of the year anytime soon, but he isn't a criminal."

"He is under investigation for murder. He jumped bail and skipped town," Teddy pointed out.

"It's not as bad as it sounds. He was arrested for unpaid traffic tickets. He wasn't cooperating with a police investigation—but he wasn't dodging them. He was out bowling."

"That hardly sounds like an excuse . . ."

I interrupted him. "When a strange number pops up on your phone, do you answer it?"

"Of course not."

"Calvin's out bowling, and an unknown person calls him. He didn't pick up. No big." I neglected to add that my sisters and I had tried calling him, too, but for all I knew, his phone had died or he had the ringer off or for one of a dozen other reasons he might not have answered. "Because my uncle has a less than stellar record with the local P.D., instead of waiting until morning and calling him again, they ran his name through the system and found he had a bench warrant out for a few measly traffic tickets." Not that sixteen hundred dollars' worth of tickets was measly, but Teddy didn't need to know that. "So they arrested him."

"And let me guess." Teddy picked up the thread. "Your buddy Detective Beauregard Russell held the bench warrant over Calvin's head to get him to cooperate with their investigation, then booked him anyway. What did you ever see in that jerk, Juni?"

I knew Teddy wasn't talking about my uncle anymore. "Beau's a good guy."

"He's a bully." Teddy had never been Beau's biggest fan. Back when Beau and I had started dating, Teddy had begged me to stop going out with him. The longer I stayed with Beau, the further Teddy and I drifted apart. By the time we both went off to college, it was as if we'd never been best friends.

But I didn't feel like unpacking any of that right now. "In any event, I just don't get how the letters fit into it. They're all nonsense."

"Let me take a look." Teddy pushed aside his now-empty plate and lined the pages up in front of him. He pulled out his phone and started tapping.

Meanwhile, I scrolled through the list of outgoing packages on the post office website. I didn't recognize any of the names. The addresses were all within a hundred or so mile radius, but none of them were in Cedar River. If each of those packages contained a letter, there were an awful lot of pieces to the puzzle to track down, but at least I knew where they were shipped. Whether or not anyone would talk to me was a different story.

The door to the diner opened and a pimply-faced kid stepped inside. He wore a white polo shirt over khaki pants, but his blue baseball cap distracted from the generic uniformity of his outfit. He approached the host stand, accepted three enormous takeout bags, and slipped them into bright orange soft-sided coolers with the Roadrunners logo printed on the side. Then he elbowed the front door open and headed to his car. Less than a minute after he'd pulled into the parking lot, he was gone, delivering food to families that wanted takeout, I presumed.

"That's it!" I exclaimed.

"What's it?" Teddy looked up from his phone to ask.

"Gimme just a sec." I double-checked my phone again, verifying that no packages were sent to Cedar River addresses from our online USPS account. My sister had recognized the man who'd brought in the first letter as a local, but there were no local packages. So how had he gotten his letter?

I dug through my bag and pulled out the mail I'd picked up at Calvin's house last night when I'd inadvertently interrupted an intruder. Most of it was junk, but one of the envelopes was from his credit card company. I picked up the butter knife.

Teddy, watching from the other side of the table, asked, "Um, excuse me. Juni, should you be doing that?"

My throat suddenly felt very dry. Out of all the people I wouldn't want watching me open someone else's mail, a postal employee was pretty high on the list. "I, uh, wouldn't want my uncle getting behind on his bills while he's, um, you know." I put the bill back down on the table, still unopened, but I could feel the heat rising on my cheeks. "You know how bad those late fees and interest penalties can be."

"And you know tampering with someone else's mail is illegal, right?" Teddy said. He shook his head. "I'm gonna excuse myself and go visit the little boys' room. When I get back, if I see anything illegal going on here, I'll have to report it."

I gave him a sheepish grin. "Noted." He muttered something I didn't hear as he walked away.

As soon as he was gone, I slit open the envelope. The irony wasn't lost on me that I'd all but decided Beau was a crooked cop when I caught him going through Calvin's mail, but this was different. Beau was looking for a reason to arrest my uncle. I was trying to help him. Conscience soothed, I pulled out the bill, unfolded it, and ran my finger down the entries. I found what I was looking for right away. There were several large charges for Roadrunners, always on Tuesday. Either Calvin was having a large amount of takeout delivered to himself or he was using the service to send out packages.

Teddy returned to the table, and I hastily stuffed the mail back into my bag. He took a sip of his drink and turned his attention back to his phone.

My mind raced as I tried to figure out how everything fit together. Calvin was hardly running around town hand delivering junk records with cryptic letters tucked inside them. His Bronco didn't look like it had been driven for a while. He wasn't using the mail for locals because he didn't have to when the local Roadrunners service was just as convenient and didn't hassle him about what his packages might contain.

The delivery driver's outfit struck a chord with me. It was far from unique, but I'd seen one just like it recently. Monica Mayhew was wearing a white shirt and khaki pants when she died. She'd been a delivery driver for Roadrunners, and there was an orange bag on the floor near the body. Had she been working that night? If so, where was her car? I didn't remember seeing an abandoned car around the shop. If it had gotten towed, there would be a record of it, but it wasn't like Beau was going to volunteer details of an ongoing investigation.

It could explain why Monica had my uncle's business card in her hand when she died, if she was making deliveries for him. Unfortunately, it also made my uncle look awful guilty. Of what, I wasn't certain.

Across the table from me, Teddy chuckled to himself.

"What's so funny?" I asked. "I could really use a laugh right now."

He pointed to the letter. "'Baby Shark,'" he said, in a singsong voice. He pointed to the other and sang, "'A tisket, a tasket, a green-and-yellow basket.'"

"Huh?" I reached for the letter. I'd run it through two different translators and tried to get it examined by a linguist, and Teddy had cracked them both in minutes.

"You know, the old nursery rhyme. It's right here. 'A tisket, a tasket, a green-and-yellow basket. I wrote a letter to my friend, and on the way I dropped it.' The translator is a little wonky, but I'd recognize that anywhere. One of my nieces learned it last week, and now she sings it incessantly."

I'd caught the "Baby Shark" reference, and the earworm had been stuck in my head all day. But I'd missed the tisket, tasket line completely. Unfortunately, the letters made even less sense now that I know what they said. "My uncle's big scheme was that he was translating campfire songs and nursery rhymes into foreign languages, writing them out longhand, and mailing them out to random people with a junk record?"

"Looks like it."

"A dead end," I muttered, collecting the notes and putting them in my bag, on top of the stack of mail. The rancher who had come to the store had been all worked up over this? Where did the money come in? It didn't make any sense. If it was one of my uncle's gag jokes, I didn't get it. But to be honest, I never really did see the humor in snakes in a can, whoopie cushions, or glitter bombs, either.

Teddy waved at our server. As she headed toward our table, he asked me, "How do you feel about dessert?"

"We had waffles for dinner," I said.

"Uh-huh."

"Covered in syrup," I added.

"Uh-huh. And yet I'm still in the mood for something sweet."

Our server arrived. She was wearing a yellow-and-white gingham checkered dress under a pink half apron. "What can I get y'all?"

"Pie?" Teddy asked me. I nodded. "Pie. What do you recommend?"

"Normally, I'd say pecan, but y'all already had the pecan waffles." She cleared our plates without spilling a drop of the messy syrup. "Triple berry?"

"Sounds perfect. Blue Bell Homemade Vanilla ice cream on top, please."

"Comin' right up!" she said with a smile.

True to her word, she returned a moment later with a large slice of pie topped with a healthy serving of ice cream. She served it with two spoons. "Y'all enjoy."

Teddy and I dug into the treat. "You're right. I needed this," I said. I took another spoonful. Then someone tapped the window next to us and I jumped, almost dropping my spoon.

CHAPTER 20

Beau stood outside the diner, tapping on the window to get my attention. As soon as we made eye contact, he nodded at me and strode away. A moment later, he entered the diner, bypassed the host station, and headed straight for our table.

"Well, howdy, folks. Mind if I join?" Without waiting for an invitation, he slid into the booth next to me. Beau plucked the spoon out of my hand, took a scoop of pie and ice cream, and popped it into his mouth. "Delish," he declared after swallowing.

"Have a seat. Help yourself," Teddy said flatly.

"Don't mind if I do. Scooch over a bit, Juni; you're taking up the whole seat."

As I slid toward the window to make room for him, I said, "Beau, we're kinda in the middle of something."

"Sorry for intruding. I was passing by and saw y'all sitting here all cozy like, and decided to pop in and say hi." He took another bite of pie. He offered to return my spoon. I waved him away. "You're welcome, by the way."

I raised my eyebrows questioningly. "For?"

He laughed. "When was the last time you'd washed that trike of yours?"

"Yes. Where are my manners?" I said, chagrined. I'd been

rude for not saying something sooner, and good Texan ladies were never rude. "Thank you for that." Then it hit me that I wasn't the only person in the booth being rude.

I'd known Beau for a long time. I'd known Teddy even longer. Maybe that's why it came as a surprise when I figured out that Beau had interrupted because he was jealous. I glanced over at Teddy, whose lips had all but disappeared with silent annoyance. I had been oblivious about so many things. "Beau," I said, in a voice that was only a hair less sweet than the pie we were eating.

"Yes, Junebug?" he asked.

"Get lost." I smiled at him to soften the blow.

He blinked at me in surprise. Beau was used to getting his own way. It had been like that his whole life. He was charming and attractive, and radiated self-confidence. He wasn't a person people said no to. "'Scuse me?"

"Teddy and I are having dinner." I made a shooing motion at him. "So, leave. Please."

He tilted his head, studying me to make sure I meant it. Whatever he saw in my face must have convinced him that I wasn't kidding. "Sure thing." He slid out of the booth and stood. "Before I go, you remember telling me that Calvin Voigt had a lady friend? I got a lead on her today. Some lawyer in Austin. Jocelyn Reyes."

"Jocelyn Reyes? Are you sure?" I asked. "I don't know where you got your information, but they broke up almost forty years ago."

Beau flashed his toothy grin. "My sources tell me that he and Reyes have been seen together a lot lately. I reviewed the footage from your grand opening, and sure enough, she was there. Could be the best lead we have so far."

Jocelyn was at the party? She'd held out on me, and I hadn't even noticed. "She's a lawyer, and a sneaky one at that. She's not gonna talk to you. Not without a warrant, and maybe not even then."

Beau nodded. "She'll no doubt evade my questions, but I can't not try, right?"

He nodded at Teddy. "Thanks for sharing your pie. See ya around, Junebug."

As I watched him leave, my head was spinning. Not only did Reyes not mention that she knew my uncle decades ago, but she also was seeing him currently and hadn't seen fit to mention any of it. What else was she hiding?

"Juni?" Teddy's voice sounded very far away.

"Huh?"

"What was that all about? Who is Jocelyn Reyes?"

"Some woman that apparently is dating my uncle. Tansy and I went to see her the other day . . ."

"Why?" he interrupted.

"Why what?"

"I mean, your brother-in-law is a lawyer, right here in town. Yet you and your sister drove all the way out to Austin to meet with this lawyer. What's going on, Juni?"

"Nothing." I sat back in the booth. "Monica Mayhew used to work for her, that's all."

"Uh-huh. Now I get it. It's one thing to be running around Cedar River trying to find your uncle or figuring out whatever those weird notes are about, but now you're looking into Monica's employment history." He shook his head. "You've got to be kidding me."

"It's no big deal," I assured him

He reached across the table to grab my hands. "No, I mean it. This is serious, Juni. You're actively investigating a murder? That's really dangerous."

"I'm not in any danger," I said. Okay, so I might have gotten knocked down by an intruder in my uncle's house, but what were a couple of bruises compared to my uncle going to jail for a murder he didn't commit?

"I can't believe your sisters are letting you do this."

I blinked at him, a little miffed that he was implying I needed to ask Tansy's or Maggie's permission for anything. "My sisters and I are in this together. We're just trying to find my uncle and bring him home before we lose Sip & Spin Records. There's nothing to worry about, Teddy."

But I was asking too much of him. Teddy was a born worrier. Back in school, he'd been class valedictorian and naturally supersmart, but he was the type that labored over extra-credit questions even when he knew he already had a perfect score.

I looked down at our hands, still clasped on the table. My sisters had teased me about going out on a date with Teddy, and despite my earlier protests, the casual setting, and the delicious waffles for dinner, I was starting to think I'd missed a clue. A lot of clues, actually. How many times had Teddy begged me to dump Beau? And why exactly had we drifted apart after I got a boyfriend?

"Is this a date?" I blurted out.

Teddy poked at the pie with his spoon, pulling out one of the berries. "I think it's a raspberry."

"Ha-ha," I said flatly. "Answer the question."

He studied me before finally replying, "I don't know. Do you want it to be a date?"

"I don't know," I said. I wasn't being coy; I was being honest. I'd never seriously considered Teddy in a romantic sense before, for all my sisters' teasing. Now that he was sitting here in front of me, I realized I might not want to entirely shut the door on the possibility. He was attractive. And smart. And sweet. The whole package, really. What did I have to lose? "Maybe?"

"Then it's maybe a date." He winked, and I blushed.

The server came by to check on us. Once we assured her

that we were done, she dropped the check on the table and told us to have a good evening. That was our cue to leave.

We walked back to the shop, which was closed for the evening. My tricycle was no longer parked out front. Despite my earlier conviction that my trike wouldn't ever be stolen, I had a moment of panic. I pressed my hands to the window of the record shop and peered in.

Sure enough, my tricycle was parked inside. Daffy was curled up in the basket, sound asleep. I had the keys to the shop in my bag, but I didn't want to disturb the cat. He might already sleep twenty-two hours out of the day, but waking a cat was a criminal offense, at least in their eyes.

"Mind giving me a lift home?" I asked. I was perfectly capable of walking, but I was having fun and looked forward to spending a few more minutes together.

"No problem."

We walked down the street toward his parking spot. A familiar blue Jeep was parked at the curb. "Wow, you really like Jeeps, don't you?" I asked.

"Why do you say that?"

"Didn't you drive a Jeep back in high school?"

"Yeah." He patted the roof affectionately as he unlocked my door. He had to wrestle the door open. "Same Jeep."

"But that was . . ." I tried to do the math in my head. It had been a decade since we graduated.

"A long time ago. If it ain't broke, don't fix it, is what I always say." He went around and got in his side of the Jeep. The interior was surprisingly neat. Back before I sold my car, there were almost always fast-food wrappers on the floorboards, a spare jacket or three in the backseat, and a double handful of coins in the drink holder that were still sticky from a soda I'd spilled ages ago and never got around to cleaning up thoroughly. Maggie would've had a stroke if she'd known about that.

My radio was usually cranked up loud enough to make my

old neighbors give me the stink eye, but Teddy's was set to a normal volume and was tuned to a local country station. We rode back to my sister's house in companionable silence, listening to the radio instead of talking. Teddy hummed along with the music. I caught him watching me in the rearview mirror and smiled bashfully.

"Thanks," I told him when he pulled up in front of Tansy's driveway. I glanced over at the house. There was a flicker of movement in the kitchen window, as if someone had pulled back the curtains and then let them fall into place. Around the side of the house was a similar movement from my mother's cottage, only she remained boldly plastered to the window, staring openly. "This was nice. We should do it again sometime."

"We should," he agreed.

I sat there awkwardly for a moment. If this was a date, was I supposed to kiss him good night? Did I want to kiss Teddy? I had a lot to think about. I settled for reaching across and squeezing his hand. "Night," I said, getting out of the Jeep and closing the door. It didn't want to close.

"You gotta slam it. Otherwise, it won't latch," he told me.

Surely, it was only a coincidence that I'd just been thinking about leaving the door open for a romantic relationship. I slammed the door harder and heard it click into place. I waved at him before turning and heading up the walk. Like a true Texas gentleman, Teddy waited until I was inside to drive away.

Tansy appeared in the hallway. "That looked like Teddy Garza's Jeep," she said.

"It was," I confirmed.

"He's had a crush on you since the third grade, you know," she said.

"Somehow, I did not know that," I replied. Although, after tonight, I was starting to suspect she might be right.

"Silly girl, it might be time for you to get new glasses if you can't see what's right under your nose. You hungry?" she asked.

"Just ate, thanks." I noticed that my sister was dressed to go out. Instead of her day-to-day slacks and pastel twinset, she was wearing a dark denim skirt, a white tank top decorated with a star made out of pink rhinestones, and a black denim jacket.

"Is that my tank top?" I asked, surprised. My sisters and I had such widely varied tastes that we rarely borrowed each other's clothes, even if we had worn the same size.

"Do you mind? I would have asked but didn't know what time you'd be getting home."

"I don't mind," I told her honestly. "It looks cute on you. You got a date tonight?"

"Nah. Just going out to the clubs."

"On a Tuesday night?"

"Best night to hear new bands that no one has discovered yet. Want to come?"

I'd always been a night owl, but the last few weeks of getting up at the crack of dawn every day had taken a toll on me. Despite it being early, I stifled a yawn. I hoped those blackout curtains arrived soon, before I turned into an early bird permanently. Plus, I had a lot to think about. "Thanks, but I think I'm gonna catch up on some reality TV and turn in early. Rain check?"

"Of course," Tansy said. "Lock up after me?"

"Sure thing."

She left. I locked the doors, leaving the hall light on for her, and headed back to my room and booted up my laptop. I settled into bed and clicked on my favorite show.

♪ ♫ ♪

I rolled over and glared at the morning sunlight streaming through the window as if I could intimidate the dawn into letting me get another hour's worth of rest. I'd fallen asleep in my glasses. Either the glasses fairy had visited me last night and put my glasses and laptop safely away on my nightstand or Tansy had checked on me when she got home and took care of everything. Gotta love big sisters.

The first thing on the agenda today was to borrow a car. To be completely honest, I felt like a mooch. Here I was, twenty-eight years old with a zero balance in my savings account, living in my sister's guest room, and wondering who I could hit up for a favor without using up all of my goodwill. I had a job, an emerging business even, but I couldn't expect a steady paycheck until it took off.

It didn't make sense, financially, to buy my own car or rent my own place. I knew that. My family knew that. So why was it so hard for me to ask to borrow a ride?

Determined to get over my hang-ups, I went to the kitchen and brewed coffee. When it was ready, I poured it into two mugs. Quietly, so as not to wake my oldest sister, who had come home late enough that I'd slept right through her tucking me into bed, I let myself out the front door and headed to my mother's cottage.

Maybe "cottage" wasn't precisely the right word. It was advertised as a mother-in-law suite on the real estate description when Tansy bought the house. But everyone in the family called it a cottage, so I went along with that. It was a stand-alone tiny home about the size of a detached two-car garage.

I knocked, and my mother opened the door. "Juni!" she said, as if she hadn't seen me practically every day since I'd moved back home. "What a lovely surprise! Come in, come in." She ushered me inside and accepted the coffee gratefully.

We settled into chairs surrounding a small café table with a mosaic tile top to sip our coffee. The inside of the cottage was one large room, with a set of fancy screens separating the bedroom area from the living room area. There was a full-size bathroom, a large closet, and a tiny kitchen that consisted of a dorm-size refrigerator, a microwave oven, and a stove top. If Mom ever wanted to host a dinner party, she'd use Tansy's kitchen in the main house, but for day-to-day meals this was more than sufficient for a woman who rarely ate meals at home anyway.

Growing up, our lives centered around our grandparents' record shop. When we weren't at school or the shop, Maggie was at volleyball practice or Tansy was at a track meet. I preferred chess club and academic decathlon to the outdoor sports. Mom somehow managed to get us all where we needed to be, keep us fed and clothed, and work at the shop. Now, instead of those responsibilities, she joined community clubs, sat on the city council, and volunteered at the animal shelter. She organized fundraisers and ran senior citizen bingo nights.

To be honest, I was almost surprised to still find her at home even though it was early. I *wasn't* surprised that she was already fully dressed in linen slacks with a sleeveless button-down shirt. She was in full makeup with styled hair, ready to face the day.

In contrast, I was still in yesterday's clothes. My hair was piled in a messy bun on top of my head. My feet were bare and my toes were in dire need of nail polish.

It scared me sometimes. When my mother was younger, she dressed almost exactly like I did now. By the time she was my age, she was married with two kids already. These days, she was so well put together there was little to no trace of the carefree teenager she once was, but I still hadn't grown out of that phase. I wasn't entirely sure I wanted to.

"And to what do I owe the pleasure of this visit?" she asked as if I'd traveled across the country to see her, rather than walked across the lawn.

"You busy today?" I asked. She reached for her organizer, which was on the counter behind us. The last time I caught a sneak peek at her calendar, my eyes had nearly popped out of my head. Every line was filled, and it was color coded. Maggie had inherited her organizational skills from Mom.

"I have a few things to do this morning but could free up some time this afternoon, I suppose."

I translated that mentally to she had a full day. "I was hoping to borrow your car, but if you're busy I understand."

"I have to be at City Hall in about thirty minutes, and I'm bringing some donations over to the clothing drive afterward. I promised Betty I'd take her to the outlet malls this afternoon. If you could wait until three or four, it's all yours."

Not exactly what I was hoping for. Four was pretty late in the day for what I had in mind, and besides, I was scheduled to work the afternoon shift at Sip & Spin. "No worries. I'll just ask Tansy."

"Why don't you just take your uncle's truck? It's not like he's using it."

"The Bronco?" I asked. "I thought it was broken down."

"Why on earth would you think that? You know Calvin. He loves that truck like it's his own kid. He keeps it in tip-top shape."

"Then why hasn't he been driving it lately? As far as I can tell, it hasn't moved an inch since I got back home."

"Don't tell your uncle I told you this, and for Pete's sake, don't tell your sisters. You know how he can get. His license got suspended a while back because of all his tickets. You know how stubborn he can be, but if he'd just taken care of it, none of us would be in this mess."

I nodded, deep in thought. Calvin didn't have a valid license. Without his phone, he would have a hard time getting an Uber. Maybe he went old school and called a taxi, but the cops had surely already checked the local company. Probably. Which means he couldn't have gone far, not without help.

I went back into the main house to change—today felt like a Violent Femmes T-shirt paired with my round rainbow glasses kind of day—and grab the keys to Calvin's house. My mind raced ahead of me on a mission. Uncle Calvin couldn't have gone far. I was gonna find him, and bring him home.

CHAPTER 21

The walk to Calvin's was short, but I dragged my feet. Truth be told, I was nervous about going into his house again. I had no reason to be. Just because the last time I was here I'd bumped into an intruder—literally—didn't mean it would happen again.

It was daylight.

It was the middle of the week.

It was the suburbs.

Nothing bad ever happened in the suburbs, in the middle of the week, in broad daylight. Right? So why did I hesitate to unlock the front door with the key I'd brought from Tansy's house?

I took a deep breath, reminded myself that I was a grown adult, and opened the front door. Inside, it was musty. The air conditioner had been off for a few days and everywhere was that stale scent of empty buildings. I opened the kitchen window to air out the house, then walked back to the bedroom to open more windows and create a breeze.

Part of me was disappointed. When I was little, my favorite game was hide-and-seek. I'd beg my sisters to play it with me over and over again. They had the advantage of being older and presumably wiser, but I had a trick up my sleeve. As soon as I heard them search a good hiding spot—like the hall closet—I'd slip out of wherever I'd been and take up residence where they'd already checked, knowing they wouldn't look there a second time. Genius, right?

If Calvin shared even half of my ingenuity, he would have snuck back inside the minute the police cleared out. He could be sleeping in the comfort of his own bed and watching television in his own living room. I knew he hadn't been home when the intruder had broken in, but a girl could dream. The stakes were a little higher now than hide-and-seek, but it was ultimately the same game. My uncle was in hiding. I had to find him and drag him back.

My phone buzzed and I jumped. Fine. Maybe I was still a teeny tiny bit nervous.

I pulled out the phone and looked at the screen. It was Beau calling. I let it go to voicemail. To be honest, it was too early to be dealing with my conflicting emotions and his unpredictable behavior. Was he calling to tell me to stay away from the investigation or to drop little tidbits that he probably shouldn't be sharing with me? I guessed I'd never know because he didn't leave a message.

Instead, there was a knock at the front door. I looked out the peephole. Standing outside was a uniformed Jayden Holt. That was fast. I opened the door. "Morning," I said.

"Morning," she replied. "Can I ask what you're doing here?"

"I have every right to be in my uncle's house." Part of me, that ingrained Texas hospitality, screamed that I should invite her in and offer her refreshments. But I heeded J.T.'s warning instead. No talking to the cops without a lawyer present. Easier said than done. "Should I call my lawyer?"

"Not necessary." She tried to peer around my shoulder. "You alone?"

I guess I wasn't the hide-and-seek genius I used to think I was. At least I wasn't the only person to consider the possibility of Calvin sneaking back home so he could lie low in comfort. "Yup. All by my lonesome."

"You've known Detective Russell for a while, right?"

I nodded. "A fair amount of years." Jayden was relatively new to Cedar River. Had anyone told her that Beau and I had history together? It was old news as far as the town gossips were concerned.

"Do you trust him?"

Did I trust Beau? What kind of question was that? Of course I trusted him. Right? Sure, he'd broken my heart, but that had been a long time ago. All sordid personal emotions aside, he was a good man.

He also thought my uncle was involved in a murder. Although, to be fair, it was becoming clear that Calvin *was* involved to some extent. I just couldn't figure out how. And yes, fine, it looked a teeny bit suspicious that he'd fled. Would Beau railroad an innocent man? Would he railroad my uncle?

And did I trust him? I didn't know.

Realizing I still hadn't answered Jayden's question, I settled for a shrug.

"Well, I trust him. He's trying to do the right thing. I've met your uncle, you know. Quite a few times, actually."

"Really? I wouldn't think you two would run in the same social circles, unless you're an avid bowler with a minor gambling habit?"

"How do you think he racked up all those moving violations? Look, Calvin never struck me as a bad guy. A good ol' boy who thinks he's a lot more charming than he actually is?" She nodded emphatically. "A hundred times yes. A murderer? No."

"We agree on that," I said, nodding emphatically.

"He's involved in something shady. And we're gonna figure out what it is. His whole life is here." She gestured in a way that seemed to encompass not only his house but all of Cedar

River, and I had to agree. "He can't stay gone forever, and the longer he tries to hide, the worse it's going to be for him. Detective Russell and I both know that, and so do you."

"Don't worry. When I find my uncle, I'm going to turn him in, even if I have to hog-tie him in the backseat of his own truck and drag him down to the station myself." That was one thing I was sure about.

"Sounds like we see eye to eye," she said.

I nodded. "Sounds like it." And I meant it. She was smart, tough, and practical. Cedar River was lucky to have her. I was just mad Uncle Calvin was making it all so complicated.

"Can you do me a favor?"

I hesitated for a second before agreeing. "Sure. What do you need?"

"The next time Detective Russell calls, can you please save us all some trouble and pick up the phone?"

I let out a snort of laughter as the pieces clicked into place. "Were you following me?" That would certainly explain how she'd shown up so soon after I did, and how Beau had known I'd gone to visit Samuel yesterday. Sounded like a waste of resources if you asked me. Didn't he have a killer to catch?

"I'm not at liberty to answer that."

"Urgh. You are almost as frustrating as Beau. You know that?"

She shrugged. "Yeah, but I'm smarter. And prettier."

"You've got me there," I agreed. I wasn't going to admit it, not aloud, and certainly not to someone I'd barely known a week, but no one was more attractive than Beau Russell. But maybe I was biased. "If he calls back, I'll pick up. As a personal favor to you. Which means you'll owe me one."

She grinned. "Deal. If I catch you going over the speed limit on that green tricycle of yours, I'll give you a warning instead of a ticket." Jayden tipped her hat to me and left.

The door wasn't even closed when my phone buzzed again.

I didn't need to check the caller ID to know who it was. I picked up. "Beau, what a surprise."

"What cha doing?" he asked.

"Hanging out at my uncle's house. But you knew that. Tell me the truth—are you keeping an eye out for Calvin or for me?"

"A little of both. Dinner tonight?"

"It's family dinner night."

"With your family, every night is family dinner night," he said.

He had a point there. "True, but tonight's special. Maggie's making tacos. Now if you don't mind, I've got errands to run."

"Be careful, Junebug," he said, and hung up before I could ask him to stop using that nickname. Or maybe I'd had plenty of time to say something and hadn't because some part of me liked hearing it. More conflicting emotions that I didn't have time to unpack.

I did a quick sweep of the house. Not literally. I didn't actually clean anything—I'm not Maggie. Well, I did take out the trash, but that was just because it was starting to smell.

The closets and drawers were as full as they'd been the day Calvin disappeared, minus the envelope of cash the intruder had taken. Calvin's boots were all lined up in his closet and his hats all hung on their hooks—all except what he'd been wearing when he went missing. His suitcases were in the closet of the spare bedroom. If he'd come back to get clothes, he'd packed light. His bed hadn't been slept in for a while. I straightened the sheets out of habit.

The medicine cabinet behind the bathroom mirror was empty. I tried to remember what all had been in here the last time I was in his house. There were pills for acid reflux, high blood pressure, baby aspirins, and something used to treat his thyroid. They were all gone now.

"Where are you, Uncle Calvin?" I muttered to myself.

There was no answer. In fact, I was starting to think there

were no answers to be found here at all. I wasn't sure if I should
be mad that he left or worried—I'd fluctuated between both
since he'd left—so I settled on an uneasy combination of the
two.

I closed and locked the windows, then dug his spare car
keys out of the credenza in the front hall. I let myself out but
hesitated at the driver's side door of his Bronco.

It did not look like much, that two-toned beast of a car. It had
tires made for bouncing over rough terrain and high-intensity
lights mounted to the roof. There were dents in the hood and
dried mud behind the wheels. It got roughly ten miles to the
gallon, and it was Calvin's baby.

I'd never been allowed to drive it, not once. He wouldn't
even let a valet behind the wheel. As far as I know, the only
person who had ever driven it besides my uncle was Samuel,
and that was only after Calvin lost a bet. He'd be spitting fire
if he knew I was about to take it for a ride.

Frankly, I wished I'd thought of it sooner. All I needed to
do was make a few passes through town and if my uncle was
still in Cedar River he'd come running out of whatever hole he
was hiding in to stop me. Maybe if I'd had more time I would
have tried that on the slim chance that it would work, but I had
places to be.

The Bronco didn't want to start; it had been sitting too long.
But I pumped the gas a couple of times, tried again, and the
old engine roared to life. I backed out of the driveway carefully. The very last thing I needed right now was to run over
his mailbox or something.

As I pulled into the street and put the car into drive, I noticed Edie and her dog, Buffy, watching me from her front
porch. We exchanged waves. I touched the gas pedal, and the
Bronco surged forward.

I missed the little Civic I'd sold before leaving Oregon, with
its backup cameras and eleventy-million mpg. It was nimble

and easy to drive. In contrast, the Bronco took every bit of concentration and coordination I could muster. Steering, braking, even changing lanes was a challenge. I didn't know how my uncle drove it.

A loud honk made me straighten out. I was used to a more responsive steering wheel and lane assist and hadn't realized that I was drifting into the next lane. I needed to pay more attention, especially as I merged onto the highway leading into downtown Austin.

Rush-hour traffic had already cleared out, thank goodness, but there was still a steady stream of cars heading into the capital city. No matter how many lanes they added to the highway, congestion continued to get worse every year. Austin had long ago overspilled its borders and began consuming surrounding towns until they became suburbs. At this rate, it wouldn't be long before it swallowed Cedar River, too.

Sure, property values would skyrocket, but so would rent at the shop. Our small-town charm would be replaced by generic chain stores and strangers waiting to get into restaurants. It would be nice to have a Barnes & Noble on Main Street and maybe a Walmart Supercenter or Target, but then what would happen to Lucy's Market and Cedar Spines Bookstore? For that matter, what would happen to Sip & Spin if we got a Starbucks and a mall?

Cedar River was better off the way it was.

Navigating downtown Austin was a trial. Maneuvering the Bronco through unfamiliar streets turned out to be too much for me, so I pulled into the first street-level parking lot I found. Luckily for me, there were several spots still open near the back, so I didn't have to wedge the monster into a narrow space between two cars that cost more than I'd ever made in a year.

I consulted my phone for directions and started walking. Navigating to Jocelyn Reyes's law firm was a breeze once I was on foot. Austin was far from the most walkable city, but downtown had good sidewalks and crosswalks. And best of all, parked out in front of her building was a burrito truck.

The line was long, which was a promising sign that it was good food. As I waited my turn I scrolled through my social media apps. I'd been so busy lately that I hadn't checked in for a while. I posted a picture of me waiting in line with a #KeepAustinWeird hashtag. When it was my turn at the window, I ordered three breakfast burritos. I had to watch my spending these days, but this was an investment, I told myself.

In the elevator up to the law office, the smell of the chorizo made my stomach growl. I crossed my fingers that the elevator would jam, just long enough that I could scarf down a burrito before my meeting. Although calling it a meeting might be a little presumptuous. I couldn't be sure that Jocelyn would sit down with me, thus the burritos. I'd considered bringing coffee from the shop as a peace offering, but it wouldn't have survived the trip. It would have gotten cold long before I got here, assuming I didn't drink it first. The delicious-smelling burritos would have to do instead.

I smiled at the receptionist as I handed her a burrito. I tilted my head toward Jocelyn's door. "Hi, Ella. She in?"

She unwrapped the foil from the burrito. It smelled heavenly. "She is," she confirmed. She took a bite of the burrito and sighed as if she was relaxing for the first time in weeks. "But I wouldn't recommend going in there. She's been in a mood all morning."

"What is that amazing smell?" Jocelyn asked as she poked her head out of her office.

"Truck downstairs." I held out a burrito. She stepped out of her office and joined us in the lobby. "I got you one, too."

She frowned at me. "You again."

"Me again," I agreed cheerfully. "Juniper Jessup. Juni."

She gave me a curt nod. "I remember. You and your sister Magnolia were here on Monday."

My smile didn't falter, but inside I was pumping my fist in triumph. When I was here on Monday, I'd been with Tansy. How'd she know I had another sister? And who was the only person I knew who called her Magnolia instead of Maggie? "I guess my uncle told you all about us," I said.

"Excuse me?"

"No need to pretend. I know everything."

Her eyes flashed with anger; then her shoulders sagged. "You might as well come in," she said, turning and heading back into her office. "Close the door behind you."

I did as she asked, knowing full well her receptionist was probably listening in anyway. In fact, I was counting on it.

I sat, passing one of the burritos across her desk before peeling the foil wrapping off my own. I took a bite. "That is amazing," I said once I'd swallowed.

"Best in the county. The state, maybe." She glanced out of her window, which framed the capitol building against a clear blue sky. "He's here every other week. I always mean to go downstairs and get a burrito, but then I get busy, and well, you know."

"I do know. I run my own business, too. Sip & Spin Records in Cedar River. But you knew that, didn't you?"

She wiped a dollop of sour cream off her bottom lip. "Yes, I know exactly who you are. Happy?"

"Not quite," I said. "The other day, when I was here with my sister, you lied to us."

Jocelyn shook her head. "I didn't volunteer any information, but I never lied to you."

"You know my uncle. You've known him longer than I've been alive. But you're not just old high school sweethearts like my mom thinks."

"How is Bea?" she asked.

That threw me for a minute, but if my mother remembered her, it made sense that she would remember my mother as well.

She'd probably hung out in the original record shop like all the other kids in the area, listening to music and combing through the stacks looking for that perfect vinyl.

"She's good. You should call her. I'm sure she'd be happy to hear from you. She'd be thrilled to death to learn that you and Calvin are seeing each other again."

She pursed her lips. "It was that darn steak house, wasn't it? I warned Cal that tongues would wag in a town like Cedar River."

"And why should you care?" I asked her. "Is my uncle not good enough for you?"

She smiled and put down her burrito. I was impressed with her restraint. She folded up the wrapper with half of the burrito still uneaten. I was almost done and had every intention of licking the foil to get every last drop of deliciousness, although I might wait until I got outside to do so, so no one would see me do it. "It's not that simple. I was going through a messy divorce. I didn't want word getting out in my Austin circle until things were settled, so I asked a colleague in Cedar River to represent me."

"Taggart and McGibbons," I said, putting two and two together.

"Actually, it was Taggart, McGibbons, and García at the time. Unbeknownst to me, my old friend Juan García was getting ready to retire, but he referred me to his son-in-law."

"Elroy McGibbons," I supplied.

"Elroy," she confirmed. "I knew that Cedar River was a small town, but I'd forgotten just how small it was until Cal walked in one day while I was in the lobby. The other lawyer in the firm is his nephew?"

"Nephew-in-law," I corrected her. "But close enough." J.T. had been a part of the family so long that the "in-law" distinction was hardly relevant anymore. He was just kin now.

"One thing led to another, and Cal and I reconnected."

"Then your husband found out somehow. It was Monica Mayhew, right? She used to work for you, and after you let her go, she started working part-time for Taggart and McGibbons. She still had a chip on her shoulder because you fired her." I felt myself gaining a head of steam. "What was it that you called her? A Goody Two-shoes? You knew she was going to dime you out to your husband, so you killed her."

CHAPTER 22

I heard a sharp inhale of breath coming from the speakerphone on the desk, but Jocelyn was too upset at my accusation to notice that her receptionist was eavesdropping. "No! That's not what happened at all! I liked Monica. Broke my heart to fire her. Turns out she's nearly irreplaceable. But I missed a court date because she was late, and that's unacceptable. She wasn't happy about it, not that I can blame her, but I'm the one that recommended her to Taggart and McGibbons."

"When we were in here the other day, you pretended to not know my sister and me," I pointed out.

"Yes. Your uncle wanted to be the one to break the news that we were seeing each other." She grinned sheepishly. "Apparently, he hasn't had a lot of serious relationships, and he couldn't wait to see the look on your faces. I wouldn't ruin that for him."

"But you still didn't say anything, even after we told you that our uncle—your boyfriend—was missing and incriminated in a murder investigation."

"I'll admit, I was shocked. I had no idea. As soon as you two left, I tried calling him, but it went straight to voicemail. He's not returning my texts or emails. I'm really worried about him."

"We are, too." I was tempted to point out how much time I'd wasted investigating her when I could have been out looking for Calvin, but if she wasn't going to hold it against me that I'd just accused her of murder, then that was water under the bridge. At least she was being honest now. "Do you have any idea where he could be?"

She shook her head. "Cal has a lot of friends, mostly good-time boys."

"Good-time boys?" I asked.

"You know the type. They want to be your best friend as long as the champagne, or, more likely, cheap beer, is flowing, but the minute your luck turns, they're gone. And let's be honest, Cal's luck was mediocre at best. These aren't the kind of guys that let you crash on their couch when the chips are down, much less when the cops are looking for you."

"Was his luck particularly bad lately? Maybe he owed money or talked trash to the wrong bookie?"

"Not that I know of. In fact, he had a pretty good run at the track last week. Said he was gonna take me out for a weekend in Corpus to celebrate."

"Do you think he went to Corpus without you?" Corpus Christi was a family-friendly beach destination that was popular with spring breakers and locals trying to beat the summer heat.

"I doubt it. Honestly, I'm surprised he suggested it. You know your uncle. He's not much of a beach person. Have you ever seen someone try to walk on sand in blue jeans and cowboy boots?"

I laughed at the image. She was right. He would totally do something like that. Calvin was more comfortable in a fishing boat on a lake or the casinos up in Oklahoma. If he was camping out, there were about a million acres of wilderness to choose from—more than I could ever search myself.

"Speaking of romantic weekend getaways, how long were you planning on sneaking around with my uncle?"

She laughed. "My divorce was finalized last week. Cal wanted to make a big announcement at the Sip & Spin grand opening, but I didn't want to steal the spotlight from you girls."

"So you *were* at the party?" I asked. Beau said he'd seen her on the security footage, which not only proved that she had been holding out on us but also placed her at the scene of the crime.

"I was. I wasn't going to go, but Cal begged me to come. I got there, and your uncle was arguing with someone. It made me uncomfortable, so I left without even saying hi."

"Who was he arguing with?"

She hesitated, as if weighing her options. "I think it was his old buddy, Samuel. I can't be sure. I haven't seen him in decades."

"Black guy, about my uncle's age? White hair, goatee, glasses?"

She nodded. "That's him."

Why had my uncle been arguing with his best friend during the grand opening? And why hadn't Samuel mentioned it when we questioned him? Not that he'd admitted much of anything. "What were they were fighting about?"

She shrugged. "Something about a game. Sorry, but I didn't stick around long enough to hear more. You have to understand—I argue for a living. And the past eighteen months have been non-stop fighting with my ex. I didn't have the energy for a confrontation. Although, now, I'm wishing I'd stuck around."

"You couldn't have changed what happened."

"No, I suppose not."

"Did you see Monica at the grand opening?"

She shook her head. "No. But it was crowded. And loud."

She had a point. Perhaps no one else noticed my uncle arguing with Samuel for that same reason.

Jocelyn stood. "Thanks for the burrito, and it was nice to get to know you better, but I have clients coming in any minute now." She handed me a business card. "I am very worried about Cal. Call me the minute you locate him?"

"I will," I promised. I handed her one of my Sip & Spin cards. "And reach out if you hear from him."

"I certainly will," she said.

As I walked back to my uncle's truck, I tried to keep my spirits up. I'd been so certain that Jocelyn was involved in Monica's death, but to be honest, now I was glad she wasn't. I couldn't remember the last time Calvin had a girlfriend. It would be horrible if the first woman he got serious about in decades turned out to be a murderer.

I knew more than I had this morning, so the meeting hadn't been a total waste of time and gas, but I still had no idea where my uncle was, who killed Monica, or how we were going to save Sip & Spin. However, as long as we were in business, I had a job to do, and right now that meant relieving my sister and starting my shift.

The drive back to Cedar River was easier than the trek into Austin. Traffic was lighter; plus, I was starting to get used to driving the Bronco. Until it started raining.

Texas can see long stretches without so much as a cloud. It was possible to go from mid-June to early September without a drop of rain. This time of year, when the rivers were full and the grass was green, a nice spring shower would still have been pleasant, but Texas doesn't do anything by halves. I leaned forward to get a better look at the sky and saw a thunderhead looming overhead. We were in for a doozy.

I drove as fast as I dared. Even so, cars zoomed past me. By the time I got to the Cedar River exit, rain was coming down so hard the windshield wipers couldn't keep up. On top of that, the windshield fogged, and visibility dropped to practically nothing. I flipped the Bronco's lights on. I might not be able to see anyone else on the road, but at least they could see me.

There was a flash of lightning followed by a loud crack. The Bronco jerked as one of the rear tires blew out and I tightened my grip on the steering wheel even as the back end fishtailed on the slick road. I eased over to the shoulder. This stretch of road was lined on either side by cattle fences around thousands of acres of pastures. I didn't want to hit a fence post or get mired down into what was inevitably a lake of mud.

When the Bronco finally slid to a stop, it took me a minute to find the hazard flashers. I pulled out my phone. The electrical storm must have been interfering with the cell towers, because I only had one bar, and that blinked down to zero. On the off chance the message would get through, I texted both my sisters that I was stuck on the side of the road with a flat but would be at work as soon as possible.

Waiting for a break in the storm, I tried to relax, but the sound of the rain beating down on the car and the fear that the driver of a car coming up behind me wouldn't see me in these conditions made me anxious. I just about jumped out of my skin when someone rapped on my window. As soon as I caught my breath, I rolled down the window.

Standing outside, rain pouring down over the brim of his hat, was Elroy. "Juni?" he asked. The cold rain blew into the window, stinging my face.

"Who else were you expecting?" I asked, then realized that was a silly question. I was driving around town in my uncle's very recognizable truck, the one he didn't let anyone borrow for any reason.

"Car trouble?"

"Flat tire," I said, gesturing over my shoulder toward the

back of the Bronco. Even as the passenger's side slowly sank into the mud, because of the deflated tire, the truck listed hard to the left.

"Let me give you a lift into town," he offered.

"Thanks!" I'd had every intention of waiting for the worst of the storm to pass so I could get out and change the tire, but the longer we sat there, the more the waterlogged pasture consumed the truck. At this rate, it would take a heavy-duty wrecker to free the Bronco. My uncle was gonna kill me.

Assuming he ever came home.

I followed Elroy through the driving rain to his car, which was parked behind me. The rain had been coming down so thick and the Bronco sat so high, I hadn't even seen him approach. "Quite the day for it, isn't it?" he asked once we reached his car. In the short dash around the Bronco, I was drenched through and through.

"No kidding." I was dripping all over his car. My clothes were soaked. Without any dry material available to clean my glasses, I was helpless. Why didn't glasses come with windshield wipers? "If you hadn't come along, I would have been stuck out here forever. I couldn't even get a phone signal."

"The storm probably knocked out the towers," he said.

"Do you think the Bronco will be all right out here?" I asked.

Elroy wiped the condensation off the windshield and stared out at it. The hazards were barely visible in the downpour. "No one in their right mind is going to be out driving in this mess."

"You and I were," I pointed out.

"True." He pulled off the shoulder and onto the road. I could feel the mud sucking at his tires for a second before he gave it a little gas and almost slid on the slippery pavement.

"What were you doing out this way?" I asked as we regained traction and started the drive.

"Seeing a client. Speaking of clients, you heard from your uncle yet?"

I shook my head. "Not a peep. I'm sorry, Elroy. You took on this case thinking it would be a few unpaid parking tickets and now look at this mess."

"Not your fault. And what brings you out on such a nasty day? And in Calvin's truck?"

"I had some errands to run in Austin, and it wasn't like he was using it." I turned around and peered through the back window. The Bronco was too far down the road now to see, but a hint of blue skies peeked through the rain. "Looks like it's almost over."

Storms in Texas were violent but rarely lasted long.

"Drop you off at record shop?" he offered.

"Could you swing me by Tansy's instead?" I needed a dry change of clothes and then I could use the landline to arrange for a tow truck. I'd figure out how to get to work later. I could always walk after the rain let up.

"No problem." A few minutes later, he pulled into my sister's driveway. "Juni? Be careful, okay?"

I nodded. "I will. Thanks for the ride." I jogged inside. The rain was slowing and I couldn't possibly get any more wet if I tried, but I was ready to be out of the weather.

Once safely inside, I left a trail of wet footprints as I squished my way to the guest bathroom. I tossed my wet clothes into the shower to deal with later and wrapped one towel around me and another around my hair. I was determined to have at least one good hair day this week, but today wasn't going to be that day.

There was a corded phone in the kitchen, a remnant left over from the previous owners. I picked up the handset and was surprised that it worked. I can't remember the last time I lived any place with a landline. I called the shop first. Maggie picked up. "Hey, Maggie, it's me. I got caught out in the rain, and I stopped by to get some dry clothes, but I'll be in as soon as I can get a ride."

"No worries," she said. "It's been slow. Hey, a customer just walked in. Talk to you later."

She disconnected. My next call was to the auto body shop. Esméralda Martín-Brown picked up the phone. She promised to pick up Calvin's Bronco within the hour and tow it to the garage. I thanked her and disconnected.

I wasn't sure where I would get the money to pay her, unless I went into debt on my credit cards. I sure wish the intruder hadn't taken the envelope full of cash from Calvin's house the other day. It was his truck, and I was only driving it because he'd up and disappeared. It made sense that he should foot the bill.

But why had Calvin had an envelope of cash hidden in his bedroom in the first place? He was the kind of man that spent money almost as quick as he made it, and if he couldn't spend it, he'd blow it on the ponies. What was it that Jocelyn said? He'd recently gotten a good win and was going to take her to the beach. But unless he'd been planning on paying for their romantic getaway in cash, why hadn't he deposited his winnings?

Then it hit me.

Of course. Uncle Calvin hadn't wanted to pay taxes on his windfall. It was the only explanation that made sense. If he'd just reported it like he should have and put it in his bank account, maybe he'd still have it instead of whoever broke into his house getting it. And now, because of that, I would have to find a way to pay for a tow truck and a new set of enormous tires out of my nonexistent funds.

But that was a problem for another day. I dried my hair as best I could with the towel, got dressed in dry clothes and shoes, and was ready to go to work. It was still drizzling outside and

I had yet to unpack my umbrella. Mom's schedule was full. Who knew where Tansy was, but she wasn't picking up her phone. Teddy was at work. I was *not* calling Beau.

Besides, everyone was reliant on their cell phones these days, and if the tower was down, no one would have service.

Before I could get too worried, Tansy's car pulled into the driveway. She honked her horn. I locked the front door and ran out to meet her. After hopping in the passenger side, I turned to my sister. "Thanks! How'd you know I needed a ride?"

"Would you believe me if I told you it was the sisters' psychic network?"

"Maggie called you."

"Yup," she confirmed. "She said you wrecked Uncle Calvin's truck? He's gonna kill you."

"Only if he comes back to town," I said. "Besides, I didn't wreck it. It was only a flat tire."

"What were you doing borrowing his truck in the first place? My car's always available for you. I appreciate that we're all in on the business. We couldn't do it without you. You've made bigger sacrifices than anyone."

"That's not true," I said, shifting uncomfortably in my seat.

"Yes, it is. You gave up a promising career, your car, and your friends in Oregon. You moved halfway across the country and invested all your savings into the family business. We're all in this together. Don't feel like you have to do this alone."

"I am worried about how I'm going to afford to fix the Bronco," I admitted.

"Charge it to the shop. If Calvin comes back, he'll reimburse us. And if he doesn't, well, a tow truck bill is going to be the least of our worries."

"Seriously, though, what if he doesn't come back?" I asked. I hadn't voiced my biggest concern aloud to my family, but I knew it was weighing on all of us.

"He will," Tansy assured me. "He has to."

She pulled up to the front of Sip & Spin and I glanced inside. Contrary to what Maggie had said about the day being slow, there was a line snaking around the store to the cash register. "What on earth?" I asked. I hadn't seen that many people in the store since the grand opening. "Are we having a sale?"

"Not that I know of. I'll go find a parking spot and come help."

I got out of Tansy's car and opened the record shop door. "Excuse me," I said to the man blocking the door. He was a skinny man in overalls without a shirt underneath. He had on a sun-bleached John Deere hat and cowboy boots that were possibly older than I was, and was holding an umbrella that continuously dripped on our floor. He wasn't holding a record. I glanced around the line. No one was. Weird. Maybe there was a run on coffee?

Today's special—All the Single Lattes—was bound to be a hit, after all. It was a simple but satisfying combination of dark roast espresso diluted with steamed milk (or milk substitute if the customer preferred), a drizzle of caramel, and a foam heart on top. But I didn't expect this kind of overwhelming response. At this rate, we would run out of ingredients.

"Get in line, girlie," the man in overalls growled at me.

"It's okay. I work here," I said. I could barely make out the Bonnie Raitt album playing through the shop's speakers over the noise of so many conversations going at once.

"Good. Maybe you can tell me why I didn't get no game piece this week? I paid for it, fair and square."

"Game? What are you talking about?"

He raised his voice and repeated himself. "The. Game." His face was turning red. He reminded me of people who are trying to communicate with someone who doesn't speak their language, so they just repeat the same things over again, but louder and slower. Only in this case, we spoke the same language. Or at least I thought we did.

"What game?"

He glared at me. "You really don't got no idea, do you?"

"I really don't."

"Well, shoot." He looked down at his feet, as if composing himself. When he lifted his head, his face was back to its previous peachy color. He raised his voice again but this time ignored me and directed it at the room. "Y'all hear that? This here girl says she don't know nothing about the game."

A murmur spread throughout the line, sprinkled liberally with words most folks around here don't use in mixed company. After a good deal of pushing and shoving, the line reversed itself right out the front door. Tansy had found a parking spot and had come back just in time to hold the door open for the departing masses.

Once they were gone, a few customers remained. "Can I help you find something?" I asked the closest person.

"Uh, I don't know. I was just walking by and saw the line and thought maybe you were giving out free stuff or something. Are you?"

"We're not," I told them. "But if you're a music lover or a coffee drinker, we can probably find something you'll like."

"But it's not free?"

I smiled and shook my head. "'Fraid not."

"Well then, y'all let me know when it's free, okay?" They left, taking another customer with them.

The one remaining customer looked at me. "I saw a band down on Sixth Street the other day that I really liked. They only had MP3 cards at their merch table, but said you carry their album on vinyl?"

Finally, a customer I could help. "We very likely do. What was the name of the band?"

"I, um, don't remember."

"That's okay. Tansy? Think you can help?"

"Of course," Tansy said. She asked a string of questions and rambled off a list of local band names as she escorted him upstairs, where the majority of our collection was housed. Right now, the very recent and the more expensive albums were on the main floor, but we might rotate that depending on sales. I didn't know about my sisters, but I was getting a little too much exercise traipsing up and down the stairs all day.

I joined my other sister at the counter. "What on earth was that all about?" I asked her.

She shook her head. "No idea. They started trickling in a few minutes ago, demanding to play some game. I told them there was no game, but they wouldn't leave. More of them kept coming, and they were starting to get agitated. Like, really agitated."

"Yeah, the guy I talked to was none too pleased. You think maybe someone is pranking us?" Maggie and I locked eyes and at the same time said, "Samuel Davis."

"What about Samuel?" Tansy asked, escorting the customer to the checkout counter. He was holding three records from three different local bands. My sister is a born salesperson.

"Think about it," Maggie said. "Yesterday we annoyed him and now a mob shows up demanding access to some game that doesn't exist. Doesn't that sound like a classic Samuel-style prank? He probably promised all those people some kind of prize to dupe them into swarming us."

The remaining customer cleared his throat from across the counter. "Um, actually, that's not what happened."

We all turned to him. "Oh yeah?" Tansy asked. "Then what did happen?"

"It's Wednesday. Game pieces were supposed to be delivered yesterday."

"What game?" my sisters and I all said, at the exact same time.

"The game. You know, The Game." I could practically hear him capitalize it. He looked around at our blank faces.

"Twenty dollars gets you a game piece. Winning game piece takes the pot, more or less. Calvin gets his cut, of course. And there are expenses."

"Wait a second, Calvin was running this game?" I asked.

He shrugged. "Yeah. Has been for ages. Used to run it out of a warehouse out by the airport, but the last few weeks, the game pieces have been coming from here. Let me tell you, getting those weird old scratched records last week was a lot more pleasant than wondering if you might get a glitter bomb by mistake."

"Tell me about it." Even now, I was still finding glitter in my hair. If several showers and a Texas thunderstorm hadn't dislodged it all by now, I might as well resign myself to finding glitter in my hair for the rest of my life.

"Well, a glitter bomb . . ."

I stopped him. "No, don't literally tell me about it. Players throw into a pot. Calvin sends out game pieces. Winner takes all. Am I missing anything?"

"Well, it's a little more complicated," the customer said. "There's usually a riddle or puzzle. You might have a winning ticket, but if you can't solve it, you don't know to come and claim your prize, and the money rolls over to the next week. Or if it takes you too long to solve it, someone else might have already won the pot. It can be geocoordinates or a crossword . . ."

". . . or lyrics to a kid's nursery rhyme written in a foreign language?" I guessed.

"Yeah, that one was a real bear. Has anyone claimed that one yet?"

I looked at my sisters. "Kind of."

Now we knew why the rancher was so angry when he'd come to collect his winnings and none of us had any idea what he was talking about. I was starting to suspect that my uncle hadn't had a streak of good luck at the ponies lately. He'd been planning on using the proceeds from the game to take Jocelyn out for a weekend getaway. I'd even bet dollars to those little cinnamon mini-muffins they sell at the bakery across the street that the envelope of cash had been this week's buy-in.

Which means there were a lot of angry players around here who wanted their money—but were any of them angry enough to kill?

CHAPTER 23

After he paid for his albums, the helpful customer left and I poured myself a coffee. "Y'all want anything?" I asked.

"A tea would be nice," Tansy requested.

"I'm good," Maggie said.

"One You Shook Me All Night Oolong coming right up," I said. I wasn't yet as familiar with our tea selection, but the stress-reducing properties of the Chinese tea, along with a generous swirl of local honey, sounded like just the thing.

We sat without talking for a few minutes, letting everything sink in. The only sounds in the store were from the barista station, a David Bowie record playing, and the distant tap-tap-tap as residual rainwater trickled down the gutters. "We need to talk to Samuel again," I finally said, breaking the conversational silence.

"Why? We know about the game now. And he wasn't very happy to see us yesterday. What makes you think he'd be more forthcoming now?" Maggie asked.

"For one thing, we know a whole lot more than we did yesterday. We know that Calvin was running the game out of the Prankenstein warehouse, and that Prankenstein's business was severely hampered when the USPS stopped accepting their glitter bombs. Sometime after that, they dissolved their partnership. Calvin invested in Sip & Spin and continued the game right under our noses. He couldn't have had much of a profit margin if he was shipping out junk records when a regular stamp costs just a fraction of that."

"Last week was a nursery rhyme, right? Music. Albums. Vinyl. Sounds to me that the record was part of the clue," Tansy suggested.

"That does sound like something he would do," Maggie agreed.

"I wonder if that's what Calvin and Samuel were arguing about at the grand opening party," I mused.

"Samuel and Calvin were arguing Friday night?" Maggie asked, at the same time as Tansy said, "I didn't see Samuel at the party. How do you know there was an argument?"

"I went to see Jocelyn Reyes again this morning, and she told me all about it."

"What? Why didn't you say something earlier?" Tansy asked.

"A lot has happened since then." I thought about it and realized that one of the reasons I'd been so suspicious of Jocelyn was because I found out she was hiding things from us. Was I doing the same thing by not keeping my sisters up-to-date? I gave them a quick summary, from the discovery that she was dating our uncle to getting a flat tire on the Bronco during the rainstorm. I knew Calvin had wanted to keep his love life on the down low, but I owed it to my sisters to tell them everything I knew.

"Calvin's got a girlfriend?" Maggie asked. She clapped her hands together and grinned. Maggie was a romantic.

"Looks that way. And she hasn't seen or heard from him since Friday. When Tansy and I showed up in her office on Monday, that's the first time she heard what was going on in Cedar River. Since his cell phone was still in his bedroom when we checked it on Saturday night, I don't think he's been able to contact anyone since he was released from jail."

Maggie's phone went off and we both looked at her. "That's my alarm," she said, gathering her purse from under the counter. "I've got to get going if I'm going to have dinner ready on time. You're both coming, right?"

We nodded. "Of course." Another great thing about being back in Cedar River was being able to sit down with the family for dinner, even if there was an empty chair at the table with Uncle Calvin on the lam.

"You want me to leave my car?" Tansy offered. "I can get a ride with Maggie."

I pulled up the weather app on my phone. Cell service had been restored; plus, we had Wi-Fi in the shop. The rest of the day looked clear. "No need. I've got my trike."

"I still don't know how safe it is for you to be riding that thing all over the place," Tansy said.

"Don't worry about me." After my sisters left, I called George's Auto Body to check on the Bronco. No one answered, so I left a message asking for a callback when Calvin's truck was ready. I hoped that it was a good sign, assuming that Esméralda was out picking up the Bronco.

I hadn't had a chance to eat anything since this morning's delightful breakfast burrito. Another coffee on an empty stomach was probably a bad idea, so I downloaded the Roadrunners app on my phone and placed an order for lunch to be delivered. While I waited, I browsed the app, looking at the variety of menus and different services they offered, but what caught my attention were the photographs of the professional-looking delivery drivers. They all wore similar white shirts with khaki pants, and all had pleasant smiles on their faces as they handed packages to their clients.

I recognized Monica in several of the pictures. Seeing her

so vibrant and happy nearly took my breath away. Life wasn't fair. A few days ago, she'd been going about minding her own business, trying to scrape together enough money to put herself through law school, and now she was dead. I'd gotten so wrapped up in my uncle's legal troubles and worrying about the financial future of the store that I hadn't let myself stop and think about Monica.

As Al Green's soulful voice filled the shop, I reminded myself that Monica was the real victim here. Not Calvin. And certainly not Sip & Spin.

The door opened and a Roadrunners messenger stepped inside. She was Hispanic and in her late teens or possibly early twenties. She was dressed in the standard uniform with her hair in a French braid and a bright orange bag slung across her body. "Juniper Jessup?" she asked.

"That's me," I confirmed.

She took my order—a grilled-cheese sandwich dripping with melted butter and an order of piping-hot French fries from the diner—out of the insulated bag and placed it on the counter. I knew it wasn't exactly healthy, but I was ravenous and it smelled so good. Besides, it came with a pickle, and that was a green vegetable, right? "That all?"

"Yup. Hey, I've got a question for you, if you've got a second."

She glanced down at her phone. "Actually, I'm supposed to pick up a coffee order while I'm here, so I've got a minute while you're making them."

"Really? But we didn't sign up for your service."

She waved a hand at me. "Customers place special orders all the time. Can I get two All the Single Lattes to go?"

"Of course." I thought about what Maggie had said about not wanting to use Roadrunners, but this was different. Sip & Spin wasn't paying the service fee, and all the customer wanted was two of the coffee specials. There wasn't a chance of upselling them, and in fact we would lose a sale if I turned them down.

Besides, in the time it took me to prepare the lattes I could ask my questions. I measured out the dark roast beans and set them to brew. "You worked with Monica Mayhew, didn't you?"

The delivery person nodded. "Yeah. She was nice. Such a shame what happened."

"Was she working Friday night?"

"I suppose she could have been. We don't have set schedules. If you're free and appropriately dressed, you log into the app and mark yourself as available. Then if any deliveries come in, your phone beeps. The first person to accept it gets the run. Friday was abnormally slow, now that I think about it. Everyone in town was here, at your big party."

That didn't exactly confirm my suspicion that Monica was working for Roadrunners on Friday, but she'd been wearing the uniform and I definitely remembered seeing their distinctive, bright orange bag on the floor of the supply closet. "Were you here?" I asked her.

She shook her head. "Nah. My parents wanted to come to the grand opening, so I volunteered to stay home and watch the little ones." She looked around the shop, taking in the various displays. "But now that I'm here, I wonder if I should have come to the party instead. Do you have any Ed Sheeran or Taylor Swift?"

"Sure do," I told her. "You have a record player?"

"No, but I think my parents have one in the attic. Is it true that vinyl sounds better than streaming music?" she asked.

"I certainly think so, but you tell me." I set down the to-go cups I'd been holding and walked over to the contemporary records display. I selected an Adele album and set it up on the turntable. As it played, I returned to the barista station, washed my hands, and finished preparing her drinks.

"I love this," she said. She paid for the drinks with a Road-runners credit card, and I made sure to tip her on the app for my sandwich. "I gotta run while these are still hot, but I'll be back to check out more music, okay?"

"Sounds good," I said. After she left, I let the record keep playing. Running a small business was stressful, but listening to a wide variety of music all day long made everything better.

I unwrapped my lunch. There were three different kinds of cheese between the thick slices of sandwich bread, and exactly the right amount of salt on the crispy fries. I turned to the com-puter, intending on surfing YouTube videos for lunch, but with poor Monica still in my thoughts, I changed my mind and de-cided to rewatch the surveillance footage from the grand open-ing instead.

Rebooting the security camera upstairs seemed to have fixed the problem, but I was annoyed that we didn't have any footage from the party. Between the failed camera upstairs and the balloons and banner blocking the ones downstairs, we had no clear visual on anything that happened inside the store. At least the camera over the register recorded sound. I cranked up the volume to hear over the album playing over the shop's speakers. I caught a couple of snatches of conversation, but it was mostly just noise.

The video from over the back door didn't have sound. I watched it several times, looking for anything I'd missed the first dozen or so times I'd seen it, but nothing jumped out at me. There was Daffy, calmly grooming himself as the stranger moved into the field of view with his head down and the cow-boy hat obscuring his face. It was almost as if he knew exactly where the camera was, which was silly because he wasn't doing anything overtly wrong. Even if I could identify the mystery man, I couldn't prove that he murdered Monica.

Finally, I queued up the footage from the front door. It, too, was silent, but the images were clear. This time around, I caught a glimpse of Jocelyn entering the shop about midway through the party and then leaving again a few minutes later. I hadn't noticed her before, but then again, I hadn't even known her the first time I'd tried to watch this video.

Now that I knew what I was looking for, I recognized Monica from her Roadrunners outfit and bright orange bag. I looked at the time stamp. It was 10:42, after my sisters and I made our big grand opening speech and before I slipped out to split a few slices of pizza with Teddy.

How long had Monica been at the party before she'd been murdered? How many people had come and gone between her arrival and when we discovered the body, just after midnight? All I knew for certain was that alibis would be next to useless when—like the Roadrunners messenger said—most of the town was right here in the shop when she'd been killed.

Between the music and multiple concurrent conversations, it had been loud and crowded inside, but I still found it hard to believe no one had heard or seen anything unusual. It didn't hurt that the beer kegs were flowing freely and the supply closet was down the hall, out of sight of the party. But it was just dumb luck that no one had needed to use the restroom or step outside for a smoke at the exact moment that Monica and her killer had entered the closet, or they might have seen something.

Wait a second. I minimized the window and pulled up the footage from the back again. The man appeared at 10:40. Assuming both clocks were correct, he arrived at the back door at almost the exact same time that Monica had entered the front door. They hadn't come together, or they would have used the same entrance, but that timing didn't feel like a coincidence.

The front door opened, interrupting my train of thought. A man a few years older than myself entered with two small children in tow. "Do you have any kid's music?" he asked. I pointed him toward the right section and then bundled up what was left of my late lunch. I had to save some room for tacos tonight.

The family picked out an assortment of records and checked out. We had a steady stream of customers for the rest of my shift. Some of them were looking to start a vinyl habit, a few were late-afternoon coffee drinkers, and there was one hard-core collector who wanted to talk in detail about the liner notes on every album he'd ever owned. Luckily, I had a dozen rare albums that he'd never seen. I pulled them, expecting him to peruse them and possibly buy one or two, but he bought the whole lot, and those records weren't cheap.

A few more customers like him and we would be a success. I couldn't wait to tell my sisters the good news.

When it finally came time to close, I locked the front door. I made sure that Daffy had fresh food and water. I hadn't seen him all day, but that wasn't much of a surprise considering how much traffic we'd had. I hoped all these customers didn't scare him away for good. I searched everywhere and saw no sign of the cat, but I knew he had ways into and out of the shop that we hadn't discovered yet. Just like I had my hidey-hole in the supply closet, Daffy had secret entrances. Well, either that, or we had a cat that could walk through walls.

I locked up the cashbox, cleaned the barista station, and turned off the record player. When I was ready to go, I still hadn't seen any sign of the cat, but it was late and Maggie's tacos waited for no one. Trying not to worry, I turned off the lights, set the alarm, and locked the door behind me on another successful day.

The ride to my sister's house was pleasant. Unlike Tansy, Maggie lived in one of the newer neighborhoods. Hers was a house built for entertaining. Now that Mom had downsized, Maggie hosted Thanksgiving dinner around her table every year, as well as throwing a Christmas party for J.T.'s clients and a Fourth of July party for the entire neighborhood. Her backyard was big enough to hold a catering tent with room left over for a dance floor on the deck.

It felt odd, parking my adult tricycle between my sister's Lexus and her husband's Beemer, especially since I now knew the cars were just for show. Between buying out J.T.'s partner and investing in Sip & Spin, Maggie was as broke as I was. Worse, actually, considering she still had two luxury leases to pay on the cars every month. If anything, it made me appreciate my trike even more.

The front door was unlocked, the usual procedure when they were expecting company. "Knock, knock!" I called as I entered the two-story foyer. At the base of the stairs was a large vase filled with seasonal flowers. The overhead lights glowed warmly, and the tastefully wallpapered walls were welcoming. Laughter spilled into the hall from the dining room.

Maybe I should ask Maggie to help redecorate my room. I could certainly use some of her design know-how.

I turned the corner into the dining room. Stretched out in front of me was a long wood table that could seat a dozen. Piled in the center were all the fixings for tacos—hard shells, soft shells, spicy meat, spiced meatless crumbles, refried beans, black beans, corn, shredded lettuce, diced tomatoes, homemade guacamole, sour cream, and two varieties of salsa. Smaller bowls held onions and jalapeños, and larger bowls held sides of seasoned rice and tortilla chips. There were three different types of cheese, including our family's "supersecret" queso recipe of half a block of Velveeta cheese and a can of RO*TEL chilis. In the center of the table was a pitcher of frozen margaritas and a plate of salt. Does Maggie know how to throw a family dinner, or what?

J.T. sat at one end of the table. He raised his margarita glass to me in a salute. "Juni! You made it!" Everyone else joined in greeting my arrival.

Although we called the affair family dinner, there was no

limit on who might show up on any given occasion. Tonight was no exception. My sisters sat nearest to J.T., across the table from each other. My mother sat at the opposite end. Elroy and his wife, Mina, sat on the far side with Maggie, nearest to Mom. Samuel sat across from Elroy, and next to Tansy was the last person I expected to see at our table.

Beau hopped up and pulled out the empty seat between him and Samuel. "Saved you a spot," he said.

"Who invited you?" I asked. Almost everyone had gone back to their tacos and conversations. They pretended to not pay any attention to us, but I could feel my mother's eyes trained on me. A friend at dinner wasn't notable. An ex was.

"You did," he said, waiting until after I'd seated myself to reclaim his own chair. "Remember? You told me tonight would be taco night at Maggie's."

"That wasn't an invitation, and you know it."

"Well, shoot. I guess that makes me unwelcome then," he said.

"Don't be silly." Mom jumped into the conversation without missing a beat. "You're always welcome at our table, Beau." She glared at me. "Be polite," she said. I can't speak for every household in Texas, but in ours you could track in mud or bring home a stranger and no one would bat an eye, but rudeness at the dinner table was not tolerated.

"Sorry," I said automatically. I focused my attention on Beau. "Of course I'm glad you're here, just surprised, that's all. Pass the margaritas?"

As he reached for the pitcher, I turned my head to address the guest on my other side. "Hello, Samuel." I pursed my lips, knowing that anything I might want to say to him right now would just get me further into the doghouse with my mom. I needed to play nice, and not just because she was watching me like a hawk. Samuel had answers that I needed. "Hadn't expected to see you again so soon, either."

He grinned at me. "Glad to see you're not holding a grudge. Girl, you should have *seen* your face when that glitter bomb went off."

I forced a smile. "Yup. Real funny. Ha-ha."

"Samuel Davis, I know you did not glitter bomb one of my daughters," my mother said, her voice stern. Though she was hard to take seriously with shredded lettuce stuck between her teeth.

"It was an accident. I handed her the wrong envelope, that's all. Right, Juniper?" he asked me with a wink.

"I'm sure it was," I replied levelly. I wasn't going to rise to the bait, not with my mom watching. "But after dinner, I'd love a word."

"I'm sure you would," he said. He stretched one arm over the back of my chair, which only left him one hand to eat with. "I always have time for the Jessup girls."

"Gee, thanks."

He patted my shoulder. I rolled my eyes at him. He laughed and removed his arm from the back of my chair so he could better hold his messy taco. "You know I love you, right, Juni?"

I smiled for real this time. "I love you, too, Uncle Samuel." I pointed one finger at him. "But you prank me again and I'm gonna fill your car with glitter and superglue. You know what they say about revenge being a dish served best sparkly."

"Speaking of dishes, pass me the guac?" he asked, holding out his hand.

I handed him the guacamole, but in my head I was calculating how much glitter it would take to fill a 1980 Pontiac Trans Am. Then it hit me that Samuel's fire-engine red Firebird wasn't in front of the warehouse when we'd gone to visit him at Prankenstein. Sure, he could have parked around back, but as bad as the roads were leading into the industrial complex, they were ten times as bad behind it. Plus, between the active loading docks and industrial-size dumpsters, there was nowhere to park back there.

His car wasn't outside Maggie's tonight, either. Then again, I hadn't been looking for it. If I had, I might have noticed Beau's truck. But a truck doesn't stand out in a neighborhood like this. A red Trans Am, complete with a firebird painted on the hood, does.

Calvin wasn't driving his Bronco because he was driving Samuel's car. I would put money on it. I muttered, "Your car . . . ?"

Samuel must have realized what I was about to say, because he put his hand over mine, pinning it to the table. He raised both of his eyebrows at me and leaned forward. "After dinner," he said, quietly.

I tilted my head. "You're not gonna run off halfway through dessert, are you?"

"What, and miss your sister's deep-fried ice cream? Not likely."

That was as close as I'd ever get to extracting a promise from him. Since I really didn't want to have this conversation in front of everyone, I nodded. "Fine."

"What are you two talking about, all thick as thieves?" Beau asked from the other side of me.

I shifted in my chair so I could look at him. He had a dollop of queso on his chin. Without thinking, I reached up and wiped it off. His stubble was prickly under my finger, and the drying cheese was stubborn. Then I realized that I probably shouldn't be touching his face without permission. Both of my sisters were openly staring at us. "Uh, you've got a little something," I said, gesturing at his chin while a blush crept across my cheeks.

Beau looked amused. Tansy and Maggie did not. "Thanks," he said, swiping at the queso with his napkin. "Did I get it?"

"Uh-huh," I said, even though there was still queso on

his chin. In desperate need of a distraction, I reached for the crunchy taco shells. After a good deal of shuffling and passing bowls, I had two perfect tacos lined up on my plate.

As soon as I took a bite, Beau asked, "So, how's your little investigation coming along?"

And just like that, I could have heard a pin drop in the crowded dining room.

While I chewed and swallowed, I considered my best course of action. Short of time traveling back half an hour and skipping family dinner, I didn't have any good options. I could pretend I didn't know what he was talking about, but I had a feeling Beau wouldn't let the subject drop. I could answer him truthfully, but then Mom, J.T., or Elroy would read me the riot act. Worst-case scenario, all three of them would team up on me at the same time.

Intent on my answer, no one said anything, but I knew what they were going to say. "Blah, blah, blah, dangerous." "Yadda, yadda, yadda, interfering with a police investigation." "Tsk, tsk, tsk, tampering with evidence."

And yet it all beat being homeless with my life's savings tied up in a business that now belonged to the bail bonds company because Calvin didn't show up for his court date.

I put down my taco, letting the stuffing spill onto my plate, and took a long swig of my margarita. Then, fighting back a brain freeze, I stood and grabbed Beau's hand. "Let's talk." Without waiting for his agreement, I dragged him out of the dining room.

There was only one place in Maggie's house that we had any chance of having a private conversation without the rest of my family eavesdropping on us. I led Beau into the half bath in the hallway, flipped on the light and noisy fan, and closed the door behind us. Only then did I realize how small the room was. It wasn't built for two people to occupy at the same time, not unless they were real friendly.

Beau put his hands on the sink, on either side of me, and leaned toward me. I pressed my back up against the sink and got a hand between us, lightly touching his chest as I said, "Don't get any ideas."

"Ideas?" he asked. "I'm just trying to wash my hands." I scooted over so he had full access to the sink. He washed his hands, then checked his face in the mirror. The flake of stubborn queso caught his attention, and he picked at it with a fingernail. "I thought you said I got it?"

"Close enough," I said.

He flicked the cheese into the sink, shut off the water, and ran a hand through his hair. Then he turned his attention to me. "You wanted to talk?"

"I don't think it's such a good idea to mention that I'm investigating Monica's murder in front of J.T. and Elroy. Lawyers are so touchy. Plus"—I shook my head—"you know how my mom gets."

Beau went still. The teasing grin on his face disappeared, replaced by an unreadable mask. "Say what?"

I blinked at him. "The investigation? That you just brought up? This can't possibly come as a surprise to you. You know me better than pretty much anybody, Beau. How many times have you caught me poking around Uncle Calvin's house? You knew I reviewed the security footage from the party, because we talked about it. I know you're okay with this, because you took me to the bowling alley and tipped me off last night about Jocelyn Reyes."

Beau looked like he wanted to raise his voice, but that would defeat the purpose of being crammed into the bathroom together. When he spoke, he sounded eerily calm, which to be completely honest was more worrisome than if he'd yelled. "For crying out loud, Juni, I thought you'd have better luck finding your uncle than I would. Rather than waste department resources we don't have, I figured I'd sic you on Calvin's trail so I didn't have to split my concentration between locating him and solving a murder."

"Wait a second. You were using me?"

"Yes. I was using you." He sounded as exasperated as I felt. "Is that what you want to hear? I thought you'd lead me straight to your uncle. I never in a million years thought you'd insert yourself into a murder investigation. Do you know how incredibly reckless that is?"

"If it's such a waste of resources to go after Calvin, why did you have me followed?"

"Believe it or not, I wasn't following you. It's a small town. People call the cops when there's a stray cat on their street that they don't recognize. I don't have to stake out a location that's got a nosy neighbor who's more than happy to call me when they see someone entering a vacant house."

Cedar River didn't need a formal neighborhood watch, not while ladies like Edie were around. "You can't expect me to believe that Miss Edie ratted me out," I said.

"Considering what happened the last time you broke into your uncle's house, maybe she was just looking out for you."

"I didn't break in," I explained. "I have a key."

"Well then, that changes everything," Beau said sarcastically. "Juni, I know how tight your family is. I assumed you'd lead me to Calvin. But I underestimated you."

"When haven't you?" I asked. Okay, that was a low blow. I'll admit it. But there would never be a better time to throw out the fact that Beau had dumped me because he didn't think I was capable of making my own life choices.

He shut his eyes and took a deep breath. I could imagine him counting to five. When he opened his eyes, he said, "I assumed you were looking for your uncle so you could talk him into standing trial for the unpaid moving violations before he defaulted on his bail and you lost the record store, but there's more to it, isn't there?"

"Who else is gonna clear his name?" I asked. "The only way I can help my uncle is by figuring out who actually killed Monica Mayhew."

"That's my job, not yours. You run a record store. I catch murderers."

"Why can't I do both?"

"Don't even joke about that, Juni," he said.

I wasn't joking, but this might not be the best time to admit that. Instead, I said, "Fine. I'll stop."

"Why don't I believe you?"

I shrugged. I guess he knew me better than I wanted to admit. After this conversation, I was more determined than ever to find out who killed Monica, to prove to Beau that I could do it if for no other reason. "What do you want me to say?"

"Promise you'll drop this. I was wrong to encourage you to go after your uncle. I know that now. I let you believe that your uncle was our prime suspect, because I thought it would motivate you to root him out faster. That was a mistake. We have evidence I can't discuss and lab results that will be in any day now. I shouldn't be telling you any of this, but I need you to understand that we've got this well in hand. So, you'll stand down?"

Nope. No way. I was too close to stop now. But if I told Beau that, I was in for another lecture, or worse, he might rat me out to my mom. "Yes."

He wasn't going to let me off the hook that easily. He took my hands and held them up between us. "Yes, what?"

"I'm done. No more investigating," I lied. I was making just as much progress as the Cedar River Police Department, if not more. They were still oblivious about the lottery game going on right under their noses, but I couldn't say anything without Beau suspecting Calvin of more wrongdoing.

He didn't believe me. I could see it in his eyes "Blast it, Juni, I'm serious."

"So am I," I promised. I tried to look sincere when mentally I was crossing my fingers.

He dropped my hands. "I'm gonna hold you to that."

"Good," I agreed.

"I better be going. I've got a murder to solve."

"Before you go, can I ask an unrelated question?" Instead of waiting for his answer, which would have given me a chance to chicken out, I barreled ahead. "Is it illegal for a private citizen to run a lottery game?"

He tilted his head. "That there's a very interesting question. I guess that would depend on if it was a non-profit charity raffle or a cash prize where the person running the lotto kept a cut. I've heard rumors about an underground game like that in the area. Do you have any specific information you'd like to share?"

Shucks. I should have figured that Calvin's lotto scheme wasn't aboveboard. "Nope. Absolutely not."

"Do me a favor and don't get involved in anything like that, okay?"

I nodded. "Don't worry, I won't," I agreed, which was at least partially true. Calvin might have used the store as a front for his game without my knowledge, but no more. I shuffled over so Beau could get to the door. "Night."

"Good night, Junebug," he replied. He let himself out of the bathroom. I turned off the fan. I could hear muffled voices coming from the dining room and wondered how much they had overheard. Not much, I hoped. I washed my hands at the sink, taking the time to compose myself. Then I walked out of the bathroom like I didn't have a care in the world.

When I returned to the table, all conversation stopped as the whole family turned their attention on me.

"What was that?" Mom asked.

"Nothing."

"Didn't seem like nothing," Tansy said. My sisters knew

about the investigation, of course. They'd been involved every step of the way and would continue to be. But that wasn't what worried my overprotective sister. She was more concerned about Beau and me locking ourselves in the bathroom. Which was ridiculous. I couldn't think of a less romantic place to be, except maybe jail.

"Y'all, can we forget about it?" I looked over at my plate. The chairs on either side of mine were empty, and my margarita had mostly melted. "Where's Samuel?"

"He had to take off," Mom said. "Said he'd call you tomorrow."

Not very likely. Not only had Beau and I gotten into an argument, but I'd let my dinner get cold and my margarita get warm. But worst of all, Samuel had slipped out before I could question him about the game or his car. All in all, not my best night ever.

CHAPTER 24

In contrast to the family dinner debacle, the next morning was looking up. When I'd gotten back to Tansy's house after dinner—the long tricycle ride did me good after all those tacos—there was a package containing blackout curtains waiting for me on the front porch. I'd hung them up on the existing curtain rods immediately, and for the first time since moving back home I slept until my alarm went off.

There was a voicemail waiting for me from Esméralda saying that I could come pick up the Bronco anytime, and that she wanted to talk to me about something she found in the tire. I groaned. In the rain and low visibility, I'd probably run over something sharp, which meant the blowout was my fault. Shucks.

But on the plus side, I could smell coffee already brewing from the kitchen. Tansy had done my laundry and there was a clean, neatly folded pile of vintage concert T-shirts for me to choose from. I even had a text from Maggie that there were taco leftovers for lunch. Yes indeedy, things were looking up.

After showering and washing my hair—I was still finding flecks of glitter every time I combed it—I selected a P!nk T-shirt and paired it with mom jeans and sneakers. I might be the only person in Cedar River who didn't regularly wear cowboy boots, but while boots were great for riding horses, they were less than ideal for a tricycle.

Tansy was spreading cream cheese on a bagel when I entered the kitchen. "Morning, sleepyhead. I thought for sure you'd get up before me," she said. "Sorry, I took the last bagel. I'll get some next time I'm at the store."

"Don't worry about it," I said. I made a beeline for the coffeepot and poured myself a mug. "Top you off?" I asked.

"Thanks, but I'm good. Ever since we put in that barista station at the shop, I've been drinking way too much coffee. I'm thinking about cutting back, maybe even trying decaf."

I clutched at my heart with my free hand. "You can't be serious. Who are you and what have you done with my sister?"

"I know, right? I never thought there would come a day when I'd had too much caffeine, and yet here we are. Got any plans tonight?"

"Nope. You?"

"Going to a baking class with some friends. It's macaron day. You should join us."

I sat across from her at the table. "Maybe you could bring me home some?"

"Sure thing. But are you certain you don't have anything going on after work?" she asked.

I nodded. "Pretty sure. What am I missing here?"

"It's none of my business, but you and Beau seemed"—she hesitated for a second before continuing—"cozy last night. Are you two getting back together?"

"No way," I told her.

Tansy let out a sigh of relief. "Thank goodness. After what happened last time, well, I was worried about you getting hurt again. I would never forgive him if that happened."

"Thanks for looking out for me, but I'm good. Beau and I are good, too." At least I think we were. Not that it would last. As soon as he realized that I wasn't going to roll over and let the Cedar River Police Department railroad my uncle into murder charges, we'd be on the outs again, but that was a price I was willing to pay for family.

"Good?" she asked, looking suspicious. "And you're not even considering giving him a second chance, are you?"

The doorbell rang before I had to think too much about the answer to that question. "Hold on, I'm gonna get that." I hurried to the door and opened it to see Teddy standing outside holding a pastry box. At first, I assumed he was making a delivery, then realized he wasn't in uniform. "Good morning! Come on in."

He followed me into the kitchen, where he set the bakery box down on the center of the table. "Donuts," he said, opening the box. A dozen donuts, each with a different glaze, filled the box. "Fresh from the bakery. Didn't know what you liked, so I got a selection."

"Thanks!" Things were getting better and better—at this rate, Calvin would show up at Sip & Spin and turn himself in by lunchtime. "Can I get you some coffee?"

"Sure." He hovered awkwardly near the doorway.

"Take a seat," I said. "Black, right?" I hoped I was remembering his preference correctly. If he wanted something steamed, foamed, iced, or flavored, he was out of luck. All of the fancy stuff was at the shop.

"Black is fine," he replied.

I poured his coffee into a mug that featured unicorns frolicking in a meadow under a rainbow-colored sky. It read: "Have a magical day!"

The donuts were calling my name. I plucked one out at random. It turned out to be a blueberry old-fashioned with a sugary glaze. It was delicious. "What brings you by this morning?" I asked between bites.

"It's my day off. I went by the record store, but Maggie said you were working the late shift today. Didn't want the donuts to go to waste, so I decided to bring them here."

"That's very thoughtful," Tansy said. She got up, rinsed her dishes, and put them in the dishwasher. "I've got to run. I promised Mom I'd help her practice her speech."

"Speech?" I asked.

"She's getting an award for one of her fundraisers."

"That sounds great. Oh, Tansy, speaking of awards, well, there are an awful lot of your old beauty pageant trophies and crowns and stuff in my room. It's like living in a shrine. I was wondering if you would mind if I moved them to the closet or something."

She looked startled. "I'd forgotten all about those! I meant to clean them out before you moved in and it just slipped my mind. I'll have them out of there before you get home from work tonight."

"No rush," I said.

"I just don't know what to do with them, you know? I don't need them, but I don't want to just toss them out. I've got some empty bins in the attic. I'll put them in there."

"Don't worry, it's no big deal," I assured her. "Have fun with the speech and all."

"I will."

After Tansy left, Teddy volunteered, "I've got nothing planned for this morning. How about you and I box up the trophies now, together?"

"I'd love that," I agreed. Packing boxes was surely platonic.

The hatch to the attic was located in the main hall. Even standing on my toes, I struggled to reach the cord. "I've got it," Teddy offered. He reached above me, pulled open the hatch, and unfolded the stairs. He climbed into the attic and carried down two large plastic tubs. "Think this is enough?"

"I'm not sure; there are an awful lot of trophies. Tansy won a lot."

"Hold on." He climbed the stairs a second time and brought down another tub. "This is the last empty one I saw up there. The rest are filled with holiday decorations."

I carried the first two tubs toward my room. Teddy followed with the third. When I opened the door, he let out a whistle. "What happened in here? Did a tornado touch down? Has anyone called FEMA yet?"

"Ha-ha," I said, eyeing the mess critically before opening the blackout curtains and letting in the morning sun. "I haven't really had time to unpack."

"Oh really?" He picked up a Red Hot Chili Peppers T-shirt from the floor, folded it, and set it on the edge of my vanity table. "How long have you been back?"

"A few weeks."

"And you still haven't unpacked?"

"I've been busy." The back wall was lined with boxes of my belongings. Books, nicknacks, and old photo albums formed the foundation of even more boxes filled with clothes and shoes. I'd sold or donated all of my furniture, cookware, and dishes before I left Oregon. I wasn't sure if it was liberating or terrifying that everything I owned fit into this bedroom, but if I was planning on staying—and I was, at least until I could afford a place of my own—I might as well start putting things away.

In the meantime, I grabbed piles of clothes and towels off the floor and tossed them in the closet to get them out of the way.

"If this is the way you clean, maybe you should be putting your services as a professional organizer instead of wasting your time selling records."

"Ha-ha." I cleared a spot on the bed and set one of the tubs down on the sheet.

"You know, normal adults make their bed when they get up in the morning," he told me.

"Why bother?" I asked. "I'm just going to sleep in it again tonight." The thought stirred a memory. Calvin's bed had been made when I'd dropped by before borrowing the Bronco. Was it like that the first time we searched his house? I didn't think it had been. But it was definitely made when I went back yesterday. Had the intruder I'd interrupted on Monday night stopped to make the bed before rifling through the drawer to find the envelope of cash? Come to think of it, even Calvin's drawer had looked conspicuously neat.

Either the intruder knew exactly what they wanted and exactly where to find it, or they were as meticulous as my sister Maggie.

"Here, I'll hand you the trophies, and you put them in the tubs," Teddy said, then, out of the blue, asked, "Are you happy to be home?"

"What kind of silly question is that? Of course I am," I told him.

"Yeah, but you've been back in Cedar River for a few weeks and you haven't unpacked. You haven't reached out to any of your old friends." He shrugged. "It almost feels like this is all just temporary to you."

"I meant it when I said I'd been busy. Everything happened so quickly, me losing my job, the perfect space opening up, and my sisters and me deciding to open Sip & Spin. Tansy and Maggie quit their jobs. I broke my lease, sold my car, and moved back. We had renovations to do, inventory to purchase, and a website to build. It's all been such a whirlwind that I haven't had much time for anything else."

"Which is exactly why I worry about you sometimes," Teddy said. "You didn't have a lot of time to think about what you wanted, so you just went along with your sisters, like you always do."

"That's not true! The record shop was Tansy's idea, true, but I've had it up to here with toxic office culture and seminars on synergy and Six Sigma and all the other nonsense. If I ever see another PowerPoint presentation, I might hurl. I enjoyed application development, but in between the constant mergers and takeovers, sometimes it felt like I spent more time updating my email signature than writing code."

Concerns alleviated, he nodded. "I get it. Corporate America wasn't for me, either. That's why I traded in my suit and tie for a mailbag and good walking shoes."

"Exactly. If I'm working ten to twelve hours a day, I might as well be doing something I love, surrounded by friends and family. And as fantastic as Oregon is, I've been homesick for Texas ever since I left," I added, honestly.

"You say that now, but wait until August."

"I didn't say I missed the summer heat," I admitted. Just the thought of it made the back of my neck tingle. I twisted up my long hair into a bun. Come summer, I'd be tempted to shave it all off. "But I did miss my friends and family."

"Well, I for one am glad you're back."

"Me too," I agreed.

Half an hour later, all three of the tubs were full. Some of the larger, oversize trophies stood on the floor next to the bed. "What do you want to do with those?" he asked.

"We can move them to the hall and let Tansy decide where she wants them." The full tubs were awkward and heavy, but Teddy had no problems carrying them up into the attic while I lined the larger trophies up in the hall. He dusted off his hands and tucked the attic stairs back where they belonged. "Thanks, Teddy. I think I can start making the room feel a little more like my own now. With all of those open shelves, there's finally room for my stuff."

"If you want, I can stick around and help you unpack."

I wrinkled my nose at that. I'd packed at the last minute, and I'd used whatever was lying around as padding or as filler when the book boxes got too heavy. Who knew what kinds of unmentionables he might find in those boxes. "Thanks, but I'll take care of it later. I've got an errand to run, and then I'm due at the store for the second shift."

"What kind of errand?" Teddy asked.

"I need to talk to Samuel. Hey, do you mind giving me a lift to his warehouse out by the airport?"

"Not at all. Like I said, I'm glad you're home, and I can't think of anything I'd rather do on my day off than to hang out together." He grinned and added, "Like we used to."

♪ ♫ ♪

When we arrived at the industrial complex, Teddy pulled into a spot and idled while we looked around. "Are you sure he's here? I don't see his car."

Like my unique tricycle, or my uncle's Bronco, Samuel's car stood out. He could always find it in a parking lot and everyone knew when he was home. If some poor kid ever decided to take it for a joyride, twenty people would tell Samuel where his car was before he even realized it was missing. It also served as a big red flag when he was inside his office and his car wasn't parked out front.

"Pretty sure," I told him. "Samuel's never missed a day of work in his life. Thanks for the lift. And for helping with the trophies."

"No worries. I enjoy spending time with you." He looked out the windshield of his car at the warehouse entrance. It did look pretty bleak. I thought I saw a faint glow of light from behind the newspaper-covered window, but I couldn't be certain. "Maybe I should go in with you."

"I'm good." To be honest, I wasn't certain that I wanted Teddy to be there for the conversation I needed to have with Samuel. Teddy was my friend, but he was also a postal employee, so technically he worked for the government. For all

I knew, he was bound by an oath to tell the police if he heard about something potentially illegal. "It's kind of family business and you know how cagey he can get."

"In that case, I'll wait here for you."

"I've no idea how long I'll be. I'll get a ride home." I had my cell phone and a long list of people I could call if I couldn't get an Uber. I got out of the car.

"Hey, Juni?"

I stopped and leaned into the car, one hand on the door. "Don't worry about me, Teddy. I'll be fine."

He grinned. "I know that. I was wondering if you'd have dinner with me again. Maybe tomorrow night? And no offense to the pecan waffles at the diner, but why don't you let me pick a nicer place this time?"

A Friday night, non-diner dinner out? That was a real date, wasn't it? It certainly sounded like one. And maybe that wasn't a bad thing. "You know what? Yeah. Sounds like a great idea. Just let me know when and what to wear."

"Do you own anything other than old concert T-shirts and jeans?" he asked dubiously. He'd seen most of my wardrobe while we were starting the long job of organizing my room, so he knew the answer to that already.

"Nope."

"Then what you're wearing now will be fine," he assured me.

"Cool. See ya tomorrow night." I closed the door to his Jeep and headed toward the Prankenstein entrance.

I knocked and waited for the door to open a crack. "You alone this time?" Samuel asked.

"Yup."

"That's Teddy Garza's Jeep," he said, looking over my shoulder.

"Yup," I repeated.

"Fine. Come on in." I turned, waved at Teddy, and followed Samuel.

Inside, Prankenstein looked more like a toy store than a place of business. The front office had two old metal desks on either side of the room. Both were piled high with balls, stuffed animals, neon-haired troll dolls, Rubik's Cubes, Slinkys, and dirty coffee cups. A shelf along the back wall held an impressive collection of Beanie Babies.

I ran my hand over the Beanie Babies, recognizing some of my favorites from when I was a kid. There was even the twin to the dragon that I'd left in the hidey-hole at Sip & Spin to guard the now-missing treasure chest. I reached for it.

"No!" Samuel said sharply, grabbing my hand. "You don't want to do that."

I raised one eyebrow at him. "I don't? Why not?"

"Those are from the new line. Pick them up wrong, and you get sprayed with blue dye, the kind they use in banks that doesn't wash off."

I pulled my hand away and stuck it in my pocket, resolved to not touch anything while I was here. "And what's the point of that?"

"You worked in corporate America. What was on your desk?"

"I worked from home a lot, but my desk at the office was about the same as yours," I said, gesturing toward one of the metal desks piled high with toys. "Significantly fewer whatsits and whatnots, but similar. Stress squeezes. Rubber balls. A couple stuffed animals."

"And did they ever walk off?" he asked.

"All the time."

"And you don't think it would be funny if a thief got their comeuppance?"

I frowned. "What if it's the night janitor, just trying to do their job? Or some toddler on Bring Your Kid to Work Day?"

"There are still some kinks to work out," he grumbled. "But that's not why you came here, is it?"

"I know about the game," I blurted out.

Whatever he was expecting me to say, that wasn't it. He stared at me with his mouth half-open, looking a little like the singing fish mounted to the wall above his desk. He gathered his wits and asked, "What game?"

"Come on, Samuel. *The* game. The lotto or whatever."

"Oh, that game."

"Is that why you two went your separate ways? You didn't want Calvin running his sketchy game out of your legitimate business?"

Samuel chuckled. "You know your uncle as well as I do. If something's not explicitly illegal, it's fair game. Everything was fine and dandy until your little mailman friend in the Jeep out there blew the whistle on us. One tiny little glitter bomb, and he narced. Can you believe that? Couldn't run the lotto out of here after that."

I went to the window and peered out a small hole in the newspaper covering the glass. Sure enough, Teddy's Jeep was still parked outside. "I don't know how legal sending a bomb—prank or otherwise—through the mail is."

"No more illegal than running an unsanctioned gambling circuit through the U.S. Post Office," he pointed out.

"Which is why Calvin used the messenger service for local players, so mail carriers like Teddy wouldn't catch on," I said. Right now it was just a guess, but if I phrased it as a question, Samuel would have sidestepped around it.

"Exactly. I doubt those Roadrunners knew what they were transporting, but they never asked, either."

"Uh-huh," I said, and I couldn't resist adding, "Thanks for confirming that. I was only guessing that he'd hired Roadrunners to deliver the lotto tickets. Was Monica Mayhew one of the couriers he used?"

"Now you look here, little lady." Samuel poked a finger at me. "Calvin would place an order for pickup and whatever driver showed up, showed up. Don't go making trouble where there is none."

"But you knew her, right?" I pressed. "According to Elroy, she applied for a job here."

"If she did, I don't remember. Certainly didn't hire her." He spread his arms out and indicated the quiet warehouse. "Does it look like I need help around here? Don't go jumping to conclusions, or trying to drag that poor dead girl into this mess. You know as well as I do that your uncle ain't never killed nobody."

When Samuel got upset, his drawl got more pronounced and his vocabulary got more country. But I didn't think I'd ever heard him use "ain't" before. On the contrary, when my sisters and I were little he used to correct us when we said it. Which meant he was more agitated than I'd ever seen him. "What are you hiding?"

"Not hiding nothing," he growled.

"You knew Calvin's lotto scheme was illegal, didn't you?"

"It's a gray area," Samuel said.

"You were in on it," I realized.

Samuel nodded, seeming to realize that I wasn't going to let this go. "Of course I was. You ever known me and your uncle to keep anything from each other? He called me after he got out on bail, freaking out. He knew if the cops took a hard look at him, they might uncover our game. He thought it would be best for everyone if he laid low until the heat died down."

"Which is why you loaned him your car."

"Girlie, your uncle is about the closest thing I have to a brother. If he needed a kidney, I'd cut mine out and hand it to him. And he'd do the same for me in a heartbeat. So yes, I picked him up after he got out of jail and loaned him my Firebird."

"Did you know he was going to skip bail?" I asked.

"Nope. But if I'd known, I still would have given him the keys to my car."

"Even after he up and walked away from the company you two started together?"

"You wanna know why he left Prankenstein?" He held his arms out wide. "Because we're going under. Got a warehouse full of glitter, glue, and permanent blue dye, and no customers. So, yes, on paper I bought him out with all the cash we had on hand. In a few months, I'll file for bankruptcy. Prankenstein will be nothing but a memory, and we'll split whatever is left."

That explained a lot. I'd assumed that he and Samuel were on the outs since Calvin didn't want to tell anyone why he quit Prankenstein. I should have known my uncle had some kind of angle, and I wasn't surprised to learn that they were running yet another scam together.

"That explains why Calvin, who's the biggest blowhard I've ever known, wanted to be a silent partner in the record shop. He wasn't putting up his own money. Which means technically, you're an investor in Sip & Spin. I'm not sure if you realize it, but if he doesn't come back, you're in just as deep as the rest of us."

CHAPTER 25

Samuel looked defeated. "I just about had a coronary when I found out that Calvin sank all of our money into the record store."

"Is that what you two were arguing about at the grand opening?" I asked. I couldn't be certain that the man Jocelyn Reyes had overheard Calvin arguing with was Samuel, but he didn't deny it.

"If you're so dang smart, why don't you tell me?"

"Your business split was just for show, but your fight at the party was real," I guessed. "A few hours later, an innocent young woman is found dead in Sip & Spin, holding one of Calvin's business cards from Prankenstein. The next day, my uncle is questioned, gets out on bail, and takes off in your car. Where is he now?"

Samuel shook his head. "I don't know. Cross my heart. If I did, I'd tell you."

I didn't believe him. "Yeah, because you've been so forthcoming up until now."

"Fine. I loaned him my car because he said he needed to get out of town for a few days, and wanted something a little less conspicuous than the Bronco," he said. A fire-engine red Trans Am wasn't what I would call inconspicuous, but if he stayed out of Cedar River, Calvin could hide in plain sight. "That was before I heard what happened to the girl."

"You can't actually think Calvin had anything to do with Monica's death?" I asked, unable to believe my ears.

"Not in a million years. But when he ran, he made himself look awful guilty. If I knew where he was, I'd drag him back myself, and if I had any way of getting into contact with him, I'd have already done it."

Now *that* I believed.

"Back to square one," I muttered. "His best friend doesn't know where he is. His girlfriend doesn't know where he is. His family doesn't know where he is. He's out there, who knows where, with no money and, as far as I can tell, nothing but the clothes on his back."

"You're not mad at him, like I thought. You're worried about him," he said.

"Seriously, am I that easy to read?"

"You could stand to work on your poker face," he admitted.

"Yes, I'm worried. Happy? The real question is, why aren't you worried?"

Samuel chewed on the inside of his cheek for a second. "I think he's got a guy."

"He's got a guy? What does that mean?"

He gave a terse shrug. "I don't rightly know. He said he was gonna lie low for a bit, but he'd be keeping an eye on things. I think he's got a guy on the inside communicating with him. Someone who knows how to get in touch with him. Someone he trusts."

"More than us?" I asked. "No way. Calvin only trusts family."

Samuel nodded slowly. "That's true."

My phone rang, and I jumped. I looked down at the ID. It was my sister. "Sorry, I gotta take this." I answered the phone. "Maggie?"

"Where are you? I've got plans this afternoon, and I expected you here half an hour ago." I looked at the clock on the wall. It was one of those flat, white industrial clocks behind a metal cage. Presuming it wasn't a prank like everything else at the warehouse, it was a lot later than I thought. Between cleaning the trophies out of my room and grilling Samuel, I'd lost track of time.

"I'm so sorry, Maggie. I'll be right there." I disconnected. "Thanks," I said, giving Samuel a hug.

"What for? I didn't do anything."

"No, but you told me the truth. That's gonna help." Or at least I hoped it would. I didn't like the idea that someone in my family was holding out on us, but it was a lead I didn't have an hour ago. "When I find him, I'll let you know."

"I'll do the same if I hear from him," Samuel promised.

"Are you telling me the truth this time?" I asked. "Or are you going to slip away the first chance you get, like last night?"

"Would I lie to you?"

I nodded. "One hundred percent you would." Samuel might be my honorary uncle, but he was also the same man who'd convinced me if I dangled a hand over the edge of the bed the boogieman would eat it while I slept. To this day, I have to sleep in the very center of my mattress with a sheet pulled up to my chin, and I blame him for that.

"Fair. But I'm not lying about this. Aren't you late for work? Scoot."

He gave me another quick hug and then practically pushed me out the front door. Teddy's Jeep was still parked outside, so I made a beeline for it. "You waited," I said as I opened the door, sat down on the passenger's seat, and buckled my seat belt.

"Told ya I didn't have any plans today." He'd been playing on his phone. He turned it off and slid it into a holder mounted to the dashboard. "Where to next?"

"As much as I'd love to hang out with you all day, I'm late for work."

"Drop you at Sip & Spin?" he offered.

"That would be very appreciated."

As he started the car, the Gin Blossoms' "Hey Jealousy" came on over the radio. I began to sing along, slightly off-key. Teddy laughed and joined in. When it was over, he said, "That song came out before we were even born, and you know all the lyrics."

"Yeah, I grew up in a record shop, remember? And now I own one. Nostalgia sells. Most of the stuff we have came out long before I was born. My dad always said that all the best music was made ages ago, and that was way back in the eighties. Besides, this is a good album."

"I'm, um, sorry about your dad." He took one hand off the wheel to reach over and gently rest it on my knee. "He was a good guy."

"He was," I agreed. The hardest part of being home was him not being here. I kept expecting him to walk into the room any minute, but of course he didn't. At least I had the comfort of knowing he passed peacefully, surrounded by friends and family.

Monica didn't have that luxury. It wasn't fair.

"Hey, Juni, did I say something wrong?" Teddy asked, snapping me back to the present.

I shook my head. "No, of course not."

"It's just, you don't really talk about your dad. Maybe I shouldn't have brought him up."

"No worries," I assured him. "I like talking about him. Dad liked you. Did you know that? He used to tease me about you all the time."

"Really?" he asked.

"He used to sing that horrible song every time you left. You know the one. 'Juni and Teddy sitting in a tree . . .'" Teddy joined in and we finished it together. *"K-i-s-s-i-n-g.'"*

"I used to think about asking you out all the time," he admitted.

"Why didn't you?" I was genuinely curious.

"I don't know. Too chicken, I guess. I mean, we were friends. Best friends. I didn't want to mess that up over a crush. Plus, we were in all the same classes and clubs. Can you just imagine how awkward chess club would have been if we'd dated and then broken up?"

"Who says we would have broken up?" I asked. His hand was still on my knee, so I covered it with my hand and curled my fingers over his. His hand was rough. "Besides, being the only girl in chess club was already awkward."

"Noted," he said.

I'd thought having a candid conversation with Teddy would have been more difficult than this, but we'd always had an easy rapport. It was hard to believe that he'd had a crush on me way back when and I'd never stopped to consider that our chemistry might be more than friendship. How could a great guy like Teddy have been there all along and I never even noticed?

Relationships were weird that way.

My mind began to wander to Monica Mayhew and her relationships. She hadn't had a boyfriend when she died, at least not one we knew about. There was nothing about her relationship status on her social media accounts. Tansy said she'd recently broken up with someone who was transferred overseas, and Mom hadn't heard anything about a new love interest from the town grapevine. Even Miss Edie said Monica told her she wasn't dating anyone. But what if there was a secret admirer who'd managed to fly so far under the radar that not even the rumor mill had picked up on it yet? Maybe he'd followed her to the party, and then . . .

That's where my secret admirer theory fell apart. Monica

was working the night of the grand opening, if her outfit was any indication. The beer and tacos were running low but had not yet run out when she showed up at 10:42, so it didn't make sense that someone at the party had placed an order for food. Even if Monica *had* been making a delivery, why wasn't her car parked out front of the shop? Parking had been a nightmare that night. A delivery person would have double-parked and we would have certainly noticed an abandoned car in the middle of Main Street. I wished I could call Beau and ask if he knew where Monica's car was, but I doubted he would be very forthcoming.

And how was the man caught coming in the back door on the surveillance video involved? Was the timing a coincidence, or did it mean something? And why was Monica holding Calvin's business card when she died?

None of it made any sense.

"Whoa, what's going on here?" Teddy asked, bringing me back to the present. He took his hand back and kept it on the wheel as we slowed to a crawl on Main Street. Getting stuck in traffic was something that almost never happened in Cedar River. All the prime parking spots along the curb were taken, and cars jammed the street. Without any streetlights to control the flow of traffic, the side streets were probably a mess, too. I leaned forward, as if getting a few inches closer to the windshield would help me see better.

"Maybe there's a sale going on that we didn't know about?" he suggested.

"I hope so." It was certainly better than the alternative. The last time I'd seen Main Street packed like this had been the night of the Sip & Spin grand opening, when an ambulance and several cop cars blocked the road. "Go ahead and let me off here," I suggested.

Yes, it was a selfish thing to do, bailing and leaving Teddy stuck in traffic when he wouldn't have been downtown at all if I hadn't asked for a ride, but I was already late for work and traffic wasn't moving.

Teddy didn't seem to mind, though. "Sure. See you tomorrow night?"

"It's a date," I said. The words slipped out before I could consider the implications.

"Or possibly a raspberry," he said, jokingly.

I grinned. After unbuckling my seat belt, I spontaneously leaned over and gave him a quick kiss on the cheek. "Thanks for the lift." I let myself out of the Jeep and started down the sidewalk toward the record shop.

The sidewalks weren't as crowded as the street, but there were more people milling about than was usual for the middle of the afternoon on a Thursday. "What happened?" I asked one of the passersby.

They shrugged. "No idea."

As I hurried toward Sip & Spin, my fears seemed to have manifested in the form of a fire truck angled across the street immediately in front of the record shop. Firefighters in full kit—thick jackets, helmets, and air tanks strapped to their backs—swarmed the entrance. I pushed my way through the crowd to get closer.

To my relief, there were no ambulances in the street and no smoke coming out of the shop.

One of the firefighters stepped into my path. "Sorry, sidewalk's closed. Go back the way you came," she said.

"But that's my shop," I said, growing more frantic by the second. "My sister Maggie's inside."

The firefighter studied me. "You're one of the Jessup girls?"

I can't say it enough. I love small towns, where everyone knows everyone. Or, at the very least, everyone knows everyone's family. "Yeah. I'm Juniper. What is going on? Is my sister okay?"

"Everyone's fine." She led me past firefighters who were rolling up hoses and arranging various tools inside cubbies built into the truck. The door was propped open. I dashed inside.

"Maggie? Maggie?"

My sister stepped out of a crowd of firefighters in bulky uniforms and crushed me in a hug. "Juni! It's okay, it's okay."

I extricated myself from my sister's arms. "What happened here?"

"No idea. I was here, helping a customer, when the fire truck pulled up outside, lights and sirens going. Someone had called in a fire. They evacuated the shop. But there was no fire. It was a false alarm."

"Or a warning," Beau said, joining us. I hadn't noticed him when I came in, but I had only been concerned about my sister. He, however, was focused intently on me. "I told you, Juni, that someone was going to get hurt if you didn't back off."

"Now *that* sounds like a threat," Maggie said, glaring at Beau. "A warning would come with some kind of message, wouldn't it? This was probably just a prank."

"A prank?" I asked. The tiny hairs on the back of my neck stood at attention. Who did I know who loved pranks? "You don't think Samuel was behind this, do you?"

Beau got out his notebook. "Samuel Davis?"

"Wait, what time did the call come in?" I asked.

Beau referred to his notes. "Twelve fifteen."

I pulled out my phone and checked my call logs. I'd been on the phone with Maggie about that time. "It couldn't have been Samuel. I was with him."

"We'll still need to talk to him," Beau said, but he didn't sound as sure as he'd been a minute ago.

"Mags! What is going on?" J.T. rushed up to join us, followed closely by Elroy.

"Where did y'all come from?" Beau asked. It was a good question. I hadn't seen them come in.

"Back door was open. Couldn't hardly get down Main Street, it was so crowded." J.T. turned his attention back to his wife. "Are you okay? Do you need to sit down?"

"I'm fine," she assured him. "What are you doing here?"

"We just got out of court when we saw all the commotion. Are you sure you're okay?"

"It's all good. Someone called in a false alarm, that's all." She turned to Beau. "Are we done here?"

"I just have a couple more questions . . ."

J.T. cut him off. "Well then, it's a good thing that her lawyer is here. Now back off and let me converse with my client."

Beau took my wrist and led me away from them. The huddle of firefighters had broken up and they were trailing out of the shop. Over the speakers, Lynyrd Skynyrd was playing, adding to the noise and confusion. "I thought we had an agreement," he said.

"What agreement?" I asked.

"Last night, you agreed to stop investigating. Looks like someone else isn't very happy with you poking your nose into places where it doesn't belong. I think this is a pretty clear message."

"First off," I corrected him, "I didn't agree to anything. Second off, I haven't even done any investigating today."

"You haven't? Then what were you doing with Samuel just now?"

"Samuel is practically family. I don't need an excuse to visit family," I said defensively, especially knowing I was more than bending the truth.

"You saw him last night," he pointed out. "I heard you tell him you wanted to question him."

I pointed to J.T. and Maggie, who were drifting toward the

back of the shop while they talked. "I saw Maggie last night, too. And J.T. And Elroy. And you, for that matter. And yet, here you all are today. It's a small town, Beau. I'm bound to bump into the same people over and over again."

"What were you and Samuel Davis discussing?"

"Family business." If I told Beau that my uncle was driving around in Samuel's Firebird, he'd update the BOLO. That car wasn't hard to spot. Calvin would be in cuffs within the hour. The only reason Beau suspected Calvin was involved with Monica's death was because my uncle ran. If I found him and convinced him to turn himself in, that would go a long way toward proving his innocence.

"Who else did you see today?" he asked.

"I was with Teddy Garza all morning. He'll confirm I was with Samuel when the prank call came in." I neglected to mention that he'd been outside in his car at the time, but he knew where I was.

Beau put his hands on my shoulders. "This isn't a game, Junebug. People have already gotten hurt. Monica's dead and your uncle's missing. And now this threat on you and your sisters? What's it going to take to get you to let it go?"

Elroy walked up behind Beau and cleared his throat. "You're not harassing our client, are you, Detective Russell?"

"Of course not," Beau replied, but he kept his eyes trained on me. "Please, Juni. I'm begging you."

"You need to take your hands off her," Elroy said, stepping closer.

Beau dropped his arms. "Please."

Elroy moved between us, blocking Beau from my sight. "If you have any further questions, feel free to call the office." He held out a business card for Taggart and McGibbons.

"I've got the number," Beau said with clenched teeth. "Juni, can I have just another minute?"

"I think you're done talking with my client for today," Elroy said. "Now, if you don't mind, the fire chief cleared the building. There's no threat. So why don't you move along?"

He ignored Elroy, instead poking his head around the taller man to ask me, "Call me later?" I shrugged. Beau left.

Elroy shadowed him to the front door and then locked it behind him, flipping the Open sign to Closed. It was eerily silent in the shop until J.T. asked, "Now will someone please tell me what on earth is going on?"

CHAPTER 26

"Can I get anyone anything to drink?" I asked. I was still shaken from finding a fire truck parked out front of Sip & Spin and seeing firefighters swarming around the shop, but no one was hurt and there was no damage, so no harm, no foul, right? Besides, I was raised to believe that any crisis could be solved with good manners and refreshments. "I make a killer coffee."

"I'll take one. Something manly," J.T. requested.

"Then you're in luck. The special of the day is Espresso Yourself," I replied as I started prepping his drink. It was a simple shot of espresso in a tiny mug. "Unless you would prefer something more *manly*. Like a bucket of fish guts and rusty nails maybe?"

"Espresso is fine," he said. He grinned at me as he hopped up to sit on the counter. I was used to his teasing and knew he was just trying to break the tension. It worked.

"Elroy?" I asked.

He was leaning against the doorway that led to the supply closet and, beyond that, the back door. "Fish guts and rusty nails sounds fine for me, but can you add some of that pumpkin spice stuff to it?"

"It's March," I pointed out. "You've got six whole months until pumpkin spice anything is in stock. Maybe seven."

"But fish guts are in season?" he asked.

"Fish guts are always in season, but we're all out of rusty nails. And buckets. However, I think you might like a Cappuccino Take Me Away." I started his drink. I layered the espresso, steamed milk, and foamed milk carefully, marveling once again at how quickly I'd managed to master our menu. "Maggie?"

"Tea?" she requested.

"One Excuse Me While I Kiss the Chai coming up." It was another drink that would have had me scratching my head a few weeks ago, but now it was second nature to whip up a dark tea infused with spices and blend it with steamed milk. I topped it with foam and a dash of cinnamon. I even managed a shape in the foam that might have been a flower. If I squinted.

I thought back to the conversation with Tansy this morning about us drinking too much caffeine. I wasn't sure that I agreed with her, but my nerves were already frayed enough without the addition of a stimulant. I refilled my water bottle instead of pouring myself more coffee.

After passing out drinks, I said, "Thanks for coming to our rescue earlier, but you two know Maggie and I are perfectly capable of not incriminating ourselves to the cops, right? Not that there is anything incriminating we can say, considering we didn't call in the false alarm. It was probably just a prank, like Maggie suggested."

"Even so, until this mess with Calvin is settled, maybe you two don't need to go locking yourselves in bathrooms with any cops without your lawyer present," J.T. suggested pointedly.

"For the record, your downstairs bath is tiny, J.T. I don't think the three of us would have fit," I replied.

"What were you two talking about, anyways?" he asked.

"If you must know, Beau got it in his head that Calvin ran off because he was involved in Monica Mayhew's death. He let that slip to me in the hopes that I would go looking for Calvin and lead him right to him. What he wasn't counting on was that while I was looking for my uncle, I'd end up picking up a bunch of clues about who actually killed Monica."

"You what?" J.T. asked, jumping down off the counter.

Ignoring his interruption, I continued, "That's what Beau was so upset about last night at dinner. He wants me to back off. Apparently, someone else had the same idea, and called the fire department to intimidate us. If I had to guess, they were sending a message about playing with fire or some such nonsense."

"Far be it from me to ever agree with Beauregard Russell, but for the record, he's right this one time, Juni. You don't need to be running around playing detective. You could get hurt, or worse. You weren't even at the shop when they called in the threat. My wife was. You could have gotten Maggie hurt. Do you understand that?"

But Maggie hadn't gotten hurt. If she had, I would have felt more guilty than anyone could imagine, especially since I was the one scheduled to be in the record shop, not my sister.

"Excuse me," Maggie interjected. "For the record, I'm perfectly capable of taking care of myself. And second off, nothing happened. It was a little scary, maybe, when the fire department showed up and yes, I was worried about the shop, but what part of *false* alarm do you not understand? Besides, Juni wasn't acting alone. I was helping. Tansy, too. Calvin's our uncle, and Sip & Spin is all of our business. You don't think me and my sisters are gonna sit on our hands while someone threatens it, do you?"

"Mags, you've got to be kidding me. I would expect this kind of behavior coming from Juni, but you're in on it, too?" her husband asked. He really seemed shocked.

"Wait a sec, what do you mean you expect this behavior

from me?" I asked. "I'm not some kind of juvenile delinquent running around causing trouble. I'm a grown woman trying to take care of her family and her business."

"No offense, Juni, but if you are all grown-up, maybe it's time you start acting like it," J.T. said. He took off his cowboy hat and set it on the counter, then ran a hand through his hair to get it to lie down evenly. "This isn't a game. A woman was murdered. No one's heard from your uncle in almost a week. And what if the next time the fire department shows up, it isn't a prank?" He shook his head. "None of us want that."

"You sound like Beau," I said, but then my voice trailed off as I stared at his hat. I hadn't paid much attention to it before. It was black with a silver band around it. Expensive, I'd wager. It was new, but I'd seen it before—in the videotape surveillance from the night of the party. From the night of the murder. The person who'd come in the back door that night had been wearing that exact same hat.

Sure, it might have been a coincidence, except cowboy hats were almost as unique as fingerprints. Even identical police-issue hats over time conformed to the heads of their wearers. Rims curled up. Bands shifted. They faded with exposure to the sun or stayed vibrant for those with desk jobs.

J.T. had seen the surveillance video. He'd reviewed it with me. He'd set the camera up in the first place. Come to think of it, he'd been involved every step of the way. He had to have recognized his hat when he watched the video, but he hadn't said a word.

"Are you listening to me?" J.T. asked.

I nodded dutifully but kept my face trained on his hat. I was afraid if I looked at him, he would see everything I was thinking as clear as day on my expression. Like Samuel said, I needed to work on my poker face.

Samuel had said something else that stuck with me. Someone was in communication with Calvin. Someone was advising him to lie low. Someone knew exactly where he kept a stash of money. Someone knew their way around his house and went so far as to grab his cell phone and his meds while he was taking the cash.

Someone in the family.

"You know where he is, don't you?" I blurted out without thinking.

"Who?" J.T. asked.

"Don't play coy with me. You know where Calvin is. You know how to reach him."

J.T. shook his head. "I most certainly do not. As an officer of the court, if I know where a fugitive is hiding I'm bound to turn him over to the authorities. Even if he's my wife's favorite uncle."

There was the pitter-patter sound of Daffy's claws on the steps as he descended the stairs from the loft and hopped up on the counter. "Daffy," Maggie said, scooping him up and hugging him to her chest. "I was so worried about you with all the commotion." As usual, the cat had made himself scarce the second strangers showed up. I worried that one of these days he'd get tired of guests intruding on his space all the time and he'd leave us to find someplace quieter.

And that's when it hit me. In the surveillance video, Daffy had calmly groomed himself as someone walked right past him and in through the shop's back door. If it had been a stranger, the cat would have disappeared before the man had come into view, but Daffy knew J.T. Why hadn't I put two and two together earlier? The cat's behavior, along with the notable hat, convinced me that it had been J.T. on the video that night.

"Why did you miss the Sip & Spin grand opening?" I asked him, my suspicions growing. If he wouldn't fess up that it was him on the video, what else was he hiding?

"I was working late," he said.

"Were you? I mean, come on, J.T. Everybody knows 'working late' is code for having an affair. Are you seeing someone? You better not be cheating on my sister, or I'll kill you."

"Of course not! I would never," he said emphatically.

"Juni, that's enough. I think I would know if my husband was cheating on me," Maggie said, moving to his side. He put his arm around my sister's shoulders.

"Where were you, really, the night of the party? Who were you with?" I didn't want to hurt Maggie, but I had a sinking feeling that J.T. was hiding something. I paused a beat as I thought about the implications. "Were you with Monica Mayhew that night?"

"I most certainly was not!" J.T. said. Ignoring me, he turned to Maggie. "I swear to you, I was working. I was at the office, by myself, until two, maybe three o'clock Saturday morning. I did not and would never betray my marriage vows."

My sister nodded. "I believe you, honey."

"But he *was* at the party, and I can prove it," I said. "J.T. was caught on video that night. In that hat." I pointed at the hat on the counter. I marched around the counter, queued up the video, and then swiveled the monitor where everyone else could see it. "Look. You can't see his face, but that's his hat. See that shiny silver band? And look at Daffy! He'd run away if that was a stranger."

"That really does resemble your hat, J.T.," Maggie said quietly.

"Not you, too," J.T. said. He jabbed a finger at the screen. "That's not me. I was at the office all night."

"Then why didn't you pick up the phone when I called you?" Maggie asked, her voice small and unsure.

"I told you. I was working. The ringer was off. I didn't

notice that I had a missed call from you until it was much too late to call you back." He seemed shaken.

"How convenient that you have all the answers," I said, torn between anger and disappointment. J.T. was like a brother to me, and I was having a hard time wrapping my head around the idea that he might be a bad guy. "You set up the cameras, J.T. Don't you think it's a little too coincidental that two of the cameras inside were covered and one wasn't working? You knew the angles. You knew exactly how to hide your face, and then helped me adjust the camera to get a better view of the alley after the fact." I rewound the video and froze the frame. "And you can't argue that that's your hat."

"Yeah, it looks like my hat," J.T. admitted, nodding vigorously. "A lot of people have hats like that. Heck, even Elroy has one just like it, don't you? A client gave us those as a thank-you gift. I think he got them at a shop over in Salado. Or was it Cameron?" He looked over at Elroy, who was white as a sheet.

Tall, lanky, narrow-shouldered Elroy.

Elroy with the fancy black cowboy hat with the shiny silver band.

Well, shucks.

I had accused the wrong lawyer.

"I'm so sorry," I said, taking a step away from the others, completely ashamed of myself for suspecting J.T. in the first place. "You're right. I was totally out of line. I don't know *what* I was thinking."

"Oh, we're gonna need more than an apology," Maggie said. I didn't think I've ever seen her so furious at me before, not even when I accidentally ruined her entire My Little Pony collection when I was four years old. Who would have guessed they would melt in the microwave? "What's wrong with you, Juni? You can't go around accusing people like that, especially your own brother-in-law."

"I'm sorry, Maggie, J.T. You've got every reason to be mad at me."

"Mad? I'm not mad at you, Juniper," my sister said in a flat voice. "I'm disappointed."

Ouch. That hurt.

I reached for my phone as I took another step back. "But hear me out. Someone came in late to the party, sneaking in the back door wearing that hat or one just like it, within minutes of Monica coming in the front entrance. And some-one convinced Calvin to lie low against his best interests, because that deflected all the attention off him. That same someone must be a person that Uncle Calvin trusts an awful lot. Someone in the family maybe." I turned to face Elroy. "Or the family's lawyer."

J.T. and Maggie both swiveled to look at him, too. "Tell me you have no idea what she's talking about, buddy," J.T. said.

Elroy shook his head, but there was a sheen of sweat on his hairline. "Of course not!" he stammered.

J.T. wasn't convinced. "You would never advise a client to skirt the law? Because we both know it wouldn't be the first time. You'd never step out on Mina? Need I remind you about Jasmine? And Shelly? For Pete's sake, you hit on Monica May-hew."

"I did not," Elroy said, but there was a hitch in his voice and a bead of sweat formed on his upper lip.

"That's not what she said when she quit, partner. Said you made her feel uncomfortable. Always commenting on her clothes, or standing just a little too close when you talked. Asking her to work late when it wasn't necessary. Inviting her to dinner."

"I did no such thing," Elroy insisted, shaking his head. "She was trying to set me up for a big payday, but she was barking up the wrong tree. Every penny I have went to buying out my father-in-law so you and I could have our names, and our names alone, on the letterhead, and I still owe the old man. Can't get blood from a stone, J.T."

"I can't help but wonder what Juan would do to you if he found out that you were stepping out on his daughter," J.T. mused. "Your debt to him wouldn't be your biggest problem. I imagine you'd do just about anything to keep that secret."

"That was you in Calvin's house Monday evening," I said. "My uncle went into hiding because you told him to, but he needed his phone and his meds. He trusted you to bring them to him. He told you where the hide-a-key was. He told you where to find the cash. Did you even bring it to him, or did you keep it for yourself?"

"Of course I gave it to him! I'm not some kind of petty thief. Yes, I know how to contact your uncle, okay? Fine. You caught me. I was protecting him. You know how cops can get. I wasn't about to let them beat a confession out of him. He's going to show up to stand trial. I guarantee it. But I was looking out for a client, and a friend. Nothing more." Elroy had stopped sweating and was starting to look pretty pleased with himself.

I guess all that practice of lying for a living came in handy outside of the courtroom, too.

"So you admit that you were in the intruder in Calvin's house," I said. "You were the one that assaulted me."

"I didn't realize it was you until it was too late. Honestly, I thought *you* were an intruder. So yes, in my haste to get out of the house, I nudged you out of the way." He was getting more smug by the second. "I didn't mean to push you so hard. I'm so relieved that you weren't hurt."

"Seriously?" I gestured at my own body. I was half his size. "You were, what, threatened by me?"

"It was dark," he growled.

"Was it really? Because you were in the bedroom, with the shades open. From my point of view, you were nothing but a shadow. But you, with your back to the windows, could probably make out the writing on my T-shirt," I said.

"It was dark," he repeated. "I was nervous. I panicked."

"Just like you panicked and killed Monica Mayhew?" Maggie asked. All her anger was now directed at Elroy, but when this was all over she and I would have a serious talk about me accusing her husband. I wasn't looking forward to that.

"I wasn't even at the record store grand opening," Elroy said. He pointed at the still-frozen computer screen. "Does that look like my hat? Maybe. It's not the only hat like that in the entire world. Two of us in this room own one just like it. But Juni has a point about Daffy. That stray is jumpier than a long-tailed cat in a room full of rocking chairs around anyone other than you girls. He wouldn't let me get that close to him without disappearing."

Hearing his name, Daffy jumped out of Maggie's arms and pranced along the counter. He leapt gracefully down to the floor and begun to weave himself in figure eights around Elroy's legs, purring loudly.

"I don't know about you, but looks like that cat's pretty comfy with you from where I'm standing," J.T. pointed out.

Elroy poked at Daffy with his boot. The cat hissed and scampered off toward the back of the shop.

"You might have snuck in the back door, but you didn't go out that way. What do you want to bet there's video footage of you leaving out the front door sometime between ten forty-five and midnight?" I asked. "That's enough to prove you were at the party at the same time as Monica."

"I swear, I didn't do anything wrong," Elroy insisted.

"You're married," I said. "Sounds like you've cheated on your wife before. You harassed Monica at work, and she quit, but you lied and told us y'all let her go."

"I don't know what you're talking about. It's all hearsay, anyway," he said, smugly.

Ignoring his defense, I continued, "What happened Friday night? I saw your wife at the grand opening, but not you. I figured you were at work with J.T., but he said he was alone. And I believe my brother-in-law."

"Oh, now you believe me," J.T. muttered.

I cringed. It was going to take a long time for me to live that one down. I hoped J.T.—and my middle sister—would find a way to forgive me, or family dinners were going to be awkward for a while. "You told Mina you had to work late, didn't you? But really you had a date. Then what? You couldn't take her out to a fancy dinner, not in a town like Cedar River. That would set tongues wagging. Calvin took a date to United Steaks and it became immediate gossip fodder. But you don't have much time. Your wife is at the grand opening party, which buys you a couple of hours, tops. Hardly enough time to get to Austin, eat dinner, and get back before Mina comes home. You ordered takeout, didn't you? Bet that impressed your date."

Then it hit me. Friday had been dead quiet according to the Roadrunners driver who had brought my grilled-cheese sandwich for lunch yesterday, but Monica was working the night of the party. She'd been wearing their standard uniform and carrying a Roadrunners bag when she died. She had probably handed out flyers for the grand opening I'd paid Roadrunners to distribute with their deliveries, so she would have known about the party. "Monica was your delivery driver, wasn't she? What did she do? Embarrass you in front of your girlfriend?"

"That ungrateful girl threatened to rat me out to Mina," Elroy said, his voice raised as the dam finally broke. "She was gonna tell my wife, all right? If she had proof I was cheating on her, Mina would have divorced me in a heartbeat. Juan would have bankrupted me. You ever heard of self-defense? Stand your ground? Monica Mayhew was going to *ruin* me. She threatened to destroy my life. I made sure she couldn't."

"That's not self-defense, you idiot," J.T. growled at his partner. "That's murder."

Elroy shrugged, recovering himself. "Not the way I see it. And not the way a jury's gonna see it, either. Monica was a tease and a liar. After all we did for her, she was trying to ruin my marriage, and my business. I was defending myself, plain and simple. Did things get out of hand after she lured me into the supply closet at your party? Sure. And I regret that. I really do. Her hitting her head on the shelf was an accident, plain and simple. If anything, y'all need to be looking at making your supply closet safer. Maybe add some padding to the sharp corners or locking the door, before you have a lawsuit on your hands."

"Seriously?" J.T. asked, advancing on Elroy. "That's the way you're gonna play it?"

Elroy threw up his hands in an exaggerated sign of resignation that seemed as fake as he was. "It is what it is, *buddy*. Have me arrested if you think it'll do any good, but I'm the only one who knows where Calvin is. If anything happens to me, he'll disappear permanently. You've got nothing. I'll get off scot-free. You'll default on the bail when Calvin doesn't show up and lose the record store. Then Rodger Mayhew is gonna sue the pants off you for creating the unsafe environment that killed his daughter."

"I don't think so," I said.

"Oh yeah? Now you've got it all figured out? A minute ago, you thought your own brother-in-law was involved with Monica's death. But yeah, let's all hear what little Juniper Jessup has to say."

"Me?" I pointed to myself. "Nah, you don't gotta worry about me." I advanced toward him and picked up my phone from where I'd left it on the other side of the coffee station, nearest to Elroy. "Hey, Mina, did you get any of that?" I asked.

His wife's voice floated out of the speakerphone. "I think I heard enough."

"You little . . ." Elroy lunged at me, but J.T. snagged him by the collar. Elroy might have had several inches on my brother-in-law, but J.T. was all muscle. Elroy gagged, reaching for his throat.

I snagged the coffeepot, full of hot, black drip coffee, and held on to it just in case I needed a weapon. Elroy might have gotten the better of me in the dark hallway of Calvin's house, but he wasn't going to get the jump on me again, with or without J.T. holding him back. "Gee, seems like Mina knows everything now, anyway."

J.T. let go of Elroy, who smoothed his shirt, buying time to get his temper under control. When he spoke again, he was as calm and commanding as he'd ever been in a courtroom. "You can't prove anything. None of you can. Tell the cops any story you want. It's all he-said, she-said. Who do you think the judge is gonna believe? You? Or me? You grew up in Cedar River, Juni, but you might as well be a tourist these days. I'm an upstanding member of this community."

"You are," Maggie said. She pointed up at the camera mounted over the cash register. "And I think a confession from an upstanding member of the community such as yourself will convince any jury."

There was a bang on the front door. We all turned to see Beau pounding on the door. I put down the coffeepot and hurried to the front entrance, unlocking it to let in the detective. He surveyed the room. "What's going on here?" He held up his phone and read the text message I'd sent when no one was watching: "911 get down to S&S. Got the killer. Got proof."

"It was Elroy."

"Elroy McGibbons?" Beau asked.

"The same," I said, bobbing my head.

"That explains why the false fire alarm was traced back to the courthouse," Beau said contemplatively.

"That son of a . . ." J.T.'s face turned red. "He must have called it in while I was in the restroom." He shook his head. "My own partner. And I never suspected a thing."

"None of us did," Beau said. "Any idea where I can find Elroy now?"

"He's right here . . ." I turned around. J.T. and Maggie were still by the checkout counter. The hallway was empty. Elroy was gone.

"He couldn't have gotten far," I said.

"You're right about that," a woman's voice said.

Elroy stumbled back into the shop. His right arm was twisted up behind his back. Behind him was Jayden Holt. She was half his size, yet handled him easily. "I caught this one slipping out the back," she said. "Figured we might want to have a word with him."

"You figured right," I said, flashing a wide grin at her. "Congratulations, Officer Holt. You just caught yourself a murderer."

CHAPTER 27

A week later, my family was gathered around Sip & Spin, drinking Papa's Got a Brand New Breakfast Blend coffees—a smooth, light roast without any fancy bells or whistles—and listening to Alanis Morissette. It was Wednesday morning, and I was in an old Rolling Stones shirt and jeans. Tansy had on a light blue cashmere sweater with dark blue houndstooth pants. Maggie was—no surprise—wearing a knee-length dress. This one had a pink top with a cutout collar and giant pink roses on the skirt.

Maggie finished up helping a couple. As they left with their purchases, Uncle Calvin and Jocelyn Reyes walked through the front door. He had his arm around her waist. Her expensive shoes clacked loudly on the floor. J.T. followed closely behind them.

"So this is why you wanted us all here," my mom said. She took Jocelyn's hands. "My goodness, Jocelyn, you haven't aged a day."

"Liar," Jocelyn said. "It's good to see you, Bea."

"Same," Mom said, drawing her into a hug. They both seated themselves at one of the café tables before Mom turned her attention to her brother. "And? How did it go in court this morning?"

"Not bad," J.T. said. He nodded hello to everyone before wagging a finger at me. I gave him a finger wave. He'd forgiven me for accusing him of murder, thank goodness, but he wasn't going to let me live that down anytime soon. Family. Gotta love 'em.

At the same time, Calvin said, "Terrible."

"You got off with a fine and a few hours of community service," J.T. corrected him.

"Like I said, terrible."

"A few days ago, you were on the run and wanted for murder," I pointed out. "This is certainly an improvement."

Calvin shook his head violently. "I still can't believe that snake Elroy thought he could take the heat off himself by convincing me to go into hiding and making myself look guilty. I'll never trust a lawyer again."

"Hey!" Jocelyn said.

"No kidding," J.T. said.

"Present company excluded, of course," Calvin added hastily.

"Ironic, don't you think, how I ended up cracking the case after I told y'all to leave it to the lawyers?" my mother said.

"Excuse me?" my sisters and I all said at the same time, turning to Mom. "How do you figure?" Maggie asked indignantly. "We did all the legwork. Juni tricked him into confessing. What did you contribute to the investigation?"

"Everything you gave the police was circumstantial. Even the security footage of his confession could get tossed out of court with a good enough lawyer, but that family photo I made us take at the grand opening was the final bit of evidence needed to place him at the scene of the crime," she said, a bit smugly.

Mom had a point. She'd posted the goofy photo we'd posed for on Facebook. No one had paid any attention at the time, but it had caught Elroy in the background. Not only did it prove that Elroy was at the party even though his face never appeared in any of the security footage, but in the photo he was walking into the supply closet also. The time stamp was right after Monica had entered the shop.

Better still, when Mom went through her phone, the picture taken just before that caught Elroy shoving Monica into the closet.

"Yup. You deserve all the credit," I agreed with her, teasing a bit. But I was so relieved that everything was wrapped up, I didn't actually care who got the credit. "Especially since you practically captured a murder in those pictures and never even noticed until Officer Holt saw the Facebook post and asked to see the other photos you'd taken that night."

"Exactly," Mom said, drawing herself up straighter. "Which is how I saved the day."

"Speaking of saving . . ." I changed the subject back to Calvin. Winning an argument with my mother was impossible, even when she was obviously wrong. "Where are you going to get the money to pay the fines?" The envelope of cash hadn't lasted long, not after Calvin paid off the last lotto winner and refunded everyone else from the final buy-in of the now-defunct game.

"I've got an idea about that," he said.

"Uncle Calvin, no. You promised," Maggie said. He'd sworn that he was on the straight and narrow from now on. No more underground lottery games. No more glitter bombs. No more bankruptcy schemes.

"Don't worry about me, Magnolia," he said.

"*Maggie*," Tansy and I corrected him simultaneously.

"Fine. Maggie. Whatever. Look here, Tansy, how much do you spend on those night classes of yours? Dancing, pottery, cooking, and whatnot?" he asked.

"I don't see how I spend my own money is any business of yours," Tansy replied.

He flapped a hand at her. "No need to get all hot and bothered. We've got all those junk records in the back, don't we? How about instead of selling them for pennies apiece to artists, we charge people big money to come in and learn how to turn them into art right here at Sip & Spin?"

"That's not a bad idea," Mom said musingly.

"Right? We can show 'em how to create bowls and vases and cutouts and whatnots. We can get one of those engraving machines and let them make their own designs."

"We can do it during one of the mornings when we're not real busy anyway, or stay open late one night a week," Maggie suggested.

"And as long as they're here, we can sell them coffee and introduce them to new music," Tansy added.

"Sounds fabulous," I agreed. "I can pull up some YouTube videos for project inspiration." I pointed at the clock mounted behind the register, the one made from a vinyl record cut to form our logo. "Wouldn't it be fun to help people make things like that?"

"That's the spirit!" Calvin said, grinning at us. "You always have been the smart one in the family, little Juniper."

I laughed. "Not hardly. Just because I figured out who the real murderer was and cleared your name . . ."

"*We* figured it out," Maggie corrected me.

Mom spoke up. "I still think I deserve the credit. If it weren't for my picture on Facebook, Elroy would probably still be walking around a free man."

"As long as everyone's patting themselves on the back, I'd like to remind you that if it weren't for my hat or the security camera I installed, no one would have figured out who actually killed Monica," J.T. said. "I mean, if you think about it, I all but delivered Elroy to you, gift wrapped."

"Sure you did, J.T.," I said, lightly punching him in the shoulder. He hadn't completely forgiven me for accusing him of murder, but we were starting to get back to normal. I should have known that my sister had more sense than to marry a bad guy.

Unable to help himself, Calvin joined the conversation. "Speaking of cowboy hats, did y'all know that cowboy hats weren't actually invented in Texas? In fact, the inventor, a fellow by the name of John Stetson, was born in New Jersey in 1830. Does that make cowboy hats more genuinely New Jersian than Texan?"

"Sure thing, Uncle Calvin," I said, cutting him off before he could entertain us with any more of his obscure knowledge. "While he was confessing, Elroy confirmed that Monica was at the grand opening to confront Mina about her husband's affair, but where did her delivery car end up?"

"I can answer that," J.T. said. "Apparently, parking was such a nightmare that night, she parked at United Steaks and walked to Sip & Spin. Elroy got lucky and found a spot in the municipal lot at the other end of the block. Otherwise, she would have probably beaten him here by a good five minutes."

We were all quiet at that revelation. If Monica had gotten to the party earlier, she would have had plenty of time to tell Mina about Elroy. She might still be alive if she had.

Calvin broke the silence. "Speaking of cars, about my Bronco . . ." I braced myself for the worst. Had I accidentally scratched it? Had the tow truck damaged the fender? Was he about to reveal the origin of the word "bronco" or explain the internal workings of a combustion engine? In all of the chaos surrounding unmasking Monica Mayhew's murderer and then finally tracking down Calvin—he was staying at a cheap highway motel next to a bowling alley, of course—the Bronco had completely slipped my mind.

Instead of charging us extra storage fees for leaving the Bronco at her shop, Esméralda had personally delivered it to Calvin's house and then sent the bill to Sip & Spin, which we promptly paid. It was pretty decent of her. If I ever got my own car, she would have a loyal customer for life. My uncle was still upset that I'd not only driven his car but also left it by the side of the road to be towed to a mechanic's garage. I didn't imagine he'd be loaning me his keys anytime soon.

"What about the Bronco?" I asked, with some trepidation.

"I figured you must have been driving recklessly to blow out the tire like that . . ."

"Seriously? You can't possibly blame me for a flat tire," I interrupted him. Then I remembered that Esméralda had mentioned something about finding something in the tire on my voicemail, and I braced myself for a lecture about paying closer attention to the road.

He rooted around his pocket and pulled out something shiny. He tossed it to me.

I looked down at a spent bullet. "What on earth?" I asked.

Maggie plucked the bullet from my hand and examined it. "You drove over a bullet?" she asked. "A nail I can understand, but not a bullet."

I shook my head as realization dawned. "I didn't drive over anything. Someone shot out the tire."

"You think you would have heard a gunshot," J.T. suggested.

"Not necessarily. It was during that bad thunderstorm last week. Lots of thunder and lightning. I might not have noticed a shot." Then I smacked my palm against my forehead. "And a minute later, who pulls up? Elroy. Maybe he thought Calvin had come back to Cedar River for his truck and he knew that if Calvin cooperated with the cops they'd realize he was innocent and start looking elsewhere for suspects. I still can't believe I got into a car with a murderer."

"Don't feel bad; he fooled everyone," Tansy said, coming nearer so she could put an arm around my shoulder.

"I mean, I invited him over for dinner," Maggie said, adding her arm on top of Tansy's. "I considered him family."

"We all did," J.T. said. "We should have seen it sooner."

"Technically, you knew him better than any of us," I pointed out. "You knew he cheated on Mina and harassed Monica, and you didn't do anything about it."

"I know, and I should have. I just didn't think it was any of my business. If it ever happens again with anyone else, I'll react different."

Mom sniffed. "You better."

"I will," he promised her.

"Speaking of family dinner, I'm gonna skip out tonight," I announced. "I've got a date."

"Oh yeah?" Mom asked. "And who is the lucky man? Teddy or Beau?"

Instead of answering, I changed the subject. "There's something I still don't understand. When I was little, I found a secret compartment in the storage closet. Someone had hidden a box, like a jewelry box, but with a lock on it, in there. I used to pretend I'd found pirate treasure, and I left my Beanie Baby dragon in there to protect it. After Monica was killed, I checked the compartment and my dragon was still there, but the chest was gone. And by the looks of the dust back there, it hadn't been gone long."

"What about it?" Tansy asked.

"Well, at first maybe I thought it was a clue or had to do with Monica's murder, but I never figured out where it fit in."

"Maybe I can help you out there," Mom offered.

"Oh yeah? I'm all ears."

"I found that hidey-hole when I was probably about the same age as you were when you found it, and put my jewelry box in it. I used to keep all sorts of things in there. Pretty buttons. Coins. A butterfly ring I'd gotten in a gumball dispenser. As I got older, I'd hide other things in there, like cigarettes."

"Mom!" Tansy and Maggie said at the same time.

"I was young and stupid," she explained. "I quit smoking once I met your dad, because he didn't like the smell of it."

"I can't believe you used to smoke," I said. "Don't you know how bad that is for you?"

"It was the eighties. Everyone smoked back then," she said, flippantly. "Anyway, when your father and I started getting serious, I used to put his love letters in the box for safekeeping. We got married and had you girls, and by the time the shop went out of business, I'd forgotten about it, frankly."

I understood how that could happen.

"Anyway, after we lost your dad, I kept thinking about that chest and the letters inside it, but I couldn't exactly walk into the dance studio and ask to root around in their storage room. Then you girls came up with the idea to lease this place and open a new record store, and I knew it was fate. First chance I got, I retrieved it, and now it's safely tucked away in my closet back home."

"That's so sweet," Tansy said. On the other side of me, Maggie sniffled. "You think we can see the letters sometime?" she asked.

"Not on your life," Mom replied. "Those are personal. I did wonder where that dragon had come from, though. Thanks, Juni, for making sure that the letters didn't get lonely."

"Anytime," I responded, but there was a strange tickling sensation in my throat. Someone was obviously cutting onions nearby, or maybe it was just springtime allergies. "Speaking of the storage closet, does anyone know why Monica was holding Uncle Calvin's business card when she died?" It was a macabre change of subject, but the question had been bugging me.

"I think I can answer that," Calvin said. All eyes turned to him. "When Monica came to Prankenstein asking for a job, there was no way we could hire her. Business was down and me and Samuel were already looking at ways we could close up shop without losing our shirts. But she told me about this dragon lady lawyer she used to work for in Austin." He squeezed Jocelyn around the waist. "I felt bad for her and gave her my card. Said if she ever wanted to play a prank on her old boss, I'd be happy to send her the deluxe glitter package, free of charge."

"You did *not*," Jocelyn said.

"I didn't know she was talking about you, sweetie," Calvin said. "I would never do that to you."

I interrupted before my uncle could launch into one of his famously long and rambling speeches. "As cute as all this is, it still doesn't explain why Monica was holding your card when she died."

"We didn't have the budget to hire any full-time help, but once I got the lottery up and running, I made sure to ask for Monica anytime I scheduled a delivery. I know for a fact that the players tipped well, because I told them it was good luck to do so."

"The business card," Maggie reminded him, trying to get the story back on track.

"Ah, yes. The night of the grand opening, Samuel and I were in the middle of an argument about something or other . . ."

"He was upset that you'd invested all his money in Sip & Spin without consulting him," I offered.

Calvin frowned at me. "Like I said, something or other, and Monica came up to me. Said she needed me to send the biggest, baddest glitter bomb I could construct to some guy that was hassling her. She waved my business card at me, reminded me that I owed her a favor. Like I wouldn't have done it just for the challenge. I told her I was in the middle of something." His face fell. "Asked her to call me in the morning. That was the last time I saw her."

"She wasn't planning on ratting out Elroy to his wife," I said, numbly. "She was just going to send him a glitter bomb. He killed her for no reason."

"Even if she had been about to expose him, that's no reason to murder her," Maggie said. "All that stuff he was spouting off about, self-defense and all that nonsense, it was all just an excuse he was telling himself to make himself feel better about what he did."

"A jury's going to see straight through him," J.T. added. "I'll make sure of it."

I nodded. "I know." I looked down at the bullet that was still in my fist. "I'll make sure to tell Beau about this, too. If they can tie it back to his gun, the D.A. can add another charge of attempted manslaughter to the charges they already have."

"It's a good thing that Elroy is already in custody, or, well, I don't know what I'd do to him," Maggie said.

"I've got a couple of ideas," Tansy said. "You mess with any of the Jessup girls and you're gonna have to answer to her sisters."

I grinned and squeezed my sisters around their waists. "Thanks for always having my back."

"Of course," Tansy said.

"Always," Maggie added.

The front door chimed as a man a few years younger than me walked into Sip & Spin. He looked at us curiously. "Sorry, am I interrupting anything?"

"Of course not," I said brightly. "How can I help you?"

Mom came by and gave me a kiss on the cheek. "I've got to run, but how about we grab lunch tomorrow, just you and me?"

"Sounds great," I told her.

"I've got to get back to work, too," J.T. said, following her to the front door. "I have to figure out how to run a law firm with just one lawyer."

"Good thing there's no crime in Cedar River," Calvin said with a mischievous grin.

"Don't even say something like that. You'll jinx us." J.T.'s gaze swept across the record shop. "Don't any of y'all go getting into any trouble, hear? I've got my hands full."

"Don't worry about us," Maggie said. "See you later, babe."

"Later, Mags."

Calvin took Jocelyn's hand and started showing her around the shop as I turned my full attention back to the customer. "What can I help you with? Looking for music or coffee? The special of the day is Shiny Frappé People, coffee blended with ice and a splash of butterscotch, topped with rich whipped cream."

"Yeah, I'm gonna need one of those. Now, this is going to sound sort of silly, but I want to ask my girlfriend to move in with me."

"Aww," Maggie said, leaning in to listen.

The customer blushed. "I already rented the apartment, so I *really* hope she says yes. I thought it might be romantic to show her the place tonight with candles everywhere, and music playing on a record player in the living room."

I bobbed my head. "Wow. Who can say no to something like that?"

"Do you have a record player already?" Maggie asked.

"Nope." He held up his cell phone. "This is all I've got, really, but it's not the same. My girlfriend is really into vinyl. She's always playing me something from her aunt's collection, and I have to admit, it's a million times better than streaming."

"We love to hear that," Maggie said. "Let me show you our record player collection, see if there's something that catches your eye."

"And I can help pick out some records. Do you know what kind of music she likes?" I asked.

"She's very eclectic, but I was thinking maybe some old-timey jazz for tonight?"

"Perfect," I said. I led him upstairs to the jazz section. Tansy joined me. I pulled out a record. "What do you think about this one?" I asked her.

"It's a great album, but it doesn't have that va-voom factor I think he's looking for tonight," she said. She pulled out another record and handed it to him. "Try this one instead. Follow me downstairs and I'll make you that Shiny Frappé People."

After he paid for his purchases and left, Tansy and I joined Maggie at the counter. Not only were we able to make a decent sale, but we all had a part in it also. Just like we all had a part in solving Monica's murder and bringing her killer to justice.

The best part about working for the family business was getting to see my sisters every day, knowing that together we could accomplish anything.

ACKNOWLEDGMENTS

Thanks for reading *Vinyl Resting Place*. I hope you enjoyed it (and the earworms) as much as I enjoyed writing it! I look forward to many more Record Shop Mysteries with Juniper and her sisters.

Writing—like solving a mystery—isn't a one-woman job. I could probably go on forever about all the wonderful people who got this book into your hands, but I'll try to make it brief.

I'd like to thank Nettie Finn, my editor at St. Martin's Press, who shares my vision for Juni and Cedar River. She's amazing to work with and, like me, she has an almost criminal love of puns. My agent, James McGowan at BookEnds Literary Agency, really gets me (and took a chance on me anyway). To all the hardworking and talented folks at Macmillan and St. Martin's Press who took a mistake-riddled (sometimes embarrassingly so!) document with lots of squiggly lines under the words and transformed it into an amazing book— Sara Beth Haring, Sarah Haeckel, John Rounds, Jeremy Haiting, Olya Kirilyuk, Mary Ann Lasher, Jen Edwards, Barbara Wild, and Hope Breeman: thank you. Y'all are the real heroes. I couldn't have done it without you!

For all the friends and family who have encouraged and inspired me—especially Toni, who had to put up with having me as a bratty little sister—and for my grandparents, who ran a family-owned business in a small Texas town decades before such things were "cool." Special shoutouts go to Dare, Ris, Liz, and La for always being there, the #Berkletes for continuing to be the best debut writers group anyone could ask for, and the amazingly talented Michelle, Ellen, and Danica for distracting me with pictures of Tom Wilson (Tomspiration for the win!) and hockey videos when I need a break. I also would like to thank Baileycakes for trying to eat every single cicada in D.C. so I could write in peace and quiet. It didn't work, but it's the thought that counts!

Finally, on a personal note, I want to credit Potassium for suggesting "Oops! . . . I Did It Americano Blend." He's a true partner, even when all he hears from me for weeks on end is "Just let me finish this chapter." His weird fits my weird, and I'll always be there when the puck drops.